BRINGING DOWN the MOUSE

BEN MEZRICH

Simon & Schuster Books for Young Readers
NEW YORK   LONDON   TORONTO   SYDNEY   NEW DELHI

SIMON & SCHUSTER BOOKS FOR YOUNG READERS
An imprint of Simon & Schuster Children's Publishing Division
1230 Avenue of the Americas, New York, New York 10020
This book is a work of fiction. Any references to historical events, real people, or real places are used fictitiously. Other names, characters, places, and events are products of the author's imagination, and any resemblance to actual events or places or persons, living or dead, is entirely coincidental.
Text copyright © 2014 by Ben Mezrich
Cover illustration copyright © 2014 by Rayner Alencar
All rights reserved, including the right of reproduction in whole or in part in any form.
SIMON & SCHUSTER BOOKS FOR YOUNG READERS is a trademark of Simon & Schuster, Inc.
For information about special discounts for bulk purchases,
please contact Simon & Schuster Special Sales at 1-866-506-1949
or business@simonandschuster.com.
The Simon & Schuster Speakers Bureau can bring authors to your live event.
For more information or to book an event, contact the Simon & Schuster Speakers Bureau
at 1-866-248-3049 or visit our website at www.simonspeakers.com.
Also available in a Simon & Schuster Books for Young Readers hardcover edition
Cover design by Krista Vossen
Interior design by Hilary Zarycky
The text for this book is set in Life.
Manufactured in the United States of America
0221 QVE
First Simon & Schuster Books for Young Readers paperback edition June 2015
4 6 8 10 9 7 5 3
The Library of Congress has cataloged the hardcover edition as follows:
Mezrich, Ben, 1969–
Bringing down the mouse / Ben Mezrich. — First edition.
pages cm
Summary: A mathematically gifted sixth-grader is recruited by a group of students to game the system at the biggest theme park in the world—and win the big prize.
ISBN 978-1-4424-9626-2 (hardcover) — ISBN 978-1-4424-9632-3 (eBook)
[1. Mathematics—Fiction. 2. Amusement parks—Fiction. 3. Genius—Fiction. 4. Conduct of life—Fiction.] I. Title.
PZ7.M5753Br 2014
[Fic]—dc23
2013027538
ISBN 978-1-4424-9631-6 (pbk)

PRAISE FOR

BRINGING DOWN THE MOUSE

"Mezrich addresses themes of loyalty and honesty
while keeping the action tight and the dialogue snappy.
Unexpectedly engrossing."—*Booklist*

"The pacing is well developed, building tension
to almost a fever pitch. . . . The plot has several
unexpected and well-placed twists, and keeps readers
guessing until the very end. A good fit for fans of
Gordon Korman's Swindle series."
—*School Library Journal*

"Fast-paced and full of behind-the-scenes detail."
—*Kirkus Reviews*

For Asher and Arya,
who make me smile every single day.
I can't wait until you're both
old enough to read this!

ACKNOWLEDGMENTS

I am indebted to my incredible editor, David Gale, and his team at S&S Books for Young Readers, especially Navah Wolfe. I am also eternally grateful to Eric Simonoff and Matt Snyder, the best agents in the business. A special thanks to Daniel Friedman, my expert on too many things to mention!

And most important of all, thank you, Tonya. Your brilliance shines through nearly every sentence in this book. And to Asher, Arya, Bugsy, and my parents—you make it all worthwhile!

BRINGING DOWN the MOUSE

IT WAS TEN MINUTES past four in the afternoon, and Charlie Lewis was running for his life.

His sneakers skidded against pavement as he barreled down the oversize sidewalk. It wound, like a flickering serpent's tail, between brightly colored storefronts, stone and marble fountains, and manicured hedges. Trickles of sweat streamed down his back. The thick straps of his heavy backpack dug into the skin of his shoulders. He'd never run so fast before, and he wasn't sure how long he could keep moving at that pace. Worse yet, the sidewalk was so crowded with tourists, he was dodging and weaving just to stay on his feet. Parents pushing strollers; little kids clutching ice-cream cones and silvery, bobbing helium balloons;

teenagers in short skirts and tank tops; everyone laughing and smiling and happy. Everyone except for Charlie, who was frantically crashing through the cheerful mob at full speed. The adults glared at him as he careened by, but there was nothing he could do. One glance back over his shoulder and it was instantly clear—*they were gaining on him.*

Loopy the Space Mouse was in front—huge black ears bobbing above the crowd, spaghetti thin arms undulating wildly at his sides, oversize hands in shiny silver astronaut gloves pawing at the air. His strange, almost manic smile seemed completely out of place as he shoved his way past a family of three, nearly upending a baby carriage as he went.

The Frog was a few steps behind his rodent cohort. Nearly a head taller, he was all gawky legs and arms, twisting and twirling as he moved like some sort of drunken gymnast. For a terrifying moment, one of his gigantic patchwork moon boots caught in the base of a vendor's hot dog cart, but he somehow managed to pull it free, and then he was moving forward again, right behind Loopy, closing the distance to Charlie with each flop of his ridiculously long tongue.

Had Charlie not known what was going to happen if the two oversize cartoon monstrosities caught up to him, he would have found the scene hilarious. A twelve-year-old with an overstuffed backpack running through one of the most famous amusement parks in the world, chased by a gigantic mouse and an even bigger mutant frog. But to Charlie, the moment was anything but funny.

A burst of adrenaline pushed new energy into Charlie's aching legs. He cut left, sprinting around a circular section of the path. A copper statue rose up at the center of the circle, protected by four of the most carefully pruned hedges he had ever seen. The statue depicted a young boy holding hands with the park's most iconic creation—Loopy. In copper, Loopy looked a lot less threatening than the fierce, flopping creature now just a few yards behind Charlie.

"Somebody stop that kid!"

The muffled cry was enough to send new shards of fear through Charlie's chest. People around him were pointing and staring, but Charlie kept on going. He didn't need to look back to know where the cry had come from. Even muffled, Loopy didn't sound like the Loopy from the cartoons; he sounded like an angry, out-of-breath adult.

Of course, it wasn't really Loopy—there was, in fact, a man beneath the mouse. Twenty-one, maybe twenty-two years old, with scraggly, spiky brown hair and a mean-looking scar above his lip. Charlie thought his name was Barry, or maybe Gary; he couldn't be sure, he'd only heard the name in passing. But the scar was impossible to forget. Charlie hadn't gotten a look at the guy in the Frog costume, but the memory of that menacing scar was enough of an incentive to keep Charlie's feet skidding against the pavement.

Eyes wild with growing fear, Charlie skirted around a pair of German tourists, too busy babbling in German and gawking at the costumed pursuers to make a grab at Charlie.

It was immediately obvious what was causing the clot of people, even at full speed. Charlie was awed by the scale alone of the architectural wonder in front of him.

Almost three hundred feet tall, Loopy's Space Station was a sci-fi movie set come to life, topped by a single crystal antenna rising impossibly high into the Florida sky. Its design represented everything the Incredo Land amusement park was supposed to be: magnificent, whimsical, and utterly impractical. The large crowd was going to take at least half an hour to file through the arched tunnel feeding through the base of the space-age structure.

Instead, Charlie cut sharply to his left, exiting the

circular path. A minute later he was crossing over a curved bridge, and it was like changing a television channel: Everything around him shifted from future Earth to the first stop on Loopy's journey through the planets. His sneakers kicked up meticulously designed clouds of reddish dust as he entered a section of the park known as Miraculous Mars at a breathless gallop.

Directly ahead, he could see people lining up for the Solar Sailboat that would take them to Mars Central Docking Station. Charlie's memory danced back to three years ago, when he'd thrown up on that boat; more specifically, he'd thrown up all over his dad, right as the boat ride ended. At least Charlie's parents had had the decency to buy him ice cream when he'd finally recovered from the trauma of barfing on a ride designed for children half his age.

But his parents weren't around to help him this time. His dad and mom were five hundred miles away, enjoying a leisurely November afternoon in what was probably the quietest suburban corner of Massachusetts. Maybe his dad was outside, raking leaves, the cold moisture in the air fogging up his glasses. Maybe his mother was reading a book in her study, something scientific and complex, with a title Charlie wouldn't even dare try to pronounce. For the first time in his life, Charlie's parents weren't going to be there to catch him if he fell. Looking back over his shoulder at those menacing giant ears bouncing over the curved bridge that connected the end of Solar Avenue to Miraculous Mars, Charlie knew there were things a whole lot worse than vomiting on his dad on a fake sailboat.

Charlie made another hard turn before he reached the Hall of Aliens—a terrifying place, full of angry-looking animatronic figures that seemed to have stepped right out of a horror movie. Now he was heading straight toward the Space Rock Carousel, which was exactly as it sounded, a revolving ride speckled with asteroid-shaped seats bounding beneath a canopy of near-seizure-inducing lights.

For a brief second, Charlie thought about hopping the low railing of the carousel and trying to lose himself in the whirl of colored rocks. But he discarded the idea almost as quickly as it came—it was a matter of simple physics. *Too many people in too small an area.* If there was anything that Charlie knew well, it was simple physics. In fact, it had been simple physics that had gotten him into this mess in the first place.

He continued forward, frantically searching for another option. His breaths had turned into gasps, and tight cramps spasmed up his calves. He wouldn't be able to go much farther.

"Charlie?" A shout suddenly shot toward him from ahead. "Charlie Numbers?"

"Holy smokes!" Another voice, close to the first, rang out. "That is Charlie!"

Charlie skidded to a stop. He quickly picked out a shock of thick dark hair near the end of the line leading up to the carousel. Heck, Dylan Wigglesworth would've been easy to spot even if Charlie *hadn't* known him since kindergarten. Not just because of that hair, piled above his oversize head like an angry storm cloud. For a sixth grader, Dylan was freakishly big all over. Mountainous shoulders jutting out of a sleeveless white tank top, hands that were more like a Great Dane's paws, and a chin and neck that seemed to blend into one single body part. Charlie knew that the way he saw Dylan was colored by the fact that Dylan and his buddies had been tormenting Charlie for as long as he could remember. Dylan had one hand on the shoulder of his ever-present co-thug, Liam Anthony, and the other hand in front of him clutching a rapidly melting ice-cream cone. Dusty Bickle, the third wheel of their malevolent bully tricycle, was never far behind the duo. Liam and Dusty could have been brothers; they both had matching curly blond hair, horselike faces, and arms that seemed to be too long for their bodies. Dylan's size and the wonder-twins' elongated limbs made them good at baseball—the three had been dominating suburban Boston's Little League for as long as Charlie could remember—but their prowess at the sport seemed to have an inverse relationship with the nature of their personalities. The more runs they scored each season, the worse they treated Charlie and his equally less-than-athletic friends.

At the moment, the look on Dylan's face was much more astonishment than malice. The only time Dylan had seen Charlie run even close to that fast was when he himself was chasing Charlie around the school playground. When he caught sight of Loopy and the Frog, Dylan's surprise turned to true shock. Charlie couldn't help but feel a moment of perverse pride. It must have killed Dylan.

Charlie didn't pause long enough to see what expression came after shock. He cut hard left, skirting the back of the line for the carousel, and headed toward a vaguely familiar building. Another space station, nowhere near as gargantuan as Loopy's; instead of a crystal antenna, this space station was crowned with jutting dioramas meant to look like recognizable landmarks from all over planet Earth: A large smiling clock, a skeletal Eiffel Tower, a daggerish Leaning Tower of Pisa. As with the carousel, there was a line of people out front, waiting to get inside. Charlie raced past the line, looking for somewhere—anywhere—to hide. The cramps in his calves had already begun extending into his thighs; a few more minutes at this pace, and he was going to collapse.

In his desperation, he suddenly noticed something that put a burst of new air into his lungs. Ten feet past the line into the building, there was a maintenance door leading inside; a man dressed in white pants and a blue work shirt was exiting, his back to Charlie. If Charlie timed it just right—

The man let go of the door just as Charlie reached it. He slipped inside, the door clicking shut behind him. He was in a nearly dark hallway with cinder-block walls. The ceiling was barely lit by crisscrossing fluorescent tubes. Steam pipes jutted out from the cinder blocks like the threads of a metallic spiderweb, connected via curved junctions to big circular gears and rusting gaskets. And above the hiss from the pipes, a dull throb of music bled into the hallway from beyond both walls; the melody could only be described as sickly sweet. Charlie mouthed the words as he jogged down the hallway: *Oh, the world keeps spinning, yes, it does.*

Beyond the music, he could hear the sound of running water.

He knew that on the other side of the cinder-block walls, little spaceships were carrying groups of visitors through a cartoonish geography lesson populated entirely by robot children: a futuristic menagerie of cyborgs populating an invented land of a time well beyond the present. As Charlie navigated between the pipes and gears, the music growing louder with each step, he imagined himself wandering deeper and deeper into the working bowels that kept that cartoon world revolving: *Rust, steam, cinder block, crackling fluorescent tubes—these were the guts that made up that spinning world, yes, they were.* . . .

Slowly, Charlie's terror began to subside. Maybe his pursuers hadn't seen him going through the maintenance door—maybe they had run right by. Maybe Charlie was free and clear. He shifted the backpack against his shoulders, taking some of the weight off his aching back . . . when he heard the click of a lock being opened from somewhere behind him, and then the sound of a door swinging inward.

He didn't look back, he just ran. Deeper, deeper into the building, the pipes and gears flashing by on either side as he went, the flickering lights casting jagged shadows as his feet skidded across the cement hallway floor. He turned a corner, then another—and suddenly, his eyes went wide. Ten feet ahead, the hallway ended in a dead end, entirely blocked by a faceless steel door.

Charlie didn't even pause. He hit the door with both hands out in front of him and felt the blow right up to his elbows. It didn't budge. Charlie cried out, throwing all his weight against the steel, every ounce of strength—and nothing. It was locked. He was trapped.

"Like a rat in a cage, kid," a muffled voice echoed from behind him. "You're not going anywhere."

Charlie slowly turned away from the door. Loopy the Space Mouse stalked down the hallway, his sausagelike, silver-gloved fingers tracing the piping along the cinder block walls as he went. The Frog lumbered behind Loopy, those huge moon boots slapping ominously against the cement floor.

Charlie pressed back against the steel, his legs trembling beneath him. *Not good. Not good. Not good.* Loopy came to a stop a few feet away, then carefully reached up and placed his two enormous hands on either side of his own orbital head. With a twist, he pulled the head off and placed it gently on the floor by his feet. The man's face, now freed from the Loopy head, was flushed, his spiky hair dripping with sweat.

He jabbed at Charlie with one of his oversize fingers.

"Hand over the backpack, kid. There's nowhere else to run."

Charlie closed his eyes, his shoulders sagging. Slowly, he reached for the backpack. In that moment, he couldn't help thinking that other kids his age were safe in their classrooms at schools across the country, taking tests, reading books, playing on playgrounds. And here he was, cornered in a dark hallway in the bowels of one of the biggest amusement parks on earth—and things were about to get ugly.

The worst part was, he had no one to blame but himself. . . .

Newton, Massachusetts, Three Months Earlier

IN THE BEGINNING, THERE were potato chips.

Well, they weren't exactly potato chips. They came in a little plastic bag and their shape was vaguely chip-like, but that was where the resemblance ended. The ingredients on the bag were printed entirely in Japanese; nobody could say for sure what they were made of. Most of the sixth grade at Nagassack Middle School was convinced it had to be some sort of soy product, though a few rebellious souls maintained that the chips were reconstituted seaweed. Since Charlie's parents were both vegetarians, he'd become pretty adept at identifying seaweed in all its variations. It was actually pretty amazing what you could make out of seaweed. For his part, he was pretty sure that the chips did not come from the ocean. Even the name matched its cartoon-ish appearance—spelled out in bright red block letters splayed across the front and back of the plastic bag with a picture of a lizard sticking its airplane-propeller tongue out at you.

Despite the mysterious ingredients, these Yum Yum Chippers were the only even remotely palatable item left in the vending machine that stood just inside the main entrance to Nagassack Middle School. The Middle School PTA had made sure of that two years earlier, banning soft drinks, sugary snacks, and high-salt treats, all of it swept away after a unanimous vote by the hand-ful of parents and teachers bored enough to spend a sweltering spring Tuesday evening locked away in a middle-school gymnasium.

Of course, the kids hadn't gotten a vote. Instead, they got a vending machine full of rice cakes that tasted like cardboard disks, celery-based snack packs you'd feel bad feeding to a goat, apple slices that went brown the second you opened the biodegradable packaging, and Yum Yum Chippers. Surely, the fact that the school had a vending machine at all, which students were allowed to visit in the brief few minutes between classes, was a luxury that many middle schools had to live without. But that didn't stop anyone from complaining. The sad state of the vending machine was an issue that crossed all class and clique boundaries.

But the political ramifications of the PTA's vote were far from Charlie Lewis's thoughts. Charlie crouched low behind a bright yellow plastic garbage can at the end of a long palisade of aluminum lockers that bisected the school's main entrance. From his vantage point, he had a clear view of the vending machine. And he was mostly hidden from the continuous slipstream of kids moving in through the glass revolving front doors of the building. Five minutes before eight a.m. was the highest traffic period of the day, which was exactly why Charlie had chosen that moment to plan his attempt. He'd never been the type of person who left things to chance.

"How does it look?" he hissed back over his shoulder. "You see any bogies?"

Jeremy Draper leaned out from an alcove three lockers back, his mop of curly red hair flouncing over his freckled face. Jeremy was an exceedingly stringy kid, with pipe-cleaner limbs and a neck that could have doubled as a garden hose. He'd been the tallest kid in their class since the second grade, which might one day be a good thing. Jeremy had been Charlie's best friend since before preschool; their mothers had met in a natural childbirth class in downtown Boston well before they were born, so

Charlie had heard every nickname Jeremy had endured: Scarecrow, Stretch, Plastic Man, String Bean, Bean Pole, Green Bean, and a dozen other variations on "bean." The names had followed Jeremy all the way until the last week of fifth grade, when his school-wide identity had gone through a radical and abrupt change. Unfortunately, the change had not been for the better.

"Watch where you're standing, Diapers!"

Charlie watched as Jeremy dodged his head just in time to avoid the soccer ball tearing by his right ear. The ball ricocheted off one of the lockers, then rebounded back toward the eighth-grade soccer player who had kicked it at him. Jeremy mumbled something toward the kid, purposely too quiet for anyone to hear. Both Jeremy and Charlie had learned early on, it was incredibly hard to fight a nickname, especially one with a backstory as good as Jeremy's.

It had happened nearly five days before the start of the last summer break: Jeremy had been rushing to beat the morning bell, and with legs as long and awkward as his, rushing was never a good idea. To this day, it still wasn't clear whether somebody had tripped him, or whether he'd stumbled over one of his own feet. What was clear, however, was that when he'd hit the ground, Jeremy's backpack had come open, spreading its contents all over the front hall of the school. Not books, not pencils or pens or any other sort of school supply. *Diapers.* At least a dozen, with brightly colored flowers speckled across their fronts, sliding mercilessly across the tiled floor. Nobody cared that Jeremy had a rapidly growing five-week-old baby sister at home, or that his sleep-deprived mother had accidentally packed newly purchased diapers instead of notebooks in Jeremy's bag; all that mattered was that a new nickname had been born. From that moment on, Jeremy Draper had become Diapers.

The eighth grader with the soccer ball dribbled by, and once again the coast looked clear. After a nod from Jeremy, Charlie started forward, inching out of the relative safety provided by the yellow garbage can.

From the long corridor of aluminum lockers, Charlie moved into the brightly lit, semicircular front atrium, which was dominated by the glass revolving doors. Five minutes to the opening bell, the doors were pretty much pinwheels of glass, spitting students into the school's main building in a steady metronome of motion. When the school had been built back in the seventies, it had seemed as good a design as any.

Like most modern interpretations of things that were very old, the Nagassack front entrance didn't make a lot of sense. The revolving door, fluorescent lights, and space-age windows made the place look like one of the high-tech firms out on Route 128. Meanwhile, the wooden rafters, paneled walls, and intensely wild brush that ringed most of the campus made you feel as if you were standing in the foyer of some sort of hunting cabin. Skulking toward the vending machine, Charlie wouldn't have been surprised to have seen moose antlers jutting out from the nearest wall.

Almost there, Charlie mouthed to himself as he covered the last few yards. His sneakers were almost soundless against the tiled floor. He could feel Jeremy's eyes on him from his secure position back by the lockers. *A few more steps.* Charlie could almost make out his reflection in the front glass of the vending machine, and a burst of anticipation moved through him. The machine was more than simply a depository for some bizarre, phenomenally healthy form of snack food. At Nagassack, the vending machine was an anchor in the chaotic, ever-changing flux of life. Only two weeks into sixth grade, the quest for Yum Yum Chippers had become an integral part of Charlie's routine.

He tiptoed the last few feet to the machine. Glancing around to make sure he was still unnoticed, he dug a hand into his back pocket, counting out the proper number of coins. His jeans were loose, which made finding the right coins significantly easier. In point of fact, all his clothes were loose; he was positively swimming in his collared long-sleeve shirt, and his socks were balled up around his ankles. Like his best friend, Jeremy, Charlie had always been too skinny. Up until very recently, that hadn't mattered. Charlie wasn't exactly sure when kids had started to notice how different other kids could be, but things seemed to be getting progressively worse. Not *Lord of the Flies*, fight-to-the-death-on-a-jungle-island worse, but bad enough.

He retrieved the coins from his pocket and quickly shoved them into the slot halfway up the vending machine. Then he hit the correct button with his palm, and watched as the corkscrew mechanism behind the glass slowly twisted the Yum Yum Chippers toward the front. *"Hurry up, hurry up, hurry up."* And then finally, the chips plummeted the few feet to the base of the machine. With a motion like a striking snake, Charlie's right arm shot out and into the machine's retrieval bin, and his fingers closed on the smooth, crinkly surface of the Yum Yum Chippers bag. Grinning, Charlie turned back toward Jeremy and the safety of the lockers.

"Well, look what we have here. My favorite little buddy with my favorite snack."

Charlie exhaled as he looked up into the oblong,

doughy face of Dylan Wigglesworth. He could hear Liam Anthony and Dusty Bickle cackling from somewhere behind their leader, but he couldn't see past the mountainous giant's hulking form.

"Dylan, doesn't this get old after a while?"

Charlie tried to sound tough, but inside, he was mostly liquid. It was true, this *had* been going on for quite a while now; after all, he, Dylan, and most of his class at Nagassack had been going to school together since kindergarten. In the beginning, they had all been roughly the same size, and Dylan had simply been a run-of-the-mill jerk, making fun of Charlie and pretty much everyone else, just for the sheer pleasure of it. But as their physical geometry changed, and Dylan grew and grew and grew, the tenor of their relationship had also changed. Dylan had morphed into an out-and-out bully. If you didn't play baseball, you were a fair target. And since Charlie had never hit or caught a ball and had basically avoided any kind of object thrown in his general direction since he was about three years old, he was extremely high on Dylan's list.

"Okay, Numbers," Dylan grunted. "You know the drill. Hand over the chips."

Charlie could feel other eyes on him, and not just Liam's and Dusty's. A small crowd had materialized in the front entrance, as it always seemed to do when something like this happened. Charlie knew that Jeremy was somewhere in that crowd, probably quivering with the urge to do something. Charlie also knew that Jeremy wouldn't dare.

If this had been some after-school special, or a movie aimed at middle-school kids, this would have been the moment when Charlie Lewis would have become a "man." He'd have said something witty, tossed the chips into the air, then given Dylan the thrashing of a lifetime. Or perhaps he would've said something charming, maybe talk about their shared childhood, and the two of them would have hugged, friends once more.

Instead, Charlie lowered his eyes as he held the bag of chips out in front of him. Dylan grunted again, disdain written across his face. To him, Charlie was nobody, nothing, just another nerd or geek or dork. He wasn't even Charlie Lewis, he was Numbers. Just some kid who was good at math but couldn't catch a baseball.

"Yeah, that's what I thought."

Dylan roughly grabbed the bag out of Charlie's hand, then showed it to Liam and Dusty behind him.

"Looks like breakfast is on Numbers," he said, laughing. The others joined in, along with some of the watching crowd.

Charlie sighed. He was about to slink away, when a flash of motion came from Dylan's left, and the scene suddenly froze like it was painted on a pane of glass.

Dylan's eyes went wide as he watched a hand reach out and grab the bag of chips right out of his pincerlike grip. Both he and Charlie turned at the same time to see two kids who had suddenly materialized, as if out of thin air, right next to them. It took Charlie a full beat to recognize the kid standing closest to them, who was now holding the Yum Yum Chippers in his extended right hand. The kid was wearing a faded leather flight jacket and stylish black jeans, and had a wide grin on his angular face.

"Looks like we got a situation here," he said through his grin. "One bag of chips, two hungry sixth graders. A real cluster jam of supply and demand. So how are we going to work this out?"

Charlie could tell that Dylan was just as flabbergasted as he was; Dylan's mouth was wide open, his lower lips starting to quiver. The watching crowd had gone silent as well.

Everyone at Nagassack knew who Finn Carter was—at least everyone had heard of the seventh grader, even if many had hardly ever seen him in person. He was one of those kids who Charlie had heard whispers about for as long as he could remember. Crazy smart, a boy genius who had been bumped up in classes since the third grade; but nobody would have ever called Finn Carter a nerd. Athletic, handsome, taller than average, with limbs as chiseled and taut as his prominent cheekbones and triangle chin. Finn had been captain of the Nagassack swim team for three years in a row and had been widely considered the best swimmer in Eastern Massachusetts since winning a state championship in fifth grade. Just last year, Finn had taken his team all the way to the national finals, himself the front-runner in four different swimming styles. The team was set to take victory at the meet. And then something happened. The final day of competition, the morning of the main team relay that would have secured Nagassack the gold medal and its first national victory in school history, and Finn hadn't showed up. It had been one heck of scandal at the time. Nobody had been quite sure what had happened. Finn had never spoken about it, never given an excuse, never given any sort of apology. Finn had simply not shown up.

And that's where most of the whispers about Finn Carter had ended. Finn had been like a ghost at Nagassack from that moment on, a kid you just didn't see in the hall or pass on your way to class. In fact, this was the first time that Charlie had seen the seventh grader up close. Dark hair in jaunty waves, falling down over his tan forehead. Ski slope cheekbones, and that knife-sharp, angled chin. Eyes the shape of almonds. Up close, Finn looked kind of like an anime character from a Japanese manga. Finn was an enigma in black jeans and a distressed leather flight jacket.

"What do you think, Magic," Finn continued, this time over his left shoulder, to the other kid standing behind him. "Should I get all Solomon in the situation, cut the bag in half and let the chips fall where they may? Or does might make right?"

Charlie looked past Finn, to the fireplug of a kid standing a few feet behind him. Finn was a mystery, a kid you just didn't see day-to-day at Nagassack; but Michael Buster, the Magic Bus, or usually just Magic, was someone you simply couldn't miss. Another seventh grader like Finn, Magic was also a standout personality at the school, but for very different reasons. Magic was a notorious class clown, a bit of a loudmouth, and sometimes even a bad seed. Even though Magic was short for his age, he was built like a battering ram, with a flat cube of a head and legs like tree stumps, and he wore a daily uniform of brightly colored tie-dyed shirts, always paired with cargo shorts. He'd been sent home for ignoring the school's dress code so many times that teachers had finally just given up. Along the way, Magic had racked up more detention hours than anyone else in the history of Nagassack. Magic had received his nickname during one such Saturday morning spent in school-ordained captivity, using the opportunity to try out a routine he had learned online—something involving a pair of chameleons borrowed from the science room and a top hat with a secret compartment sewn into the lining. Of course, the trick had gone horribly wrong; to this day, the lizards were thought to be living somewhere in the rafters of the school. And Magic had earned himself three more weeks of detention along with his brand-new nom de plume.

At the moment, Magic was grinning almost as widely as his friend Finn while he stepped forward, poking a stumpy finger into Dylan's chest.

"We could wrestle for it. I'm not sure I'm in this one's weight class, but I'm willing to make a go of it."

There was sweat beading on Dylan's upper lip. Charlie could see that his nemesis was more than a little bit put off by the presence of the two older kids. Even though Dylan was bigger than both of them, and he had his two buddies behind him, the two seventh graders were an imposing sight. Magic was thickly built and, more important, didn't seem to care about getting in trouble. And Finn was a mystery. At the moment, there was a frightening spark in those almond eyes. Something was going on here that Charlie did not understand. And if Charlie didn't understand it, Dylan certainly would be beyond lost.

"Keep the chips," Dylan finally growled. He stepped away from Magic's finger, then gave Charlie a final look. "We'll talk again later, Numbers."

With that, Dylan turned and stalked away. Liam and Dusty follow dutifully behind. Eventually, the crowd of onlookers disbursed. Charlie wanted to leave too. Really, he wanted to turn and run as fast as he could, but the two seventh graders were still standing in front of him. So he just stood there, waiting.

When the crowd was mostly gone, Finn showed him an amiable smile.

"Here you go, champ," Finn said. "But you really should be more careful about what you put into your body."

He tossed the bag of chips to Charlie. It hit Charlie in the chest, and he made a grab for it, but of course the bag fell right through his fingers. As he bent down to pick it up, he noticed Finn's military-style boots, and Magic's flip-flops. *Another Saturday detention waiting to happen.*

"Uh, thanks."

Charlie straightened back up, clearing his throat as he tried to think of what to say. It was a bizarre situation, the two seventh graders acting like Good Samaritans in a place that was pretty short on random acts of kindness. Charlie glanced past them and caught sight of Jeremy. Jeremy was shooting him a look that was easy to read: *Get the heck out of there, man, before something else happens!* But Charlie was frozen in place.

"Don't let that jerk get you down," Finn responded, still smiling. "Guys like him spend their lives trying to prove something. Guys like us, well, we don't have anything to prove."

Charlie raised his eyebrows. *Guys like us?* Up until this moment, he would never have imagined that Finn would even know who he was. And even if the older kid somehow recognized Charlie from some school photo album, what could they possibly have in common?

"Well," Charlie murmured. "I certainly appreciate the help. I'm just glad you happened to be walking by."

"With a name like Numbers, you can't possibly believe in coincidences, can you?"

Charlie's mouth opened, but he didn't know what to say. He wasn't sure what Finn meant by the question. He glanced up at the clock fixed into one of the wooden rafters near the ceiling, saw that it was barely a minute before the morning bell, but he still felt rooted in place.

"Numbers isn't really my name."

"We know who you are, Charlie. And we know why they call you that. We're just here, making conversation."

And suddenly, at that moment, the shrill sound of the morning bell reverberated through the front atrium. A shiver moved down Charlie's spine, not entirely due to the metallic vibration from the bell. The situation was getting stranger by the second. Charlie cast another look at Jeremy, saw his friend waving his spindly arms, gesturing that they were going to be late. Maybe Finn and Magic didn't care about getting detentions, but Charlie had never been in trouble in his life.

"Okay, then. We should be on our way to class. Thanks again, and I guess I owe you guys."

"If you really mean that," Finn said, sliding his hands into the pockets of his leather jacket, "there is a way you could pay us back."

"It's just a bag of potato chips," Charlie started, but Finn laughed. Magic reached out and gave Charlie's shoulder a friendly squeeze.

"Relax, kid," Magic said. "We're not here to give you a hard time. We just want to invite you to join us on a little excursion this Saturday."

"I assume you're free?" Finn added, arching an eyebrow.

The morning bell went silent, the metallic sound still echoing in Charlie's ears.

"This Saturday?" he asked. "I mean, I've got a lot of homework, and I think my parents might have something planned—"

"I totally understand," Finn interrupted, shrugging amiably. "But if you change your mind, or somehow find some free time—the Sherwood Halloween Fair. Ever heard of it?"

Charlie blinked. Of course he had heard of the Sherwood Halloween Fair. The annual fall carnival was one of the highlights of the season. Although it was a weak little sibling to the larger carnivals in places like Salem or Concord, the Sherwood Fair was less than twenty minutes from Nagassack, and certainly worth the brief car trip and the five-dollar entrance fee.

"Sure," Charlie said. "What about it?"

Finn smiled again—then suddenly turned and headed toward the revolving glass door that led out of the school, Magic right behind him. Two minutes *after* the morning bell, classes already probably starting, and the two seventh graders were heading outside.

"If you finish your homework," Finn responded as he

entered the glass revolving door, "meet us at Sherwood, and you'll find out. By the midway games, say two p.m."

With that, in a swirl of glass and distressed leather, Finn was gone. Magic gave Charlie a final wave, then followed his mysterious friend into the revolving door.

"Enjoy your chips, Charlie."

Charlie watched Magic's flip-flops as they vanished within a whirl of motion. Alone by the vending machine, he could barely feel the bag of chips against his palm. He shook his head, then quickly rejoined Jeremy by the lockers.

"What was that all about?" Jeremy asked as they started toward their first-period class.

"I have no idea," Charlie answered truthfully.

But deep down, Charlie was more than a little curious. He thought about what Finn had said, about there being no such things as coincidences. If Finn and Magic hadn't run into him by the vending machine randomly, well, the whole scene didn't make much sense.

"We're going to be late," Jeremy grumbled, propelling himself forward on his giraffelike legs.

Charlie followed two steps behind, still lost in thought.

He couldn't shake the feeling. Something big was about to happen.

3

GREEN.

A lush and brilliant interlocking tapestry of green, flashing by at close to thirty mph. Charlie felt himself disappearing into that deep well of color as he pressed his face against the cold glass window. Ten days after Labor Day and the trees had not yet begun to change, but the colors seemed all the more intense because they were now so temporary. A few more weeks and the green would give way to an entirely different palette, reds and yellows and browns, nature's fireworks painted in strokes of leaf and daggers of bark.

"The turn should be right up here," Charlie's dad interrupted. "Unless we passed it already. I mean, I guess we could have passed it. But if we passed it, we can just turn around at the next mile marker. Still, I'm pretty sure it's right up here."

Charlie closed his eyes, pressing his face harder against the glass. An unintentional smile flickered across his lips. Even with his eyes closed, he knew that his dad was poking at the GPS control panel with one hand while tapping nervously at the steering wheel with the other. The GPS, of course, had been turned off the entire drive over from their house. His dad never used it until they were within spitting distance of their destination. Not because he had confidence in his sense of direction—in fact, quite the opposite. Charlie's dad could get lost trying to find his way out of a cardboard box. It was just that he didn't seem to remember the car even had a GPS until it was usually too late.

That was the thing with genius; it often had zero application in real life. His dad was a double PhD in physics and engineering, a tenured professor at MIT, one of the top scientists in New England, and he still had no idea how to work the most basic functions of his two-year-old Volvo. Even worse, he had made this trip at least once a year since Charlie was five. Usually, Charlie's mom was in the front passenger seat, navigating. Today, Charlie was glad that his mom has been too busy getting her latest paper ready for publication, because it was going to be a lot easier to ditch his dad, rather than both his parents together, when they reached the fair. Not that his mom was any less oblivious than his scientist father. She was Charlie's dad's equal in most respects. Two PhDs, in biology and virology, and just as much difficulty in dealing with the most basic elements of day-to-day life. Charlie's mom could write papers that led to lifesaving drugs for cancer patients, but the last time she'd packed Charlie's lunch for school, he'd opened up the brown bag to find two uncooked eggs and a piece of toast buttered with cottage cheese.

Even so, the two parents together might have wondered why Charlie had been so insistent on going to the Sherwood Halloween Fair that particular Saturday afternoon. There were still a good eight weeks until Halloween, and though the fair opened on Labor Day, it didn't really get going until halfway through October. Luckily, Charlie's dad hadn't bothered to ask why Charlie had wanted to make the trip. He'd just smiled and retrieved the keys to the car.

"Of course," his dad continued, still tapping the steering wheel and the GPS, "we could always stop at a gas station and ask directions. But then we'd have to find a gas station. I'm not even sure there is a gas station this close to Sherwood."

Charlie watched more green go by. There really wasn't much of anything in Sherwood. The center of town, which they'd passed a few miles back, consisted of a tiny little diner, an even smaller general store, a brightly lit Dairy Queen, and a pair of competing real estate offices. The whole place had a blink-and-you'll-miss-it sort of feel, and the only time anyone mentioned Sherwood was around Halloween.

"Dad!"

Charlie pointed toward the windshield, just in case his father somehow didn't see the banner a dozen feet ahead, stretched out between two telephone poles. The words themselves, SHERWOOD COUNTRY HALLOWEEN FAIR, fit on the sign because someone had drawn the letters too large, but the orange and black colors made it crystal clear that they had arrived at the right place.

Charlie's dad relaxed, navigating the Volvo the last few yards, and then he turned onto a packed dirt road. A makeshift parking lot opened up in front of them. At two in the afternoon, the lot was about half full; as the season progressed, the place would become so jammed with cars, they would eventually start turning people away. The fair didn't have anywhere near the cachet or reputation of the much bigger Halloween carnivals, but for this leafy area, it was pretty much the only game in town.

After they parked, Charlie followed his dad toward the front entrance to the fairground. A picket fence ended in an open barn-style gate, next to which sat the windowed ticket kiosk, run by a handful of teenagers in matching orange-and-black T-shirts.

"Five bucks," his dad mumbled as he paid the entrance fee. "Seems like it goes up every year."

Actually, it had been five dollars a ticket for as long as Charlie could remember, but complaining about the fee was one of his dad's favorite rituals. Charlie's parents often complained about money. With two tenured professor salaries and only one child, they were far from poor, but they'd always found comfort in the practice of living on a strict budget. Charlie had definitely inherited some of their conservative ideology; he had been saving most of his weekly allowance for years, and now there was a cardboard box under his bed with almost nine hundred dollars hidden inside. Jeremy, the only person who knew about the cardboard box, had often asked Charlie to take the stacks of five- and ten-dollar bills out when he came over, just to see what they'd look like piled up together on Charlie's bed. Most months, Jeremy didn't get an allowance; Jeremy was one of a handful of kids at Nagassack Middle School who was there on student aid. Jeremy's dad was an assistant manager at the local

Shaw's supermarket, and his mom had left nursing when she had given birth to Jeremy's baby sister.

"You can't put a price on fun, can you, Dad?" Charlie responded as they stepped past the ticket booth and looked out across the fairground.

And indeed, if you were putting a price on fun, the Sherwood Halloween Fair would've been on the low end of that monetary scale. Aside from the assorted booths hawking cotton candy, roasted peanuts, foot-long sausages, and Halloween friendly balloons depicting everything from ghosts and witches to cartoon characters, the only two true highlights of the fair were readily visible even from the front entrance.

Directly to Charlie's left, just inside the gate, was the Haunted Hayride. Basically the hayride consisted of a tractor hauling an oversize wagon piled with hay. The ride lasted about ten minutes and followed a figure-eight dirt track that stretched out across the farmland adjacent to the parking area. Assorted papier-mâché dioramas dotted either side of the track, things like skeletons hanging from trees and scarecrows dangling from iron hooks. But the real haunting was enacted by a handful of teenagers dressed as ghosts, who were getting paid to run alongside the wagon, shouting at the passengers inside. The ride was actually pretty scary—until you turned about eight years old; then it was just plain uncomfortable, bouncing around that hard flatbed, hay jabbing at any exposed skin, while teenagers yelled at you.

The second main attraction was on the far side of the park; Charlie could just make out the top of the enormous Ferris wheel from where he was standing next to his dad, and he had to admit, it was pretty impressive. Strung with thousands of multicolored lights, at night you could see the Ferris wheel through the trees from miles away. The fact that the carnival even had a Ferris wheel was pretty surprising; there weren't any other rides to speak of, unless you counted the ponies in the petting area off to Charlie's right. But the Ferris wheel was enough to keep people coming back, even if they had to wait thirty minutes in line for the eight-minute journey.

"What time did Jeremy say he was going to meet you?" Charlie's dad said as they both moved through the open gate.

"Two," Charlie answered. "He's probably already on line at the wheel. We'll wave to you from the top."

Charlie didn't feel good about lying to his father, but he wasn't quite sure how to explain what he was really doing at the Sherwood Fair. The truth was, *he* didn't even know why he was there. The more he thought about the strange meeting at the vending machine, the less he understood. More than once, he had decided to ignore the whole incident. But eventually, his curiosity had gotten the best of him.

"And you have enough money to enjoy yourself until we meet back at the car?"

Charlie patted his jeans pocket. He'd brought thirty dollars from his stash, more than enough for a hot dog, ice cream, and maybe a couple of rides on the wheel. Although he couldn't imagine that Finn and Magic had invited him to the fair to take a ride on a Ferris wheel.

"Okay, man. You know where to find me when you're done."

Charlie's dad gave his shoulder a squeeze, then wandered off toward the concession tent. Charlie felt another pang of guilt as he watched his dad go; he knew that lots of kids his age didn't have nearly as much independence as he did. Part of that was probably because he was an only child; sometimes his parents went out of their way to make him feel like they were his friends and not just authority figures. And the other part was because his dad was on the older side; he'd had Charlie when he was in his early forties. Or maybe it was just his dad's "absentminded professor" personality. Whatever the reason, Charlie had a lot of freedom, and he didn't usually abuse the privileges that came with it.

Charlie waited until his father had reached the concession tent and had become absorbed by the menu hanging over an ice-cream counter before he started on his way deeper into the fairground.

The farther he went into the carnival, the more crowded the place became. Mostly kids—mostly teenagers, at that, in pairs and in groups. A large portion of the other kids were dressed like him, jeans and sweatshirts, light jackets, but a few were definitely getting into the spirit of the thing. From face paint, all the way up to the kinds of costumes you had to go into the city to buy. Television characters, political figures, and then all the standards: witches and goblins and monsters of various sizes and shapes.

Charlie was so busy looking at all the costumes, he almost walked right past the wooden sign hanging between two poles, set about eight feet off the ground, pointing toward the entrance to a brightly colored tent. Charlie almost laughed out loud, thinking that he was more like his father than he realized; really, the sign should have been hard to miss. It was at least five feet long, and the letters emblazoned across the wood were in a font that was supposed to mimic Old English:

Midway Games

Being the kind of kid that he was, Charlie had headed straight to the school library after his chance meeting with Finn. He'd heard the word before, "midway," and he had a vague idea of what it meant. Midway games were essentially carnival games, the things he'd been playing since he was little, the games that most kids looked forward to when they went to fairs and carnivals. The ring toss, baseballs thrown at milk bottles, coins thrown at ceramic plates, fishing poles used to catch plastic fish, water guns shot into the mouths clowns, etc., etc., etc. But even knowing the definition of the word— well, it seemed like such a strange thing for Finn to have mentioned as a meeting place at the Halloween Fair. So Charlie had decided to add to his knowledge with a little extra research.

It hadn't taken him more than twenty minutes at a computer in the library to find out pretty much all there was to know about midway games. He had been surprised to find that they dated a whole lot further back than he'd realized, all the way to the Renaissance, a time period near the end of the Middle Ages that conjured up visions of lavish artwork and royal courts often throwing elaborate masquerade parties. At some point during those elaborate royal parties, it turned out, jousting and swordfights had given way to simpler games involving cards, wheels, balls—things that people could play that didn't lead to loss of limbs.

Hundreds of years later, these games made their way to America. Then, in the late nineteenth century, the city of Chicago was home to a World's Fair, during which the first Ferris wheel debuted. The modern versions of the Renaissance games had been set up to entertain the people waiting for their turn on the wheel, and from that moment, the name Midway stuck, in tribute to the area of Chicago where the fair had taken place.

Midway games had become standard at every fair, carnival, and circus. Charlie didn't know anyone who hadn't tried his hand at tossing a ring around the neck of a bottle at least once, or knocking a pyramid of milk bottles down with a baseball.

Stepping through the threshold of the tent, Charlie felt a familiar tweak of excitement as his eyes took in the various games spread out across the tent's vast interior. The first thing that struck him were all the colors, from the huge stuffed animals that hung in tethered clusters above the various gaming booths, to the lights that were strung along every table, post, and pole in the tent. So much color, it was almost hard to concentrate on any one thing for very long. Adding to the visual cacophony, the air was thick with the mixed scent of cotton candy, spilled soda, and sawdust from the floor.

Once he'd gotten acclimated to the scene, Charlie began to chart out the area around him. Ever since he was little, he'd had the strange habit of seeing the world numerically; looking around the tent was like looking at a scene as if it were drawn on graph paper. Three squares to his left was a ringtoss setup, a waist-high counter overlooking a low platform covered in dozens of empty soda bottles packed tightly together. Three kids were playing the game at the same time, tossing plastic rings toward the tops of the pins, as a carnival worker, a "carny," watched with a bored smirk. Hanging from the ceiling, three imaginary graph paper squares above the pins, was one of the many elevated jungles of stuffed animals: monkeys, lions, tigers, and even a couple of oversize giraffes, a few swinging so low on their plastic tethers that the kids playing the game had to toss the rings at ridiculous angles just to avoid hitting them.

Two squares to Charlie's right, there stood a standard milk-bottle game: another waist-high counter, this one facing an expanse of dirt that ended in a small stage, on which stood a pyramid made up of six oversize milk bottles, three on the bottom, two above that, and one on top. A teenager was standing by the counter, holding three baseballs in his hands. As Charlie watched, he threw the balls one at a time at the bottles. His first two throws missed entirely. His third caught the bottom left bottle directly in the center, and the kid shouted with joy. For a brief second, it looked like he'd win the game, that all six bottles would go down, but when the dust cleared, one of the three bottom bottles was still standing, and the carny shrugged. As the kid turned away from the counter, dejected, the carny began restacking the bottles.

Charlie moved deeper into the tent, passing more games, mentally graphing everything he was seeing. Next to the ringtoss was a horse race waiting for players, consisting of eight water guns lined up next to one another above another low counter, each facing a target that, when hit with water, made a little wooden horse move across a scoreboard hanging along the back wall. A teenage carny with a microphone stood by the dormant horses, ready to announce the game. Just beyond the horse race, Charlie saw a basketball toss, a hoop high up on a wooden frame, in front of a group of teenagers arguing over who was going to chance a shot first. Charlie watched as they finally came to an agreement, and the biggest of the group took aim, hurled a basketball in a perfect arc at the hoop, only to shout in anger as the ball ricocheted off the rim with an ugly clang.

"Don't feel bad for him, Charlie. LeBron James couldn't make that shot in ten tries."

Charlie turned to see Finn off to his left, lounging back against one of the waist-high counters, which overlooked what appeared to be a coin-toss game. Charlie could hear oversize coins bouncing off ceramic plates on the other side of the counter as a pair of older kids with their backs to him played the game a few feet to Finn's left.

"It doesn't look that tough," Charlie finally responded. "The basket isn't nearly as high as a real one."

"Oh, it's not tough. It's *impossible*. Or nearly impossible. The hoop isn't a circle, it's an oval. An optical illusion, really. Makes you think it's closer than it is, and that the ball is small enough to go through easily."

Charlie watched as another shot clanged off the rim, this one bouncing so high, it smacked another group of stuffed animals hanging from the ceiling. Then he crossed to where Finn was standing.

"I guess I never noticed," Charlie said. He could feel his nerves going off, and he felt incredibly self-conscious around the older, more self-assured kid. Finn was dressed pretty much the same as he had been before, leather jacket, dark jeans, but this time he was wearing a Red Sox baseball hat low over his eyes, and his hands were jammed into the pockets of his coat. He looked different, somehow, but Charlie couldn't quite put his finger on why.

"You're not supposed to notice. You're supposed to think you can win. That's how all these games work, Charlie. It's all about perception."

Finn glanced toward the two teenagers a few feet over at the counter, their backs still toward Charlie. Charlie followed his gaze. The teenagers were leaning forward, taking turns tossing gold-colored coins at the shiny porcelain plates that were glued to multi-tiered platforms spread out across a large rectangular area below. No matter how the teenagers tossed the coins, the results seemed to be the same; the coins were noisily bouncing and ricocheting all over the place and eventually landing on the packed dirt floor beneath the platforms. A carny was standing beneath another hanging bloom of stuffed animals, watching with a smirk on his face. The teenagers didn't seem to mind that they kept losing; they were both laughing as they played, and when one ran out of coins, he reached into his pocket and pulled out a pink ticket, which the carny exchanged for three more of the oversize coins.

"So," Charlie said when Finn finally turned his

attention back in Charlie's direction. "What exactly are we doing here? And where's Magic?"

Finn smiled.

"He's around. We're here to win prizes, like everyone else. Maybe a nice giraffe to keep you company on the ride home?"

Charlie wasn't quite sure how to respond to that, but before he had to think of something to say, Finn leaned in close.

"Oh, and when you see Magic, you don't know him."

At first, Charlie thought the older kid was joking, but the look on his face was completely serious.

"I don't know him?"

"Nope. And his name's not Magic."

Charlie cleared his throat.

"It's not?"

"And I'm not Finn."

This was getting stranger by the minute.

"Who are you?"

"I'm Billy Logan. I go to Ashbury Middle School in Wellesley."

Charlie watched as one of the teenagers exchanged another ticket for more coins.

"So you're Billy," he said to Finn, who nodded.

"Yep."

"And who am I?"

Finn raised an eyebrow beneath the rim of his baseball hat.

"You? You're you."

"I don't get a fake name?"

"Why would you need a fake name?"

Charlie paused.

"I don't know."

Finn laughed, then turned suddenly and gestured toward the carny manning the coin toss game. The carny strolled over, and Finn handed him a pink ticket, getting three of the gold-colored coins. Then Finn looked at Charlie.

Charlie started to reach into his pocket.

"I need to go to the ticket booth," he started.

Finn stopped him with one hand, holding his other hand down at his waist, low enough that the guy working the game couldn't see. In his palm was a roll of pink tickets at least three inches thick.

"This should cover you for a while."

Wow. There had to be enough tickets in the roll to play fifty times. Charlie looked at Finn, wondering if he should really take them. Finn's face was unreadable, but there was something in his eyes that told Charlie to just go with it. So he took the tickets, tore one off, and handed it to the carny.

The gold coins felt cold against his palm. They were slightly larger than quarters, with some heft to them.

"You go first," Finn said, stepping back to give Charlie room.

Charlie looked out over the field of plates. He'd played the game before, on previous visits to the fair and at other carnivals over the years. Of course, it was easy to hit the plates—you didn't even really have to aim to hit a plate—but to win, you had to actually get a coin to stay on the plate, which was really hard. In fact, Charlie had never actually won anything at the game. A chart on the wall showed the prize list. One coin on a plate got you the smallest-size stuffed animal, which was little bigger than his hand. Two coins won a medium-size critter, one of the monkeys or skunks. Three coins got you a giraffe. Charlie had never seen anyone walk out of the midway games with a giraffe. But who knew, maybe today would be his lucky day.

He licked his lips, concentrating on the nearest set of plates. Focusing all his attention on the glossy center of the highest one, he took a deep breath and tossed the first coin in a nice soft arc toward the plate.

There was a loud clack, and the coin bounced up

into the air, twisting and turning, then dropped off toward the floor. Charlie cursed to himself, glancing at Finn. Finn shrugged, and Charlie turned back toward the plates, readying his second coin. He narrowed his eyes, aimed right for the same plate, and *clack*, again, his coin bounced up into the air, ricocheted off the bottom of one of the hanging giraffes, and disappeared to the floor.

He didn't even concentrate on the third throw, he just let fly. The coin clattered from plate to plate like a stone skipping across a lake, then vanished off the edge. Charlie sighed, stepping back. Finn patted his shoulder.

"Hey, at least you hit the plates."

Finn took Charlie's place at the counter, and gave him a little wink.

"Like I said, it's all about perception. To me, those plates are as big as the moon."

His right arm shot out, and with a flick of his wrist, he let fly one of the gold-colored coins. The coin arced almost straight up, then came down at a very sharp angle. There was a tiny clack as the coin hit one of the plates—and stopped dead, flat against the porcelain, directly in the center. The two teenagers, still watching from a few feet away, applauded, and the carny gave Finn a smile.

"Nice shot, kid. That's one. Good luck on your second—"

Before he could finish speaking, Finn's wrist flicked again, and a second coin flashed through the air. Up, up, up, arcing so high, it seemed to almost disappear into the jungle of stuffed animals hanging from the ceiling. Then it reappeared, heading almost straight down toward the plates. It landed on the same plate as the first coin, just a few centimeters from the center, and stuck just like the other coin, dead flat against the plate. The teenagers cheered. Charlie stared at the two coins, then looked at Finn.

"That was amazing."

Finn laughed.

"Why, you think it's hard to hit the moon from a few feet away?"

He tossed the third coin from his left hand to his right, held it up to show Charlie how it gleamed in the colored lights strewn along the tent struts, then flicked his wrist a third time. The coin shot through the air, again a nearly vertical path, and descended onto the same plate once again, clacking right between the two other coins. It didn't bounce or ricochet, it just stuck there, planted like a flag on the moon.

"Holy smokes," one of the teenagers croaked.

The carny stared at Finn, then reached above his head and pulled one of the stuffed giraffes free from where it was hanging. He crossed to Finn and handed him the stuffed animal. Finn took it with both hands. It was so big, Finn had to crane his neck to see past the thing's body.

"Pleasure doing business with you," he joked. The carnival worker gave him a steady look.

"Everyone gets lucky once in a while, kid. What's your name?"

"Billy," Finn said, smartly. Then he turned and walked away from the counter. Charlie followed.

"How did you do that? You landed your first three coins. Was that some sort of trick?"

Finn waited until they were far enough away from the coin-toss game before he leaned past the giraffe, close to Charlie's ear.

"It's not a trick. It's math, chemistry, and a little physics."

"What?"

"There he is. This should be fun to watch."

Finn pointed with a giraffe foot, and Charlie saw Magic leaning up against another counter. This game was just as familiar as the rest, a balloon-popping game that consisted of a high wall covered in brightly colored balloons. Kids behind the counter, located about five feet from the wall, threw darts at the balloons, trying to pop them for prizes. Charlie counted four kids taking turns tossing darts, but no matter how hard the kids were throwing them, the results were always the same. The darts either missed the balloons, or hit them and bounced right off. As far as Charlie could tell, you had to hit the things straight on with enough force, and nobody seemed to be able to do so.

Magic was standing a foot back from the other kids, just watching them throw. He had three darts in his left hand, down low against his side. He looked like he was waiting his turn.

When there was a lull in the throwing, he stepped forward, passed one of the darts from his left to right hand, and took aim. His hand jerked forward, and the dart whipped through the air. It hit one of the balloons dead-on and there was a loud pop.

All the other kids turned to look. Magic just smiled, took aim with a second dart, and tossed it just like the first. There was another pop, a second balloon bursting into nothingness. Before anyone could react, the third dart was in the air. And again, *pop!* A third balloon disintegrated.

There was a moment's silence, then applause. The

carny running the game gave Magic a look very similar to the look Finn had gotten from the coin-toss carny, then yanked an identical oversize giraffe from the jungle hanging above his head.

Magic grabbed the stuffed animal from him, slung it over his shoulder, and turned toward Finn.

"Hey, Billy," he said, rather loudly. "Just finished up here. Mom and Dad are probably waiting in the parking lot, so we better get going."

He and Finn headed for the exit to the tent, giraffes in hand. Charlie had to skip to keep up, they were moving so fast. His mind was whirling. As the carny had told Finn, everyone got lucky sooner or later, sure. But was it just a double display of luck that he had just witnessed? Charlie's number-obsessed mind was constantly calculating odds: little things, like what were the chances a particular color bird might fly by at a particular moment, or what were the chances of seeing someone he knew in a particular department store. Calculating these odds, well, it seemed really improbable. And the sure way both Finn and Magic had approached the games, the seeming ease in which they had thrown the coins and darts, it didn't make sense. Then he thought back to what Finn had said right before they'd run into Magic. *It's math, chemistry, and a little physics.* What did that mean?

He caught up to the older kids just as they passed through the threshold of the tent, and cleared his throat.

"You use math to win stuffed animals?" he asked.

Finn stopped, then turned and suddenly handed him the giraffe.

"We use math to win a whole lot more than stuffed animals. Or at least, we will. With your help."

Charlie felt his heart pounding in his chest. He had no idea what the older kid was talking about, but he could feel the electricity on his skin, the way Finn's words seemed to charge the very air between them. Before he could respond, Finn and Magic were moving away. Charlie finally found his voice.

"Why me?"

The two seventh graders just kept on moving. Magic gave Charlie a little wave over his right shoulder as they went.

"We'll be in touch, kid."

And with that, they were gone. Charlie was left standing, bewildered, at the entrance to the midway games, bathed in the colored lights of the circus tent, an oversize stuffed giraffe held tight against his chest.

4

HEY, JUST BE GLAD it's not snowing. And if we die out here, at least we won't have to take Mr. Marshall's social studies exam."

Charlie grimaced as he yanked the collar of his down jacket up as high as it would go. He was shivering so hard that he could hear his teeth clattering together, and it felt like the bones in his cheeks had turned to ice. It wasn't supposed to be this cold so early in the fall—but then again, growing up in New England, the seasons had always seemed to rage over the calendar like hurricane-driven white-water rapids. The best you could do was dress the part. Today, for Charlie, that meant a navy blue down coat that made him look like a blueberry Michelin Man, thick jeans tucked into thermal socks, and stiff work boots that kept his toes warm but left blisters on his heels the size of golf balls. All things considered, he'd rather have dressed normally and stayed inside.

Unfortunately, staying inside wasn't an option at eleven thirty a.m., because that was the beginning of the sixth-grade lunch period. Which meant that if he wanted to eat, he had to line up outside, single file, on a covered double-wide sidewalk, and wait his turn to pick up a plastic tray from a stack by the propped-open double doors leading inside. It seemed crazy, having an outdoor entrance to a lunchroom in New England, and every year, the school administration made plans to shift the waiting area to somewhere more reasonable. But for some reason, these plans never came to fruition. There was always some other construction project or school addition that took precedent. Charlie secretly believed the school wanted them put on ice before lunch—better to keep them from turning into wild animals in the relatively free time between classes.

Once Charlie claimed a tray and a battered fork and knife, he'd get to make his way inside. But for the moment, from where Charlie was standing—still twenty feet from the double doors, wedged between Jeremy and a British exchange student named Niles who was quietly cursing to himself as he bounced from foot to foot in a useless effort to stay warm—it seemed like they'd be stuck outside forever. Charlie would have gladly taken three of Mr. Marshall's notoriously tricky social studies exams in exchange for a trip to the front of the lunch line—or a pair of better fitting boots.

"If you die first," he said, eyeing Jeremy's high-top Converse sneakers—obviously a hand-me-down from some cousin somewhere, so scuffed and worn they looked as comfortable as cotton, "can I have your shoes?"

"Don't you get your allowance next week? Make me an offer. I don't need all my toes."

Charlie laughed. The thought of his allowance cheered him, because it meant another month had gone by, and the deeper he moved into sixth grade, the more routine and comfortable middle school was beginning to feel. It was already the last Thursday in September. After the bizarre and electrifying afternoon at the Halloween fair, life had almost instantly returned to the uneventful and warmly monotonous rhythm of another school year. Middle school felt just like elementary school, from the bus picking him up at his suburban home in a leafy cul-de-sac near the Newton-Wellesley line, to Jeremy and Charlie's daily assault on the vending machine. And then after homeroom, the relentless hop from class to class, most of it mindless swatches of time to Charlie, because he was too far ahead of the curve and too smart to open his mouth when the teachers asked questions. He knew what it was like to be the kid who gave the right answer too many times.

As fascinating as the Halloween Fair with Finn and Magic had been, that had seemed to be the end of the bizarre episode; despite Magic's farewell words, the two seventh graders had made no attempt to contact Charlie, nor had he seen either kid in the hallways in school. And the further away from that afternoon Charlie got, the more okay he was with the idea that it was just some strange moment in his life, insignificant and soon forgotten. After two weeks, the thrill of that moment had begun to fade. The more Charlie thought about what he'd seen, the more reluctant he was to delve much deeper into the matter.

It's just math, chemistry, and a little physics.

In Charlie's mind, there were a few too many problems with what Finn had implied with that cryptic statement. To use math to beat carnival games suggested the games had a predictive nature about them—that the games themselves had a set, mathematically precise way they were supposed to be played, and that you could somehow figure out mathematical or physical formulas that gave you an edge. Throwing a coin at a plate seemed to be a game of skill and luck, not math. And popping balloons with a dart? Wasn't that just about how good your aim was and how strong your biceps?

Either Finn and Magic were just messing with him, or they were involved with something much more complex than Charlie could imagine. And of course, there was one other possibility—that somehow Finn and Magic had figured out a way to cheat. Charlie wasn't a saint, but he tried to be a good kid most of the time, keeping the lying to his parents to a minimum. Telling his dad he was going to meet Jeremy at the Halloween Fair was about as bad as he got. But cheating a carnival game—that seemed plain wrong. He'd never cheated on a test—not that he'd ever felt the need to—and he'd never taken anything that wasn't his. So if Finn and Magic were involved in some scheme to cheat at carnival games, well, that just seemed like something he didn't want to know more about.

Whatever the case, Charlie had finally decided to put all his ruminations aside, and he'd gone back the business of being a regular sixth grader. Hanging out with Jeremy and the rest of his friends during his free time, avoiding Dylan and his gang in the halls and on the playground, studying for his classes, doing his homework, having regular dinners with his parents when they weren't off writing papers or playing with their test tubes, beakers, and pipettes in their respective labs.

"Finally, here we go," Jeremy interrupted Charlie's thoughts, gesturing with a spindly arm. "We seem to be moving. If we can just get our muscles thawed enough to make it to the front of the line, we might survive another day at this prison camp."

Charlie rubbed his hands together to get life back into his fingers, then followed as Jeremy and the rest of the line lurched forward toward the trays. A few more minutes went by in grim silence, broken only by the sound of a few dozen boot soles scraping against the near-frozen sidewalk, and then they were working their way through the double doors, both gripping lime-green plastic trays and tarnished silverware. Charlie had found a fork with three tines intact—a coup!—but the only spoon he'd managed to track down had been flattened into something resembling a miniature shovel. No matter, Charlie was inside, his skin prickling as the heat brought life back into his zombified outer cells.

They made quick work of the food dispensary. Choosing matching cartons of whole milk from the industrial-size coolers just inside the doorway, lining up again to slide their trays down the aluminum shelving tracks that allowed the lunch ladies—flabby-armed doughy women with hairnets and white-and-pink short-sleeve buttoned coats that made them look like dental assistants—to dollop out huge spoonfuls of vaguely identifiable slop into the different hexagonal compartments dug into the trays. As usual, one of the compartments got a heavy glob of beans and rice; next to that, some sort of meat, drenched in sauce that seemed to glow beneath the fluorescent ceiling lights; and in the last compartment, bread, orange, rectangular, and mushy, that could have once been bananas, corn, or wheat.

And then they were through the line and out the other side, facing a wide room that had once doubled as a gym—until a grant from a wealthy alum with fond memories of dodgeballs and rope climbs had led to the construction of a fairly ridiculous monstrosity on the far side of the school complex, complete with fiberglass bleachers and an Astroturf track. Charlie was certain the alum had spent less time on the receiving end of those dodgeballs than he and Jeremy, but even so, you had to applaud his generous spirit.

In short, the lunchroom floor was still shiny cement covered in fading blue and red lines that had once designated a basketball court. There was still a scoreboard attached to the far wall, though the digital screen had long since faded into a gray cloud of dead pixels, and the clock had frozen in time—2:55, numbers that seemed apocryphal in that they mimicked the idea of a school day that never ended, a final class that never let out, never reached the holy, buzzer-blessed moment of 3:00.

Spread across the basketball court were a dozen long rectangular steel picnic-style tables, with circular stools attached along each side. The stools were green, blue, and yellow, in no particular order. For some reason, the guys usually preferred the green and blue stools, while the girls preferred the yellow. Charlie had his theories, but he'd never tried to analyze the preference scientifically, though he was sure his mother would have attacked the problem with statistical fervor, compiling data charts and conducting blind polls. For Charlie's part, he didn't really care about the color of his stool. His main goal, like most of the other kids, was to get through lunch as fast as humanly possible.

As Charlie moved out of the food dispensary and past the first few steel tables, he could see that most of the other kids in his grade were already way ahead of him; the tables closest to the food were already full, the kids hunched over their trays, focused on shoveling the nameless slop down their throats. Many of the kids hadn't even bothered removing their heavy coats, scarves, and even gloves, because lunch bled into recess. The faster you ate, the more free time you got to hang out with your friends in the much more preferable indoor/outdoor playground that was attached, via a side door, to the lunchroom. The playground was pretty state-of-the-art—an indoor section full of donated toys, electric trains, puzzles and board games, and a nicely manicured yard dominated by a prefab plastic jungle gym contraption with built in slides, swings, and climbing apparatus, all connected by tubes that were designed to vaguely resemble some sort of space station. From afar, the jungle gym looked more like a habitrail built for giant hamsters, but nobody was complaining—it beat the aging tire swings and warped steel slides that had previously littered the play area.

Beyond the habitrail/space station, there was a field for pickup soccer next to a triangle for either baseball or kickball—but Charlie and his group usually avoided those high-risk areas. With Dylan's crew continually roaming that part of the recess geography, it was much safer to stay near the front of the playground, in full view of the open doorway leading back into the indoor section of the recess area. Mrs. Patchett, who had been drawing recess proctoring duties since the school year began, never actually set foot outside the indoor section, but even though she looked to be in her mid-hundreds, she had eyes like a hawk. Dylan wouldn't bother anyone within range of her seemingly bionic vision; he was content lording over the fields, if not all the flies.

In short, lunch was really just the opening act for recess, which meant you got in, you got out, and if you were lucky, nobody got hurt in the process.

"Ah, the other inmates are already plotting our jail-break. Sharpen your spoon, Charlie, we go over the wall as soon as we choke down our radioactive mystery meat."

Charlie followed Jeremy's gaze and spotted their group at their usual place—the last table, farthest back in the room, tucked into a corner on the left side of the basketball court. The far edge of the table was positioned right up against a locked door that used to lead to the old boys' locker room, and the center stool—green, at the moment empty and waiting for Charlie—was directly beneath a fluorescent ceiling panel that had gone dark at least four years ago. Charlie had once heard that the bulb that had flickered inside the panel had been recalled for leaking unnamed chemicals; Bobby, the school janitor, had assured him the yellow goo that Charlie could still sometimes see pooling in the corners of he ceiling panel was perfectly innocuous. Even though Bobby had never graduated high school, Charlie wanted badly to believe him. Better a little noxious chemical than giving up the table he and his friends had spent most of their lives around.

It wasn't exactly preferred real estate, but it was home. Since third grade, Charlie and his friends had been eating together at that table, and even though now they were in middle school, there didn't seem any reason why they should shake things up.

"Looks like Crystal is way ahead of you, Jeremy. She's distilling the bread down to its acids and bases, and she's going to use the runoff to tunnel our way out."

Crystal Mueller, the only girl at the table, looked up from her tray as Charlie came around the corner and chose the free green stool next to her. Jeremy took the seat directly across from him, his back to the rest of their class, and pointed at the impressive contraption Crystal had built across two of the plastic compartments of her tray. From Charlie's vantage, it looked like she'd cut a plastic straw in half, attached one end to a rubber party balloon, and placed the other end in two spoons that looked like they'd been melded together under intense heat. Everything on her tray had come from the lunchroom, but seeing it all put together like that was bizarre—if you didn't know Crystal Mueller.

"Is Charlie right?" Jeremy asked once they'd settled into their seats. "Are you building a still?"

Crystal's cheeks flushed as she pushed her brown bangs off her forehead, then steadied her chunky, zebra-rimmed glasses on her nose. She was constantly read-justing those glasses—a nervous tick that Charlie found equal parts charming and annoying, depending on his mood. Then she rolled her eyes behind the quarter-thick lenses.

"It's nothing of the sort. It's a simple pipette and a vinegar well. I've siphoned the vinegar out of some salad dressing, and now I'm going to test the corn bread for calcite deposits."

Charlie stifled a laugh, because with Crystal, it was impossible to know if she was joking or completely serious. He'd been friends with her since second grade, and her obsession with geology sometimes seemed to bleed into every aspect of her daily life. She'd been col-lecting rocks for so long that she'd run out of room in her bedroom to display them, so she kept boxes in all their lockers. As the only girl in their little group, they gave her a fair amount of slack—even though Charlie would have been the first to admit that she was quite possibly the smartest of them all. But he'd never have told her so to her face; he wasn't that shy a person, but with girls, he often clenched up like he was trying to swallow something particularly large. Usually, he didn't think of Crystal as a girl, but sometimes, when she did something particularly impressive, or when he noticed her pretty features, her little nose and brown doe eyes, he found himself losing words. Then again, more often then not, he thought of her the same way he thought of Jeremy and the rest of them. After all, he'd seen her rock collection.

"I read somewhere you can use the same trick to identify warts," Kentaro Mori mumbled from the far end of the table as he stuffed his mouth with his own piece of bread. "Maybe you should spray some of that stuff on Marion. He's looking a little froggy today."

Crystal shot Kentaro a look, then turned back to her makeshift pipette. Kentaro was a head shorter than Crystal and weighed even less than Charlie. Compared to Jeremy, he was the size of a toddler. It wasn't his fault, really; he was the youngest of the group by far, only ten years old. He'd been skipped forward twice already, and if his parents hadn't been concerned about the social results of bouncing the only Japanese kid at Nagassack Middle School into an even older class, he'd have been on his way to high school before any of them knew it. Rumor was, he'd been reading in five different languages before he was out of kindergarten. He'd won two state spelling bees in consecutive years and had also placed in a regional Scrabble tournament while still too young to play peewee soccer.

"They aren't warts, they're hives," Marion Tuttle sniffed from next to Kentaro, completely missing the joke. "I think there might be cantaloupe in the bread."

The last of their gang, the unfortunately named Marion, had always been plagued by allergies. Ever since Charlie had met the kid at a neighborhood playground, he'd been suffering from one breakout or another. Sometimes it was as simple as a rash covering his face, arms, and legs because of something he'd eaten. Other times it was worse, an asthma attack or a weird near-seizure, which meant a trip to the school nurse, and sometimes a quick ride to the nearest emergency room. In fact, by sixth grade, Marion knew the nurse so well, he called her by her first name, and more than once a week she drove him home so he wouldn't have to brave the uncontrolled atmosphere of the bus. Life, for Marion, was a constant battle with the elements. There was an

EpiPen in his book bag and a chart taped to the inside of his locker door listing all the medicines he was on and who to call in case he, say, swelled up like a blowfish.

Marion was also an incredible artist; give him a piece of chalk and a blank board, and soon you'd have the Sistine Chapel in chalk dust. As long as he managed to avoid the errant peanut, wisp of gluten, essence of shellfish, or twist of coconut, Charlie was certain Marion would one day be designing a new wing of the Museum of Fine Arts.

And then there were Charlie and Jeremy rounding out the table. This was the only group of people that Charlie had ever really called best friends. To be sure, Charlie had other groups of friends. There were kids who lived in his neighborhood who he'd grown up with: Johnny and Michael Massweller from next door whom he played kickball on the lawn with and chased lightning bugs after barbecues; Davey Colbert, who was in his swim class at his father's gym, who came over after school once in a while to play video games; but those friendships had never really transformed into anything deeper than a series of scheduled playdates. Charlie thought of them as surface friends; from a mathematical perspective, there was no deeper connection between him, Johnny, Michael, and Davey than there was between the numbers on a ruler.

But Jeremy, Crystal, Kentaro, and Marion were something much more. To the rest of the school, they were known as the Geek Squad, or sometimes the Dork Brigade, or even the Nerd Herd. Charlie's parents called them the Whiz Kids, which seemed extremely dated but was at least a little kinder than the other nicknames. To his parents that was a good thing, and sometimes even to Charlie and his friends, it really was. None of them feared tests or homework or the random gaze of a nearby teacher. But day to day, their reputations were a continual challenge.

Charlie had no illusions as to his own personal social standing at Nagassack. He was skinny, clumsy, horrible at anything involving kinetic motion of any kind. But he was also the kid most likely to use the word "kinetic" in common conversation. His parents had been calling him a genius since he was three years old, and though he never thought of himself in those terms, he knew that his mind worked fast, and that he was especially good with numbers. At four, he had been able to do long division, and by seven, he'd been joining his dad in the MIT engineering department, observing and sometimes participating while his dad puttered away at some odd circuit board or digital device. And day to day, he knew he was different; he really did often think of the world in terms of numbers. Waiting for the bus each morning, he'd watch the cars go by, and unconsciously calculate each vehicle's deceleration time as it approached the stop sign by his house. On the rare occasion he was forced to play kickball with Johnny and Michael, every pitch was more than just a big rubber ball rolling across grass; it was a mathematical formula come to life, a lesson in rotational physics. Even the flight of a lightning bug could freeze him in his tracks, an incredible study in lift, aerodynamics, and chaos theory.

Everyone outside of the Whiz Kids had started calling him Numbers, a nickname he'd earned after getting a perfect score on a national math test that had been targeted at ninth graders, but had mistakenly been handed out on the first day of fourth grade by a language-impaired substitute teacher. To Charlie, the Numbers name always evoked nothing more than the feeling of being a prison inmate—just another number.

But the truth was, he wasn't. Nor were any of the other Whiz Kids. Even the location of their lunch table was a function of their brain power and their social status. They certainly hadn't chosen it because it was in the far back of the lunchroom, located under a poison-spewing, busted light tube by a door that smelled of ancient sweat and liniment oil. They'd chosen it because it was the table closest to the where the teachers ate. Fifteen feet away, on a low dais that had once housed a gymnastics area, squatted a circular table with chairs instead of stools. At the moment, as usual, there were four teachers at the teachers' table: Mrs. Fawler, who taught sixth-grade English lit; Mr. Doughtry, who taught both algebra and physics; Mrs. Collier, French and Spanish; and Mr. Tom, who taught shop. The teachers had trays, just like the kids, but instead of little cartons of milk or juice, they had coffee mugs and Styrofoam cups. The mugs were self-evident, but nobody really knew what was in the Styrofoam cups, something that had been the subject of debate for many years.

For the most part, during lunch the teachers kept to themselves. At the moment, the four teachers were huddled around a laptop that one of them had brought along, probably watching a movie or a television show. Having parents who were professors allowed Charlie to see a bit behind the curtain, and he knew better than most that when teachers weren't teaching, they were kind of like everyone else.

"I'm not going to waste my good vinegar on Marion's nasty warts," Crystal said, slowly spreading drops from the pipette on the orange bread. "I'm only interested in the advancement of science."

"Our own little Madame Curie," Jeremy said, digging into his meat with a fork that was shaped like an *L*.

Charlie was about to chime in and point out that Curie was a physicist and a chemist, while Crystal only cared about rocks, when he suddenly saw a flash of motion over Jeremy's right shoulder. In that split second his mind went into reflexive overdrive, calculating angles and arcs, comparing the bulky white thing that was spinning through the air—on what he instantly calculated was a collision course with the back of Jeremy's head—with a meteor charging toward the earth, but before he could say anything, the thing slammed into Jeremy and exploded in a rain of mushy brown globs.

"What the heck?" Jeremy shouted, reaching back with his hand. He pulled the thing off his neck, held it in front of them, and groaned.

It was a diaper, sprung open by the impact. Dripping down his wrist, and smeared all over his neck, shoulders, and hair, were mounds of rice and beans. Jeremy's cheeks turned bright red as he dropped the diaper onto his tray.

Laughter broke out from the tables closest to their own, and Charlie couldn't help but glance past his embarrassed friend at the row of kids who were pointing and high-fiving one another as they enjoyed the moment. Of course Dylan was in the middle of the pack, half off his stool and pointing with a thick finger at the mess covering Jeremy's shoulders.

"Direct hit!" he shouted. "That's gotta hurt!"

Charlie glanced back at the teachers' table, but none of the teachers had even looked up from the computer screen. They weren't likely to do anything, anyway. Sure, bullying was wrong and even illegal in many states, but it was also a constant reality. Charlie was pretty sure smart kids had been getting picked on by athletic kids since the dawn of time. The caveman drawing pictures on the cave walls probably had to dodge rocks thrown at him by the bigger cavemen who went out hunting every morning. It was another curve on the circle of life.

"He's such a jerk," Charlie said as Jeremy picked rice out of his shirt collar.

"Yeah," Kentaro added, helping sweep beans off the table. "Nobody thinks he's funny."

Jeremy pushed his tray back, then shrugged.

"Yeah, well, the joke's on him. I was going to go back for seconds, and he's just saved me the trip. He turned in his stool and shouted back toward Dylan's table. "Thanks, Dylan—"

And then he paused midsentence. Charlie looked past his friend to see what had stopped him, and then his eyes went wide.

To his utter shock, he saw Finn and Magic strolling right up behind where Dylan was still half standing. In Finn's hand was a tray fully loaded with food. Mounds of the radioactive looking meat, moguls of beans and rice, and a pile of the orange bread. As Finn passed Dylan, he tipped the tray ninety degrees—spilling the food all over Dylan's oblong head.

"Hey! What the hell!"

Dylan sputtered, grabbing at the chunks of meat that were now running down his face. He whirled and found himself staring up at Finn, who opened his mouth in mock concern.

"Oh, man, I'm sorry, I can be so clumsy sometimes."

Dylan's table went silent. The other nearby tables were all staring as well.

"You're not supposed to be in here," Dylan finally managed.

"You're absolutely right," Magic butted in. He dropped his own tray on the table in front of Dylan, sending more meat and rice spraying into Dylan's lap. "Can you bus this for us? Thanks, we owe you one."

The two seventh graders kept on walking. Dylan stood there, his skin beet red, as he pawed the food from his cheeks. The other kids nearby were still staring. A few laughed, but most just seemed in shock.

Seventh graders didn't eat until the next period, and they never came in when the sixth graders were still in the lunchroom. And no one had ever shut Dylan down in the middle of his antics before.

Charlie was just as shocked to see the two seventh graders as everyone else. They were completely out of place in the lunchroom, and yet neither of them seemed at all uncomfortable. Finn was still in his leather jacket, slung over a denim button-down shirt with a high, stiff collar, and there was a pair of sunglasses jutting out from his shirt pocket. Magic was wearing one of his signature tie-dyed shirts and his regular cargo shorts, but he'd exchanged his flip-flops for what looked to be moccasins. Both of them were smiling as they suddenly approached Charlie's table.

Charlie threw another glance toward the teachers' table, but none of the authority figures in the room seemed to have noticed the older kids, or the interruption. They were still bending over the laptop, watching whatever was on the screen.

"Is that Finn Carter?" Crystal finally said, breaking the silence. Her brown eyes were wide behind her thick glasses. "And is he coming over here?"

Before Charlie could respond, Finn and Magic had reached the table. Magic brushed an errant clump of rice off Jeremy's shoulder, while Finn glanced amiably at the group.

"Hey, guys. I'm Finn, and this is Magic. Charlie, it's been a while. You have a free minute?"

Charlie could feel all his friends staring at him. His cheeks were pale, but he tried to sound as cool and collected as possible.

"It's recess, so yeah, I mean, I guess so."

Finn smiled.

"Good. If we can pull you away from your friends for a bit, there's someone we'd like you to meet."

With that, the two seventh graders headed toward the exit on the other side of the teachers' table. Charlie watched them go. They left the cafeteria with such audacity and confidence that there was no shred of evidence that teachers would even mind the older students intruding on the lower grade's lunchtime. Charlie turned back to his friends, who were still staring at him. Then he shrugged.

"I guess I'll see you guys later."

Without another word, he rose and followed Finn and Magic toward the door.

TEN MINUTES LATER, CHARLIE was still following Finn and Magic. The anticipation that had been building since he'd left the lunchroom was slowly being replaced by a more potent sense of annoyance. He'd expected them to lead him down a rabbit hole, but he'd thought it was going to be a much shorter trip.

He glanced past his two tour guides at the long industrial-looking hallway that extended out in front of them for what seemed like forever. Charlie hadn't been in this part of the school building in years. In fact, he wasn't really officially *in* the school building anymore; the hallway actually bisected an adjunct building the students affectionately knew as Old School, because it had once housed the art and music departments.

Since the renovations that had begun with the new gym and had since grown to touch nearly every facet of the school, Old School had gone into disuse. Like with the outdoor waiting area for the lunchroom, there was always talk of how Old School would eventually be restored into everything from a computer center to a theater department, but for the moment the place was pretty much abandoned.

The carpeting beneath Charlie's feet, which no doubt was once a brilliant orange, had faded into a nameless shade of yellow, and the wooden, windowless doors that lined either side looked scuffed, heavy, and foreboding. Charlie had to remind himself that he wasn't being kidnapped, he was voluntarily following the two seventh graders into the depths of Old School—even if he couldn't exactly say why.

For their part, Finn and Magic had remained silent for most of the walk. Charlie had fought the urge to ask them any questions. He could tell they were enjoying the building suspense—Finn was as much a showman as his stockier friend. Charlie was willing to humor them for the time being. After what Finn had done to Dylan in the lunchroom, it was the least he could do. And truthfully, he was curious; what did any of this have to do with him? Why had they singled him out?

Without warning, Finn came to a stop in front of one of the nameless, numberless doors, and gave the solid wood a double knock with the knuckles of his left hand. There was a brief pause, and then the door swung inward on creaky hinges. Magic grinned at Charlie, then waved him inside.

"You first. Mind the tiger; she only bites if you make sudden movements."

Charlie looked at him, and Magic laughed.

"Kidding. She's not a tiger. She's more like a Cheshire cat. But she's certainly got claws, so keep that in mind."

With that, Magic gave him a little shove, and Charlie was through the open doorway.

After Charlie's eyes adjusted to the surprisingly dim lighting, he realized that he recognized the room; he'd taken art classes there in first and second grade, though the place had obviously gone through some changes since he'd last stepped inside.

The first thing he noticed was that someone had taped black construction paper over all the windows, cutting out most of the natural light that had once bathed the semicircular front area in an orange, comforting warmth. The handful of bare bulbs hanging from what used to be blown glass light fixtures were barely enough to illuminate the hardwood floors, and though the room had no corners, there seemed to be plenty of shadowy alcoves between the long waist-high counters that ran along most of the curved walls.

The second thing Charlie noticed was that someone had hung a thick velvet curtain right down the center of the room, cutting it in half. From Charlie's vantage point, he couldn't see what was behind the curtain, but he knew from memory that the room extended at least twenty feet beyond the dark velvet; like an iceberg, most of the place was now hidden from view. And like an iceberg, what Charlie couldn't see seemed way more ominous than what he could.

Directly in front of him, the room looked more like he remembered it. Two rows of little plastic drafting tables with chairs attached to them, white-topped with flat surfaces resting at an angle of about twenty degrees. Instead of a blackboard, the drafting tables and chairs had been set up facing a rather large flat-screen television. Standing directly beside the flat-screen TV was a woman, her back to the room. She was tall, angular, with long black hair hanging straight down the center of her back. She was wearing dark purple boots with exceedingly high heels. Even so, the woman would have been tall in bare feet.

She turned as Charlie entered the room and gave him a wide, extremely white smile.

"Charlie, we've been waiting for you. Come on in and take a seat, and we can get started."

Despite the smile—and those magical, perfect teeth, made twice as large by her pencil lips—there was something terrifying in the angular contours of her face. Her cheekbones were so high, Charlie felt like he could rappel down them, and her eyes were like ice chips, glowing an unnatural shade of blue. Though her hair had seemed to flow freely down her back, like some sort of sable waterfall, her bangs were like a knife edge, styled so severely he could see every perfectly coiffed strand. She was pretty, but definitely much older than Charlie, and much older than Finn and Magic; she looked to be college-aged, though she could have passed for someone in the later stages of high school. She gave off an air of confidence that seemed to fill up the room. Even if the curtain had been made of lava instead of velvet, she would have remained the focus of attention. It took all Charlie's inner strength to shift his gaze back to the rows of drafting tables and the four young faces looking back at him.

Because of the curtain and the somewhat terrifying woman, Charlie hadn't even noticed the four kids seated in the front two rows when he'd first stepped into the room. Two of them he recognized from his own class at Nagassack: a redheaded boy named Daniel who had been in most of his math classes throughout elementary school, whose wide face was such a morass of freckles, it was hard to pinpoint where his hair ended and his forehead began; and Jake Tucson, a soccer player in a Nagassack team sweatshirt who always seemed to have his eyes closed, even when he was looking right at you. Jake had been in a lot of Charlie's classes over the years, but he'd always sat in the back row with the other jocks, never seeming to pay any attention. In fact, Charlie wasn't sure he'd ever heard the kid say a single word to anyone.

The other two faces were complete mysteries. Near the front of the room, closest to the flat-screen TV, was an African-American boy with shortly cropped hair and an unreadable smile. The kid's clothes were impeccable; his jeans were a designer brand that Charlie's parents would never have let him buy, and his shirt was charcoal-colored, made of a material that Charlie would have guessed was at least partially cashmere. He was also wearing a gold watch, the kind that Charlie had seen in magazine ads, the ones that usually featured tennis players or windblown guys on sailboats.

But it was the last face in the room that caused Charlie to look twice, because if she was a student at Nagassack, he couldn't understand how he'd never noticed her before. Silken blond hair raining down against the shoulders of her snowy white sweater. Round red cheeks perfectly balanced by a button of a nose, above a slash of red lipstick that couldn't begin to conceal lips so plump, they could have come right out of a cartoon. And eyes, those eyes—well, if the woman at the front of the room had eyes like ice chips, this girl's eyes looked like they were made of pure smoke. Gray on gray on gray, and yet somehow, when she smiled, as she was doing right then, they gave off a warmth that could have lasted Charlie through three days on the lunch line.

"Charlie," the woman at the front of the room continued, "meet the gang. Finn and Magic you already know. Jake and Daniel are in your grade, so you might have met them before as well. Greg Titus is in the seventh grade and lives in Weston. And this is Sam Ashley. Sam is transferring into Nagassack in a couple of weeks. Her family is moving into the area from New York City, where I grew up, so I've been showing her around, helping her get acclimated."

Charlie turned back to the woman by the TV, feeling heat rising up the back of his neck, which he attributed to the fact that everyone in the room was still looking at him.

"And you, well, I mean, you . . ."

"Who am I, right?" The woman laughed, but even the sound of her laughter seemed tight and controlled, like the skin taut across her cheekbones. "My name is Miranda Sloan. I'm a teacher's aide in the master's program at Northeastern. I'm doing a semester here at Nagassack, working with Mr. Glendale, helping out in algebra and basic statistics."

Charlie nodded. Mr. Glendale taught seventh- and eighth-grade math and physics, and was also sometimes a homeroom monitor subbing in for the sixth graders when one of their regular teachers was out sick. He was a nice guy, a little clueless, midfifties, with almost no hair left on his head and a paunch that fought daily battles with the buttons of his usual uniform of a stiff white shirt and black slacks. He also wore ties that were way too wide and spent most of his classes with his back to the students, writing unintelligibly across the blackboard. Sometimes, when it was particularly hot outside, he sweated so much that the back of his shirt became nearly transparent, revealing so much back hair that some of the students called him Mr. GlenBear when he wasn't listening.

Mr. Glendale didn't seem to have anything in common with this woman. Nor did it make any sense that a seventh- and eighth-grade teacher's aide would be gathering students together in an out-of-use art room to talk about algebra and statistics. The deeper Charlie went down this rabbit hole, the more confusing it all became.

"So what exactly are we doing here?" he finally blurted, deciding to take the direct approach.

Finn and Magic took seats in the back row, Finn gesturing toward an empty seat next to him. Charlie shook his head, opting to stay closer to the door.

"If it's okay, I'll stand."

Miranda laughed again, then pointed to the door.

"That's fine. Would you mind closing the door? Wouldn't want just anybody dropping in."

Charlie fought the sudden urge to run down the hall. What was the worst that could happen? He shut the door, then turned back to watch the woman flick the television on. He saw that beneath the TV, she'd hooked up an iPad. She hit the screen, and the black TV screen was replaced by the familiar frame of a YouTube video.

"Some people like to begin at the beginning, but I'm more the 'begin at the end' type of gal," Miranda said, and then she hit play.

Charlie found himself looking at an enormous wheel that dominated most of the television screen, standing upright on a huge triangular frame. The wheel was broken into five sections, like a vertical pizza pie. Each section was brightly colored and contained a cartoon character. He recognized all the characters, because he was twelve, had access to a TV, and had eyes in his head.

Loopy the Space Mouse. His sidekick, the Frog. Dandy the Squirrel, with his bowler hat. Boots the Kangaroo. And Maddy the Turkey Hawk.

You pretty much had to have grown up in a cave not to know the pictures on the wheel, a constant presence on TV and in movies. They were the central characters associated with one of the biggest amusement parks in the world. Incredo Land, based outside of Tampa, Florida, was built around a futuristic theme, and was a place every kid dreamed of going. Loopy the Space Mouse was imprinted on more T-shirts and coffee mugs than the rest of the characters combined, but they were all familiar to Charlie, like a set of cartoon childhood friends.

But other than the recognizable characters, he had no idea what he was looking at. Then the camera panned back, and Charlie saw that the wheel was up on an enormous stage. And in the background—well, he certainly recognized the building that rose up behind the stage, disappearing right out the top of the screen.

"Is that Loopy's Space Station? I mean, at Incredo Land?"

Magic shushed him. Charlie glanced from him to the other kids in the room, who were all intently watching the TV screen. If they were surprised to be watching some YouTube video shot at Incredo Land in Tampa, Florida, none of them was showing it. Unintentionally, his eyes shifted to the blond girl, Sam, but she was concentrating on the screen just like the rest. He forced his gaze back to the TV.

The view continued to pan back, and he saw that on the stage next to the wheel were two people. A middle-aged man in a suit and tie, with curly gray hair and wide, friendly eyes. And a kid, about Charlie's age, in shorts and a T-shirt, red-faced and nervous. The man said something to the kid, who reached forward and grabbed the side of the wheel with two hands. Music started up from an orchestra somewhere offscreen. Then the kid gave the wheel a solid thrust downward, and it began to spin.

As it spun, Charlie focused in on the edge of the wheel. He saw that at the top of the frame, a little finger of plastic shaped like an arrow hung down against the front of the wheel, and that as the wheel spun, the finger flicked against tongs that marked the edge of each of the slices of pie-shaped sections. Although he was too far away to hear the clicks, he guessed that the wheel was making noise as it went, clicking away as the cartoon images blurred together in a swirl of wonderful color.

Charlie had seen wheels like that at carnivals before, and knew how they worked. Usually there was a picture of a prize on each of the wheel's sections. You spun the wheel, it went around for a while, eventually slowed, and whatever the arrow was pointing at was what you won. But this seemed a little different, because instead of prizes, there were pictures of Incredo Land characters. Which made sense, because obviously from the giant castle rising up behind the stage, the wheel was in Incredo Land.

Charlie felt his natural curiosity rising up, and he was about to ask another question, when the man on the screen said something to the kid, and the kid shouted audibly: "Loopy!"

There was applause from somewhere offscreen. The wheel went around again and again, and eventually began to slow. Soon Charlie could make out the characters, still blurred, but distinct. Then the wheel slowed a little more, and he could see the colors separating, the bulbous eyes and rounded ears. His eyes could follow each cartoon as they went around and around, Dandy then Maddy then Loopy, etc., etc., etc.

And eventually the wheel slowed all the way to a stop. Charlie's eyes moved to the arrow, and saw that the wheel had landed on Dandy. There was an audible groan from the offscreen audience, and then the video went dead. The TV screen returned to black, and Miranda spun back toward the classroom.

"Any questions?"

Charlie stared at her. She had to be kidding. Any questions? He didn't even know where to begin.

"That was Incredo Land," he started, which seemed like as good a place as any. "A stage somewhere on Solar Avenue . . ."

"Wow, he really is a genius," Greg jibed from the front row. "Hard to believe someone that smart is still in the sixth grade."

"Quiet, Greg," Sam said, swatting his arm. "Give him some time. Remember what we were like two weeks ago."

Charlie looked from one to the other, then back at Miranda.

"Yes, Charlie, the video was shot at Incredo Land, exactly one year ago last November first. It's part of an annual promotion that the park has been running for the past few years. One kid, age fourteen or below, gets to spin the wheel each November, and if he picks the right cartoon character, he wins a pretty nice prize. They call it the Wheel of Wonder, but it's actually a pretty standard carnival game, usually called a wheel of fortune."

"A wheel of fortune," Charlie said. "Like the game show."

"If you want to get technical," Greg chimed in again, and Charlie could tell he wasn't the sort to keep quiet for very long. "The game show stole the name from the carnivals, not the other way around."

"And the carnivals stole the wheel," Finn interrupted, "from an ancient Greek and Roman army tradition."

"Greek and Roman?" Charlie asked. It had been a long time since he was the least knowledgeable in a classroom full of his peers, and he couldn't help noticing that he was enjoying the sensation.

"Yes," Sam answered, before Greg could. "Greek soldiers used to draw numbers on a shield, turn it on its side, and give it a spin. They would bet on which number would come up. Eventually, they traded the shield for a chariot wheel, but the idea remained the same. Then it worked its way into carnivals, and eventually casinos."

"The roulette wheel," Charlie said. He'd seen them

on TV before, and had even once had a discussion with his dad about how they worked. But the wheel of fortune, or Wheel of Wonder, seemed much simpler than a casino roulette wheel, because there were far fewer segments to spin through, and there was no ball dropped onto the spinning surface that would bounce chaotically from segment to segment. Just a wheel with an arrow and a few cartoon characters.

Interesting stuff, but he had no idea what it had do with him. Or why these kids were in an abandoned art room during his recess period. Then a thought struck him: *Incredo Land*.

He knew that once a year, Nagassack offered students from grades six and up the opportunity to sign up for a class trip that was partially sponsored by the PTA, and that for the past few years, that trip had been to Incredo Land. His parents being as budget conscious as they were, Charlie had never really looked into the trip, but he was pretty sure it took place around the first week of November, because the kids that went often had to take make-up tests during their Thanksgiving break.

Curiouser and curiouser.

Miranda must have noticed the look on his face, because she grinned.

"Yes, Charlie, the class trip this year is to Incredo Land, and happens to fall right when this promotion is going on. Which means that a student from Nagassack, if he or she is really, really lucky, might just have a chance to spin that wheel and win that prize. Which, if you're interested, happens to be eight lifetime tickets to all the Incredo Land theme parks. There's also a little cash prize, which can go to the charity of the winner's choice."

Charlie raised his eyebrows.

"Eight lifetime tickets, that's a pretty incredible prize. But really, I don't know what any of this has to do with us."

Finn leaned toward him.

"It has everything to do with us, Charlie."

"Why is that?"

"Because this year, six weeks from now, actually, we are going to beat that wheel."

Charlie looked at Finn, and saw that he was dead serious. Then Charlie shifted his attention to the other kids, and they were all nodding in agreement. He shook his head.

"It's not possible. I mean, even if one of us was lucky enough to get to spin the wheel, it's random, there are five possible outcomes, you'd have to guess right and there's no way you could know. It's just not possible."

"Oh yes it is," Miranda interrupted. "And there won't be any luck involved."

Charlie paused.

"You know how to beat the wheel?"

"No, actually. You do."

Charlie rocked back on his feet. He was stunned by her simple words and the matter of fact way she'd said them. At the same time, something clicked in the back of his mind, just an inkling, but he was beginning to understand why he was there. Why they had chosen him.

Like Finn had said, there weren't any coincidences.

But before he could respond, Miranda was moving to her left, toward the edge of the vast purple curtain that closed off the back part of the room. She reached for the material, then turned back toward Charlie.

"But first we have to get to the wheel. Which isn't easy. Thousands of kids try to get to the wheel each year, but only one gets to give it a spin."

Part of Charlie wanted to walk right out of there, but his feet felt like they were glued to the floor.

"And how do we get to the wheel?" he asked.

Miranda smiled. With a flourish, she yanked back the velvet curtain.

"First, we're going to need to win a game."

IT WAS THREE GAMES actually, or one game broken
into three parts.

Charlie stood frozen in place as the curtain swept
all the way back to the blacked-out windows, revealing
the far half of the art room. All the furniture had been
removed, and in its place, well, it took a few minutes
for Charlie to believe what he was seeing.

Carnival games. Just like in the tent at the Sherwood
Halloween Fair. Life-size and seemingly reconstructed
with the utmost precision, the three games were spaced
out from each other to fill nearly every inch of the semicircular area. Two of the games—a balloon-dart game
like he'd watched Magic beat at the fair, and a coin toss
like the one Finn had decimated—were to his right, and

to his left, a common rope ladder game. Charlie had seen the rope ladder before, had even tried it once or twice. Basically, it consisted of an angled rope ladder that started at the floor and ran up, at a forty- or fifty-degree angle, to where it was affixed to the wall. At the peak of the ladder was a little bell; the object of the game was to climb up the ladder and ring the bell. It sounded much easier than it actually was; the ladder would twist and turn under your weight, and Charlie had never seen anyone actually make it to the top of the ladder—other than the people who worked the game, who usually performed the feat to get you to believe it wasn't rigged, that it was indeed possible.

"You guys must really like carnival games" was all Charlie could think to say.

There was a moment's pause, then laughter.

"We really like to *beat* carnival games," Magic said, rising from his chair. He strolled past Miranda and pointed to each game in turn. "Balloon darts, plate coins, and rope ladder. The three pillars of the carnival, and all of them completely beatable."

"What do you mean, beatable?" Charlie asked.

Miranda smiled.

"What do you think it means, Charlie?"

"I think maybe you guys figured out a way to cheat."

"Cheating is a strong word," Miranda responded. "If a game is set up unfairly, would you consider evening the odds cheating? We don't intervene with the design of these games, and we don't break any printed rules. So, is using your brain to beat a game cheating?"

Charlie didn't know how to answer that. Of course, using your brain wasn't cheating, but there were plenty of things that were unfair. That didn't give you license to break the rules. Then again, if there really was a way to beat these carnival games that wasn't explicitly against the rules, well, would that really be so wrong? He'd watched Finn land three coins on those plates, and it definitely hadn't looked like cheating to him. And Magic popping those balloons, it hadn't seemed like he'd done anything against the rules.

"Maybe not," Charlie finally said. "But what do these games have to do with Incredo Land and the spinning wheel?"

Miranda strolled over to the low counter facing the balloon-dart game. She lifted one of the darts off the counter, inspecting the metal point as she turned it over in her hand. Her bright red, manicured nails seemed much sharper than the end of the dart.

"These games are the gateway to the wheel. They've set up a Midway Center right on Solar Avenue at

Incredo Land, full of every kind of fair game you can imagine. By playing these games, you win tickets, and the kid who wins the most tickets in a single day gets a shot at the wheel. They count the tickets by weight right at the park's closing time, and the winner gets to spin the wheel the very next morning. The rules don't say anything about a group of friends pooling tickets; whoever shows up with the most tickets at the end of that promotion day gets to spin."

"And that's going to be one of you?" Charlie asked.

"No," Finn said, still in his seat, putting his feet up on the drafting table in front of him. "That's going to be you."

"Me?"

Charlie still hadn't moved from right in front of the door. He didn't know whether to turn around and just get the heck out of there, or move deeper into the room to check out the three games up close. He was certainly intrigued. He felt like he was being asked to join some secret club. He'd joined clubs before: a chess club, a math club, an astronomy club, but never anything like this. Still, it didn't seem real to him. The idea that he was special enough to be asked to join—not just to join, but to star in this bizarre endeavor—it simply seemed like an elaborate, practical joke.

"Are we going to beat the claw game too? You

know, the one with the claw on a crane, where you try to pick up toys or stuffed animals. I think there's one at Chuck E. Cheese's with Star Wars action figures in it. I'd love a Chewbacca to go with the R2D2 I won at my last birthday party."

The blond girl from the front row, Sam, shot him a look that would wither a rosebush.

"I know you're trying to make a joke, but the claw game, it's a sucker's bet."

She flipped an errant strand of her long hair out of her eyes.

"A sucker's bet?" Charlie asked, his voice sounding a bit choked as he tried not to avoid her eyes. That shy feeling he got around most girls felt amplified a hundred times, but he wasn't going to shrink away in front of all these people.

"A sucker's bet. Which means that if you take that bet, you're a sucker before the game gets started. See, the claw games are rigged. Picking up a stuffed animal takes a certain amount of pressure applied over a certain amount of surface area. Picking up a golf ball with your fingers, for instance, is actually the application of pressure using the muscles in your hand, via the friction created by the pads of your fingers, translated to the surface of the ball."

Charlie loved the easy way she spoke about complicated science. He found himself instantly enrapt, his shyness overwhelmed by her obvious intelligence.

"This pressure," she continued, "or force, is known scientifically as PSI, pounds per square inch. It takes a certain amount of PSI for a claw to lift a stuffed animal—and the PSI applied by those claws isn't fixed. It changes based on whether the owner of the machine wants you to win or lose. Turns out, in the state of Massachusetts, there's an archaic law that says coin-operated vending games must pay out once every twelve tries. So the claw machines are set to only exert enough PSI to grab a stuffed animal in one out of twelve attempts. No matter how good you think you are, no matter how hard you try, you can only win one in twelve times."

Charlie leaned back against the door. He was duly impressed. Not just by the science of what she had said, but by the way she had said it. Her cheeks were flushed, her eyes sparkling. She was passionate about this, the science behind a game. It wasn't just some stupid claw machine at Chuck E. Cheese's; it was something she could mentally take apart and understand.

"A sucker's bet," Charlie finally said.

"Now you're getting the feel for this," Finn commented, picking at his shoelaces. "Claw games, basketballs thrown at hoops that are too small or wrongly shaped, baseballs thrown at milk bottles—"

"The milk bottles are rigged?"

"That's right." Sam nodded. "The milk bottles look like they're all the same weight, but it turns out one of the bottles is usually way heavier than the rest. When that bottle is put on the top of the pyramid, it's really easy to knock them all down with a single throw. That's what the carnival workers do to 'prove' to the players that the game is fair. Then, when they restack the bottles, they put the heavy one on the bottom as one of the lower bottles in the pyramid. Suddenly, it becomes almost impossible to knock them all down in one throw. Again, it's about force versus friction, kinetic energy versus inertia—"

"The bottom line is," Miranda interrupted, putting the dart back on the counter facing the wall of balloons, "we don't play games we can't win. We only play games that are beatable. And when we find beatable games—"

"We beat the heck out of them," Magic chimed in, grinning.

Charlie felt the door against his back. His head was spinning. The words Sam had used, *force, friction, kinetic energy, inertia*, of course he knew what they all meant, not just from his science classes, but from his own reading and research. His friends—his Whiz Kids—used words like that all the time. But Charlie had thought they were the only kids who ever talked like that. Sam, Finn, Magic, the rest, these weren't losers; these were cool sixth and seventh graders who had chosen to hang out with one another, had chosen to talk about math and physics in an abandoned classroom.

"With physics and math," Charlie said, "you beat carnival games."

"And that's where you come in," Miranda said, bringing the attention back to her. The fact that she was older, a college student, a teacher's aide, gave her a natural authority. There was definitely a divide between her and the rest of the group; there was no question, she was the boss, she was running the show.

"Because I'm good at math," Charlie said, trying to finish her thought.

"No," Greg joked, "because you're so handsome."

Miranda shushed him with a look, then turned back to Charlie.

"Not just because you're good at math, but because you understand something important. You know that math isn't just something you learn in a classroom. You know that math is something you can use in real life. Knowing math, and how to think mathematically, scientifically, doesn't just make you smart—"

"It makes you win." Finn said, pushing his boots off the desk and rising to his feet.

"Charlie," Miranda said as she stepped away from the dart counter, reached out for the curtain, and yanked it closed with a swirl of purple velvet. "Here's our offer. We'll cover the cost of your trip to Incredo Land. We'll teach you our secrets, and make you part of our little team. And when we win, we'll split the lifetime Incredo Land tickets. We've already agreed, each of the group will get one, and you'll get the remaining two. They're pretty much priceless. And the little cash prize will go to my teacher's aide program at Northeastern."

Charlie swallowed, running through it in his head. Two lifetime tickets to Incredo Land—he couldn't even begin to imagine what they would be worth. But still, what would he be getting himself into? What Sam had said, the way she'd said it, he was fascinated by how brilliant it seemed. Just the idea of spending time with her and the rest of this group, talking about science, beating games using math, was truly compelling. But something about it also seemed a little frightening. And maybe even wrong.

"And what do you get?" he finally managed, using every ounce of courage to get the words out. "I mean, no offense, but you can't be doing this for Incredo Land tickets."

Miranda laughed.

"Amusement park tickets, at my age? I must be like a hundred, right? No offense taken. I'm actually writing my thesis about this. The math involved, but also how you guys work as a group."

Charlie nodded. Having two parents in academia meant he knew what a thesis was, and how kooky some of the subjects that PhD and masters students chose to write about could be. His mother had written her own PhD thesis on hummingbird flight. It wasn't that bizarre to think that Miranda would be writing a paper on a group of middle-school kids banding together to beat carnival games. And if a few hundred bucks, or whatever the cash prize might be, ended up going to her university teacher's aide program, that would probably benefit her as well. Her motives were understandable.

Still, it wasn't an easy decision for Charlie. He'd never been involved in anything remotely like this. And if it wasn't cheating, well, then why did Finn and Magic use fake names at the Sherwood Fair? Charlie knew he didn't have the full picture yet.

"I guess I need to think about it," he said.

Finn opened the door behind him and gestured with a hand.

"That's as much as we can ask. I'll walk you back to the last few minutes of your recess."

Before Charlie got through the doorway, Miranda crossed the room, fast and quiet as a cat, and leaned in close.

"One more thing. We do ask that you keep this discussion just between us. This is an invitation that isn't open to everyone, and the fewer people who know about us, the better it is for everyone. I'm sure you understand."

Charlie nodded. Up close, her perfume was strong, something floral and sweet, but beneath it was the slightest tinge of sweat. When she turned away and headed back into the room, her long hair flicked at him, silken strands gently kissing the skin of his cheeks.

Finn closed the door behind him, and then they were alone in the long corridor. Finn smiled.

"Quite a lady, isn't she? She put this whole thing together about a month ago, recruited us one by one. Pretty sure she used school transcripts to decide who to approach. I think she's made some pretty good choices, don't you?"

Charlie nodded, but he didn't know enough about

the group to judge any of them. Daniel and Jake hadn't said a word the entire time. Sam was obviously smart, and Greg, though he seemed kind of an jerk, seemed to know his stuff. Finn and Magic were strange, but also confident enough to do just about anything.

And that left Charlie. Well, Charlie knew he was smart and good with numbers. If Miranda had really read his school transcripts, she knew he had always been at the top of his class, especially in the maths and sciences.

But deep down, Charlie knew it wasn't as simple as that. Even if she had recruited the rest via their school records, he knew with him, it was different. In fact, now that he'd seen what they were up to, he had a feeling he knew exactly why she had chosen him.

Charlie started down the hallway, Finn right next to him.

"It does seem like she knows precisely what she's doing," Charlie said, nodding.

Finn had been right all along. There was no such thing as coincidence.

7

THE DINOSAUR WAS HUNGRY.

Charlie could see it in her glazed, intense, prehistoric eyes; she was ravenous, down to her core, and every genetic instinct imprinted in her soul by those still-evolving random twists of DNA within her cells was telling her that it was time to feed. The ultimate prerogative, the definition of imperative, her body had been built for this moment. Her long prehensile neck jutted forward, muscles rippling beneath her thick, almost rubbery skin. Her sharp, bony, beaklike mouth opened wide, as if on hinges, revealing a sliver of bright red tongue. Her entire body lurched forward on legs as thick as mini tree trunks, her rapier-sharp claws curling forward against the gravel floor of her terrarium—and then it happened. Her beak slammed shut with a crunch that echoed against the terrarium's thin glass walls.

Charlie leaned close, watching her jaw work as she pulverized the head of lettuce. Of course, the creature in the terrarium wasn't actually a dinosaur, it was a twelve-year-old painted turtle named Greta. Charlie hadn't traveled a hundred million years back in time, he'd just gone across to the main building, to the second floor science lab, room 231.

Over the past few years, Charlie had spent a lot of time watching Greta wander around her terrarium. Since third grade, he had been visiting room 231 on a pretty consistent basis; all his science-related classes had met in the brightly lit second-floor "lab," and he felt comfortable and at home beneath the recessed fluorescent panels that covered the domed ceiling.

The dome was an accident of architecture; Charlie's father had told him that the original plans for the second floor of Nagassack Middle School had actually called for a cantilevered, environmentally friendly sunroof that would help heat the building during the cold winter months. But somewhere between blueprints and buttresses, the Nagassack Building Committee decided alumni funds would be better spent on a four-hundred seat theater, which, it turned out, was just as swelteringly hot in winter and summer, because of its unfortunate location right above the main boilers that fed super-heated steam through the school's vascular system. In any case, the sunroof was out, the dome went up, and Nagassack was the only middle school that Charlie knew of that taught science in the round.

The table setup was perfect for a thirty-student class, which was the norm. The far half of the room was reserved for special projects, and for the preserved samples that lined the metal shelves above the micro-scopes: fish, bugs, frogs, snakes, mostly sealed in plastic containers with cork tops, some stuck right to display boards with brightly tipped pins. Next to the shelves, tucked into the farthest curve of the circular room, was Mabel the skeleton. Mrs. Hennigan, who taught science from fifth to seventh grades, never tired of telling her classes that Mabel was the most expensive specimen in the entire school. At Halloween, she got a jack-o-lantern sidekick, placed right beneath her dangling, bone-white toes. Around Christmas, Mabel was dressed up with a red Santa hat and a cotton-ball beard.

The room itself smelled of hamster wood shavings, though there hadn't been a live hamster in the room for as long as Charlie could remember. A lot of kids attributed the smell to Mrs. Hennigan herself; a heavyset woman with curly white hair and poorly applied blue eyeliner, she had a penchant for sacklike outfits that seemed to be made of burlap. Everything she wore was beige, down to her hospital-style tights and outdated platform shoes. Her hand always shook when she wrote on the chalkboard at the front of the room, which made her mostly illegible handwriting even more impossible to decipher, and the glare from the fluorescent panels in the dome only amplified the effect.

As usual, Mrs. Hennigan was at that chalkboard, scratching away with a piece of chalk as small as a pencil eraser, while Charlie watched Greta devour her lunch. Every now and then, Hennigan's nails hit the blackboard as she wrote, sending an awful screech reverberating through the wood-shaving-scented air. Most of the kids groaned at the sound, but Charlie remained focused on the turtle.

He'd often found solace watching Greta; seeing her roam around her tank in the slow-motion manner of her species helped him think, and at the moment, he certainly had a lot to think about. A casual observer might wonder how a turtle could aid a twelve-year-old's meditation, but for Charlie, it made perfect sense. One of his most significant childhood memories revolved around a turtle just like Greta.

It had happened just a few days past his eighth birthday. He and Jeremy had been outside playing and had discovered a little creek that ran parallel to Jeremy's backyard. They'd never seen the creek before, because it was past the invisible line that Jeremy's parents had drawn beyond which they hadn't been allowed to play, but that morning they'd decided to push those boundaries and explore. They followed the creek through the dense underbrush, finally coming to a little clearing where the water swelled to what almost could be described as a pond. And in the middle of the pond, they spotted a turtle sitting on a rather large log. Before either of them could even react, they heard laughter from the other side of the pond, followed by a rain of rocks, all aimed at the hapless reptile. A bunch of older kids, maybe age fifteen or sixteen, were hurling stones at the poor creature. Most were poorly aimed, but a few were finding their target, and Charlie could see the red splotches where the rocks were cutting through the turtle's shell, finding the soft meat beneath. Slowly, painfully slowly, the thing was trying to get off the log and into the safety of the pond, but with every second, the rain of stones became heavier, the moment more dire.

Charlie and Jeremy had watched in silence, unable to do anything. Charlie had never felt so helpless. Eventually, he'd just turned and made his way back along the creek to Jeremy's yard. He liked to imagine that the turtle had made it off the log, injured but alive, and disappeared beneath the surface. But he knew, realistically, that the turtle had probably never gotten off that log.

Greta, safe in her terrarium, made Charlie feel secure in a world that seemed every day less in his control. After a day like this, even a moment with Greta seemed unlikely to put it all in perspective.

"Okay, Charlie, I'm ready for another try."

Charlie turned away from the terrarium to see Jeremy grinning at him from behind their shared lab table, most of his face obscured by a pair of oversize safety goggles. He was wearing rubber gloves and had in his right hand, held delicately between two eel-like fingers, a shiny red marble.

"You don't need the goggles, Jeremy. Or the gloves."

Charlie tried to keep his voice soft, although there was little danger of Mrs. Hennigan turning around any time soon. Once she started scrawling against the blackboard, she was in for the duration.

"Safety first," Jeremy responded. "Wouldn't want a marble popping up and taking out my eye."

"It's a bowl and a ball. Nobody's going to lose any eyes."

Charlie crossed over to where Jeremy was standing and glanced down at their shared science project. Really, on the surface that's all it was, a bowl and a ball. The marble was from Charlie's collection, one he'd been adding to since early childhood—he'd always been fascinated by the mathematically perfect little spheres, and the many ways you could use them to turn boring textbook physics and math concepts into fun, illustrative paradigms. Toss one in the air, hello gravity. Roll one down a ramp, potential energy meets friction. Smash two together, kinetic energy and the second law of thermodynamics. Roll one down a bowl, and you got all three paradigms for the price of one.

The bowl was pretty good for the job, ceramic and smooth, although Charlie could have done without the brightly colored petunias that covered most of its inner and outer surface. Charlie had borrowed the bowl from his kitchen cabinet at home; once upon a time, it had been the family salad bowl, in use at least twice a week for many years.

Though it still carried the vague, pungently vinegar smell of salad dressing, the smooth inner surface of the petunia bowl was exactly what Charlie had needed for his and Jeremy's shared science project. He watched as Jeremy dramatically placed the marble at the top edge of the bowl, right beneath a little black line Charlie had etched to mark the theoretical entrance point. Jeremy gave the marble a little push with his finger, and the marble rolled around the lip of the bowl, then began its descent, rolling in tighter and tighter circles as it traveled down, inch by inch, toward the bottom.

"Houston, we have entry into the upper atmosphere," Jeremy exclaimed. "T-minus twenty seconds until impact!"

Charlie glanced at the digital timer attached to the top of the bowl a few inches from where Jeremy had started the marble. The device was his own construction; it was actually just a Casio watch with a simple timer application. Charlie had removed the watch's strap and had superglued the remaining square section of the device to the ceramic bowl. Jeremy had engaged the timer with his left hand just at the exact moment he'd pushed the marble off on its spiraling descent. He had presumably also made a mental note of the time on the watch as the marble passed the entry point, completing its first revolution around the interior lip of the bowl. He'd make another mental note again as the ball finished its second roll around the bowl, and the rest, as Charlie liked to say, was math, math, and more math.

The real science behind the marble's descent to the

center of the bowl was actually so sophisticated that Charlie wouldn't have been able to explain it without the help of a textbook, and maybe his parents. You had gravity pulling the marble down toward the bottom of the bowl, the horizontal velocity of Jeremy's initial push fighting that downward motion, the curve of the bowl adding another horizontal element, the friction from the bowl's surface slowing the descent, the revolutions of the marble itself causing more chaos along the way—but none of this really mattered in the scope of Charlie and Jeremy's project. Their project was actually quite simple, a ball and a bowl, even if it was an illustration of something incredibly complex.

"And there it goes," Jeremy continued, squinting down into the salad bowl as the marble spun down to the bottom, then finally rolled to a stop. "Splashdown!"

Charlie grinned at Jeremy's dramatics. When they finally presented their project, they would certainly use terms like that—splashdown, impact, upper atmosphere—because it was a lot more fun than just talking about a marble rolling around a bowl. Pretending that the marble was a satellite breaking orbit and plummeting to the earth made the project interesting and, really, was where the idea had come from in the first place.

It was actually the continuation of an experiment

that Charlie had been working on over the summer, the results of which he'd submitted to a statewide science competition a few weeks before school began. Charlie had only won second prize with his research; first prize had gone to a kid who'd built a functioning volcano using modeling clay, baking soda, and food dye, as clichéd a project as you could find, but admittedly pretty compelling to watch. Still, even second place had inspired Charlie to continue working on the project, so when Mrs. Hennigan suggested that her sixth graders pair up and do an independent project to show to the rest of the students at the end of the semester, it had seemed natural for Charlie and Jeremy to delve into the ball and bowl.

"Splashdown is a good guess," Charlie commented, "because in real life, there'd be an eighty-five percent chance it would land in water."

It was Charlie's dad who had first told him the story of Skylab, a space station/satellite that back in the late seventies had become a front page headline when it had broken orbit and crash-landed off the coast of Australia. As it fell, predicting where the satellite/station was going to impact the earth had become a nationwide sensation, and a couple of magazines had even offered prizes to anyone who got their hands on a piece of the wreckage. Charlie had immediately seized on the story as an inspiration for his science project.

It was that event that Charlie was trying to illustrate with his ball and his bowl. Jeremy was along for the ride; he was a good partner because though he wasn't quite as skilled at math as Charlie, he was sharp enough to quickly follow along.

"In real life," Jeremy responded, "this marble would be the size of a speck of dust and this bowl should be as big as the entire room. And in real life, Finn Carter wouldn't have kidnapped you from the lunchroom and dragged you off to god knows where and then sworn you to secrecy."

Charlie rolled his eyes as he opened a notepad on the desk next to the bowl and held up a pen.

"He didn't kidnap me, he just wanted to talk in private. Give me the first and second time marks."

"It's 4.3 and 3.2. Yeah, right, he wanted your advice on swimming the backstroke. Oh, I forgot, he doesn't swim anymore, right? Maybe he's some sort of super-hero now, protecting kids from bullies and making the world a better place for geeks like us."

Charlie understood Jeremy's frustration. He'd been peppering Charlie with questions for the past twenty minutes about where he'd gone during lunch and what

Finn had wanted. Charlie had never kept anything secret from Jeremy before; they had shared everything with each other pretty much since they could both talk. But Charlie had essentially made a promise in front of Finn and the others, and beyond that, well, he had to admit, he was a little scared of Miranda. Not just because she was basically an adult and had invited him into a secret world, but because he was pretty sure he knew why she had invited *him*, specifically, and it wasn't just that he was really good at math and was under the age of fourteen.

"Jeremy," he said, as he continued scribbling on the notepad, pretending to ponder the two numbers Jeremy had given him while he was actually thinking about something else, entirely, "you know anything about the fall school trip? Incredo Land?"

Jeremy raised the thick safety goggles and ran a hand through his mop of red hair.

"I know I won't be going. And neither will you. My parents can't afford to send me to Incredo Land, and your parents are way too cheap to send you."

"They aren't cheap—"

"Okay, *practical.* That's the word I'm looking for. Your parents are so practical, they'd never send you to Incredo Land. They didn't buy you a bike until you were ten, and even then it was so used the tires were practically elliptical."

Charlie wanted to argue, but Jeremy was essentially correct. His parents didn't like to spend money unless they had to, which meant things like trips to Incredo Land were pretty unlikely.

"Can you imagine it, though?" Jeremy mused, his eyes glazing a bit. "Flying in an airplane. Staying in a hotel room with no parents around? Ordering room service and swimming in some giant, rodent-shaped swimming pool? All those rides? The Space Drop, and that one that goes underwater on Jupiter's moon, and Saturn's Rings—and all the freaking candy you can eat?"

Jeremy's excitement at the idea was infectious. Charlie couldn't manage the pure ecstasy he was seeing in Jeremy's eyes, but he didn't deny that the thought of a week in Incredo Land sent sparks up his spine. It was true, the school trip would be sans parents, though there would be teacher-proctors, of course, three at a minimum. But the rest of Jeremy's musings probably weren't that far off. Charlie had flown in planes before with his parents, strapped in between them in a middle seat with an iPad on his lap. This would be different, this would be flying like an adult. And the hotel, the pool, the rides, well, all that would be pretty incredible.

Still, he did his best to temper his thoughts. Incredo Land was a dream that he wasn't supposed to be able to have again, at least not yet. His parents had talked about going there again when he was older, and only during the summer, when it would be cheaper, and way, way hotter. Nobody wanted to go to Florida in the middle of the summer, when it was *practical*.

He pretended to concentrate on the notepad in front of him. And part of his brain really was playing with the two numbers Jeremy had given him, the two timer marks that told him how long it had taken the marble to go around the inside of the bowl on its first and second revolutions. Those two numbers were the key to their project and were also the key to the paper that Charlie had submitted to the state science fair earlier that summer. Because those two numbers were all you really needed to tell you when a ball would get to the center of a bowl, or where a satellite would hit the earth. Everything else, you already knew.

Those two numbers, when plugged into an equation that took into account the circumference of the bowl, or the earth, and the height at which the ball, or satellite, made its entry, gave you the rate of descent, and the change in its deceleration on the way down. Once you knew how fast the ball was going around and around, and how that velocity changed as it got closer to the bottom, you could figure out where it was going to end up. The equation was complicated, but the procedure of the experiment was not. All Jeremy had done was drop the marble and hit the button on the timer twice.

With the notepad and enough time, Charlie could figure out the rest. On his dad's iPhone—which is what Charlie had used for the paper he'd submitted to the state science fair—Charlie could do the calculation almost instantaneously. His dad had helped him write an app for just that purpose. If he'd had his dad's iPhone with him in the science lab, he could have plugged the numbers in as the marble rolled down the bowl and had a pretty accurate idea of when it would stop before it actually did.

And if the bowl had been a spinning wheel cut into five triangular sections, and instead of a marble the satellite was represented by a little arrow clicking along the outside of the wheel—

Jeremy interrupted Charlie's thoughts, leaning close over the salad bowl.

"So Finn's interest in you has something to do with the school trip? Is that what you're trying to tell me?"

Charlie didn't immediately respond. Jeremy reached into the salad bowl and grabbed the marble, then tossed it into the air. Charlie managed to catch it before it hit the table, then glanced toward Mrs. Hennigan, who was thankfully still screeching and scribbling her way across the blackboard. Jeremy laughed, poking Charlie with a gloved finger.

"I doubt he's interested in you because you know how to calculate how long it takes a marble to roll down a bowl."

Charlie laughed, but inside, he was suddenly sure.

Jeremy couldn't have been more wrong.

MARION TUTTLE WAS HAVING a moment. Hunched over the piece of notebook paper, halfway out of his plastic institutional-style chair, his rounded, spotted cheeks puffed out around his pursed lips, beads of sweat rising in the creases of his doughy forehead and jowls. The Bic pen gripped in his right hand was moving so fast it was a purple blur, the point riding back and forth across the paper in strokes that would make an Olympic swimmer blush. He had been going at it for minutes, but still nobody spoke, nobody said a word, all caught in the awe of the moment, the miracle, the art.

And then, finally, Marion stopped. Pen poised in the air a few inches above the page, breathing hard, the sweat now running freely down the sides of his face.

Then he grinned, settled back in his chair, and crossed his stubby arms against his potato-shaped chest. Their corner of the school library had gone dead silent, save for the creak of the heating pipes that crisscrossed the low ceiling and the occasional scrape of a plastic chair leg against the hardwood floor.

"Magnificent" was all Charlie could say, breaking the quiet as he peered down at the drawing from his perch at the end of the rectangular table that the Whiz Kids called their summer home. The library was as safe a haven as the Whiz Kids could ever hope to find; Charlie doubted Dylan and his ilk could even find the place without the help of an angry teacher.

"Might be your best work yet," Jeremy agreed from Charlie's left. "You really captured his soul. The way the light ricochets off his hair, creating that little halo effect. Really top-notch."

"A masterpiece," Kentaro agreed, directly across from Marion. Kentaro was on his knees on his chair, better able to see over the table. He pointed one of his tiny fingers toward the drawing and grinned. "You better sign it, because when it ends up in a museum, you're going to want all the pretty girls who see it to know where it came from."

Marion glared at him, indignant.

"Why would I care what a bunch of girls think of it? I'm an artist, I don't do this for the accolades. It's my calling."

Crystal laughed, hunched low over the table next to Kentaro.

"Yeah, this is your *Mona Lisa*. But it's not finished. I know exactly what it needs."

She reached into the pocket of her jeans and pulled out a little plastic bag filled with something that sparkled, even in the dim track lighting of the library. She opened the bag and carefully sprinkled the substance onto the piece of paper. It was granular and soft, somewhere between dust and salt, and the way it stuck to the paper reminded Charlie of the glitter his mother used to decorate all their holiday cards, most of which were still stacked in the front closet of their house, because she'd absentmindedly forgotten to send them, even though the whole family had spent hours sticking stamps to envelopes and culling addresses from multiple contact lists.

Jeremy raised his thick red eyebrows, then gave the plastic bag in Crystal's hand a little flick.

"You keep a baggy of sand in your pocket? Like, a snack, or something?"

"It's not sand." Crystal huffed. "It's quartz. Finely ground. For your information, quartz is the most common mineral in the Earth's crust. A perfect mix of silicon and oxygen, which binds well to most surfaces, and it's very beautiful because it has a high refraction index, which, for you Neanderthals, means it sparkles extremely brightly in any kind of light. Just like Mr. Scar's hair."

Although Charlie was a nerd himself, he still found amusing the matter-of-fact way Crystal spouted geological information. He knew she wouldn't have gotten the joke. Sometimes it seemed that the whole world, to her, was a laboratory to be processed and explained in precise scientific terms. It could be annoying at times, but it could also be cute; sometimes Charlie found himself laughing about something she'd said hours earlier. Sometimes he'd even wake up in the morning still cracking up about something she'd done the day before. Jeremy had teased him a few times about having some sort of crush on her, but Charlie didn't see it that way. She was just so unique, it was hard not to be charmed by her quirks.

In any event, when the rest of them looked on the piece of paper at the drawing Marion had made of the school librarian, Mr. Scarborough, they saw a perfect caricature. Superman shoulders stuffed into a light-blue oxford shirt, buttoned so high and tight up his neck that his Adam's apple looked like a big meal being digested by a little snake; Clark Kent glasses perched on a diamond sharp nose; a blond—yes, arguably sparkly—hairline receding up a slope of shiny forehead like an alpine avalanche in reverse. It was an amazing drawing, especially done so quickly with a Bic pen in dim lighting. But that was the miracle of Marion, a kid who had once spent a week in the hospital because of an ant bite, not even a bee—just a simple garden variety ant; give him a pen and a piece of paper and he could capture your soul. He wasn't going for *precision*, he was going for something bigger. As smart as she was, Crystal never quite got that; Charlie had once spent a Saturday afternoon with her and the rest of the Whiz Kids at the modern art wing of the MFA, and at the end of the day, she'd simply commented: "Well, some people really do have trouble coloring within the lines." With Crystal, you just had to understand, the world was supposed to live within the lines too.

But Jeremy, for his part, wasn't going to let Crystal off that easy. He got too much enjoyment out of baiting her. He put his hands to his mouth in mock surprise.

"You have a crush on Mr. Scar? Should we call him over so you can inspect his beautiful blond locks up close?"

Crystal glared at him from behind her zebra-rimmed glasses.

"I don't have a crush on anyone. I just think his hair looks a little like quartz. While your hair has the distinct glow of hematite. Which is the brittle mineral form of iron ore. If a rock could be stupid, it would be hematite."

Jeremy cocked his head as if thinking it through.

"Isn't hematite magnetic? Yep, that sounds like me. I've been told I've got a very magnetic quality."

"Well," Kentaro chimed in, peering up at Jeremy, "like a magnet, you are kind of sticky."

"That's true," Crystal agreed. "I've seen you after gym class. You bind to your T-shirt even better than the quartz binds to paper. In fact, I'm surprised you aren't stuck to your chair right now."

Now Charlie couldn't keep himself from laughing out loud. You could talk in hushed whispers at your own peril, but turn Mr. Scar's library into a banter-filled locker room, and you were in for a world of trouble.

Although to be fair, the place kind of *was* shaped like a locker room. Rectangular, with white cinder-block walls, low tiled ceilings, and windows that were little more than the sort of unopenable slits that you'd expect to find in the basement of an inner-city gym, or perhaps a prison. In the direct center of the room sat a round wooden gazebolike structure, supported by brightly decorated turquoise pillars, containing a single round table with multiple built-in chairs.

With the gazebo as its physical and emotional center, the rest of the library consisted of low aluminum bookshelves that fanned out in a sunburstlike pattern. Closer to the gazebo, the shelves were packed tightly together, with barely enough room between them for a regular-size student to browse. The Whiz Kids had claimed the table closest to the library's entrance, for the simple reason that it was also farthest from Mr. Scarborough's desk, which was all the way on the other side of the room. At the moment, even as Charlie craned his neck back and forth, he couldn't catch sight of Mr. Scar's impressive shoulders or the waves of his receding hair. In fact, at first glance around the library he didn't see anyone at all, but then he saw a flash of motion from the other side of the gazebo. He waved his hands at Crystal and Jeremy, who were still jawing on about ferrous minerals and sticky substances, urging them to quiet down, when he suddenly realized that the motion he was seeing wasn't Mr. Scar at all.

It was three people, actually, strolling briskly between the library shelves directly toward the gazebo.

Charlie didn't fully comprehend what he was seeing until they seated themselves at the table in the direct center of the room.

Miranda Sloan was at the head of the Gazebo table, her back to Charlie, that cascade of pitch-black hair dancing down the bare skin of her neck. She had placed a large hardcover book on the table in front of her and was pointing out chapter headings with one of her talon-sharp, manicured fingers. To her right, leaning forward over the book to get a better look, was Greg Titus, the cocky seventh grader. And across from him, vaguely facing in Charlie's direction, though not looking at him all, was Sam Ashley. She was smiling at something Miranda was saying, and she shook her silky golden hair out of her smoke-colored eyes. Charlie couldn't help thinking that it would take more than a single bag of Crystal's quartz to get that hair right.

"What's up?" Jeremy whispered, looking at Charlie. "Is it Mr. Scar? Is he coming over? Because if he is, Crystal could sign the picture instead of Marion, maybe save us from detention when she confesses her undying love."

"Shut up," Crystal hissed back, shoving her bag of quartz back in her pocket like it was some sort of contraband. "If anyone is in love with Mr. Scar, it's you, iron head, the way you keep going on about him."

"It's not Mr. Scar," Charlie responded simply, staring at the gazebo and its occupants. Miranda still hadn't turned around, but now Sam was glancing his way, and he thought he saw the slightest hint of a smile in the gray of her eyes.

Another coincidence? Charlie didn't even have to think it through, because he knew the answer. He looked over at Jeremy, who was busy flicking quartz dust at Crystal while Marion did his best to protect his Mona Lisa from the fallout of their escalating battle. Jeremy hadn't noticed the group in the gazebo, and even if he had, he couldn't possibly have connected them to Charlie. Which was good, because Charlie was having enough trouble keeping from explaining his association with Finn. He couldn't imagine what sort of trouble he'd get in trying to explain away Ms. Sloan, Greg, and Sam.

On the other hand, sitting there with his Whiz Kids, going about their regular routine in their desolate, safe corner of the Nagassack equivalent to a gulag, he found himself unnaturally attracted to that gazebo. His entire body seemed to be pulling him in that direction. And deep inside, Charlie felt something click.

Without a word, he rose from the table and started

down the aisle between the two nearest bookshelves. He moved so fast that Jeremy and the rest of the Whiz Kids didn't even look up from Marion's picture and their rapidly expanding quartz war. Before Charlie could take three breaths, he was at the steps that lead into the gazebo. He took them two at a time; he didn't want to give himself a chance to change his mind.

When he reached the table, Ms. Sloan looked up from the hardcover book. Before she could say anything, Charlie leaned low so that his friends across the room wouldn't see or hear him from behind the gazebo's pillars.

"You read my science paper. The one I submitted to the Massachusetts State Science Fair, on predicting a satellite's descent to the earth."

Ms. Sloan's smile didn't move. Her lips looked like Marion had drawn them across the porcelain skin of her face, perfect and precise.

"Yes. By accident, actually. I was a volunteer judge, and when I saw your project, I knew you would be perfect for our endeavor. You have the brains for this, Charlie. With a little work, you'll take us exactly where we need to go."

Charlie took another breath, then nodded slightly.

"I'm in. But I have one condition."

Ms. Sloan waited. Charlie could feel Greg and Sam

watching him as well, but he didn't break focus.

"Jeremy Draper goes with me to Incredo Land. All expenses paid."

"Diapers?" Greg blurted out, laughing. Charlie glanced at him with narrow eyes.

"Jeremy *Draper*. Yes. He goes or I don't go. He doesn't have to know anything about what we're really doing there. He won't be involved in this. But he gets to go on the class trip. This is a dealbreaker for me. He goes, or I don't go."

Although he hadn't fully realized it until he'd seen the three of them in the gazebo, Charlie had come to the decision in the science lab, when Jeremy had waxed poetic on the perceived joys of Incredo Land. Charlie wasn't going to do this just for himself, or because it seemed like an amazing adventure, or because it was math turned into something powerful and profitable. He was going to do this for himself and Jeremy, two kids who didn't get things like this dropped in their laps every day.

Ms. Sloan waited a full beat, then shrugged her angled shoulders.

"Okay."

Charlie didn't wait for her to say anything else. He quickly turned and headed down the steps, breathing hard like he'd just run a marathon. His face felt flushed, and he couldn't feel his feet within his boots. Just as he stepped off the last stair and out of the shadow cast by the gazebo's high, turquoise pillars, he heard Sam's voice trickle after him, her words like fingers of velvet against the back of his neck.

"Welcome aboard, Charlie. Brace yourself, it's going to be a wild ride."

IT HAPPENED SO FAST, Charlie never had a chance to react.

One minute he was standing in front of the purple curtain, Finn next to him, Miranda reaching for the heavy velvet, and the next thing he knew, strong hands grabbed him by the waist and he was suddenly up in the air, the world spinning around him. He was vaguely aware of the curtain being pulled back and the sound of laughter mixed with applause, and then he was upside down, his head inches from the hardwood floor. He looked up toward his feet and saw Magic grinning down at him, thick hands around his ankles.

"First rule of the Carnival Killers," Magic said, "always be aware of your surroundings."

Magic lowered him gently to the floor, then helped him back to his feet. Finn was in front of him, Sam and Greg right behind Finn, and the redheaded fellow sixth grader, Daniel, standing next to Jake Tucson, the soccer jock, right beneath an oversize banner that read, in big block letters: WELCOME TO THE TEAM.

The whole scene was kitschy and stupid and fairly ridiculous, and it filled Charlie with a warmth he couldn't begin to describe. No matter how much comfort he got from his Whiz Kids, as an admittedly geeky kid he'd always had trouble shaking the feeling of being a little different, a little lonely. Being welcomed into a group of kids like these gave him a palpable rush. It certainly took the sting away from the fact that he'd had to lie to his parents for the second time in a week to get them to drop him back at school after dinner—seven p.m., the latest he'd ever been to the Nagassack campus. They hadn't even balked when he'd told them he'd been elected the head of a new math club that would be meeting three days a week in Headmaster Walker's—or Warden Walker's, as most of the kids called him—office to prepare for a statewide quiz competition after Christmas break. A pretty elaborate lie, but even though Charlie was new at deceiving his parents, he'd come to the conclusion that an elaborate lie was probably more believable than something simple and straightforward. After all, a simple and straightforward road was easy to see down, while one filled with twists and turns was much more obscure.

"The Carnival Killers?" he finally managed, when the heat went out of his cheeks. "Is that what we're calling ourselves?"

"That's not set in stone," Finn grumbled. "Personally, I kind of hate it. I wanted to go with something a little subtler. Like the Magnificent Seven. Or why not the Numbers Gang, in honor of our newest member?"

"But the Carnival Killers has such a nice ring to it," Magic responded, giving Charlie a friendly little shove forward. "And that's who we are, that's what we're going to do. We're going to kill the biggest carnival on earth."

The group parted as Magic guided Charlie out of the front, semicircular section of the art room, past where the curtain had hung. Charlie could see that the three mock fair games were exactly as they had been when he'd first seen them, the coin toss to his right, the dart-balloon game to his left, and the rope ladder directly ahead, attached to the back wall. He also noticed that the windows were still blacked out with construction paper, even though it was obviously dark outside this late into September.

"Hyperbole aside," Miranda said, "I think it's a good fit. But we'll have plenty of time to argue about the name over the next five weeks. In the meantime, we need to get our newest member up to speed."

Five weeks. Charlie felt a burst of adrenaline at the mention of the deadline, because he knew what she was referring to: the trip to Incredo Land, something he couldn't have even imagined two days ago, something he still couldn't really envision because it seemed so unreal. But the other kids in the room obviously felt differently, because they immediately broke into action, moving to the various games set out across the orange-lit room. Greg and Sam went right to the rope ladder, quietly discussing some aspect of the game as they went. Daniel and Jake stepped over to the balloon-dart setup, immediately arguing about who was going to play first; Jake seemed to make the argument moot by getting to the darts first. But before he made a toss, Charlie felt Magic's hand on his shoulder again, and he found himself right up in front of the coin-toss counter, staring out at the sea of shiny white plates that covered much of the floor ahead of him.

Finn pointed to the three oversize gold coins that were neatly stacked up on the counter and gave Charlie a nod. Charlie glanced over his shoulder, but Miranda had crossed back into the front half of the room, taking a seat in one of the institutional-style plastic drafting chairs. Maybe it was an act, maybe she was watching everything out of the corners of those exotic, frighteningly intense eyes. Maybe the team was such a well-oiled machine, she could hang back and let them bring Charlie into the fold without her. It was too soon for Charlie to judge the dynamics of the group yet. Either way, it was obvious what he was expected to do: *Dive in, headfirst.*

He picked up the first coin, shrugged, and tossed it at the plates. Clink, clatter, clunk—just as it had happened at the Sherwood Fair, the coin ricocheted off a couple of plates and landed with a thunk on the floor.

Finn folded his arms against his chest and cocked his head to the side.

"Charlie, what is the object of this game?"

Charlie looked at him, then at the plates, then back at Finn. It seemed like a pretty stupid question.

"To get a coin onto a plate."

"Wrong!" Magic shouted, startling Charlie. Magic grinned again, but Finn shushed him with a hand.

"The object of this game is to get a coin to *stay* on a plate," Finn corrected. "It sounds like a minor difference, but that difference is everything. It's real easy to get the coin onto a plate."

He reached forward, picked up one of the coins, and flung it at random toward the closest plate. Much like Charlie's coin, the little gold piece clicked and clacked through the field of plates at random, ending up on the floor with a clunk. Then he turned back toward Charlie.

"But to get a coin to stay on a plate? That's something else entirely."

He picked up the last coin, then centered himself in front of the counter. His back was to Charlie, so for a brief second Charlie couldn't see what he was doing, but then with a flick of his wrist, Finn sent the coin in a high arc, up toward the ceiling, where the gaggle of stuffed animals hung, just like they had at the Sherwood Fair. The coin barely missed the lowest hanging animal—a Zebra with googly eyes—at the top of its arc, then dove straight down, hitting a plate in the direct center of the field. This time, the coin didn't ricochet or hop from plate to plate. The coin hit the plate and stopped dead, planted firmly against the porcelain.

"How did you do that?" Charlie asked.

"Magic," whispered Magic with a laugh.

Finn turned back to Charlie. His face was completely serious.

"Science looks a lot like magic when it's applied correctly."

Winking, Finn suddenly pulled himself up onto the counter where the three coins had previous been stacked, then flung one jeaned leg over the top. Reaching down, he grabbed one of the plates off its base and held it up to show Charlie its smooth, shiny front surface.

"The plates that they use in carnivals are usually polished porcelain or ceramic. Exceedingly smooth and shiny and slippery; in fact, sometimes the carnies even oil them up to make them even more so. Anything that hits them with any sort of horizontal force is going to slide or roll right off."

"And when you toss a coin forward," Magic butted in, "you're giving it a lot of horizontal force. The harder the toss, the more forward force. Which means in this game, the stronger you are, the worse you actually do."

Charlie nodded, taking it all in. Horizontal force, what Finn and Magic were talking about, in physics terms was forward velocity. The speed of an object moving forward multiplied by its weight. The coins didn't have much weight, but even so, any reasonable amount of forward velocity was going to add up to enough force to make it hard for one of them to avoid sliding off the slippery surface of an oiled plate!

Which is why Finn had obviously avoided as much forward velocity as he could.

"So you arc the coin up, toward the ceiling. The more of an arc you give it, the less horizontal force, and the more force on the vertical, or up and down, axis."

"Give the kid a gold star," Magic said. "Or maybe a gold coin. But see, there's a problem with your solution, isn't there?"

Magic pointed toward the ceiling with a thick finger, and Charlie looked up, immediately seeing the jungle of stuffed animals.

"That's why they hang the stuffed animals right above the game," Charlie murmured, a little awed at realizing something he'd never thought about before. "They're trying to limit your vertical throw."

"Right," Finn said, still straddling the counter. "You can't get really good height at most carnivals because the doggone stuffed animals are hanging right there, like some chaotic zoological piñata. But with a little practice, you can still arc it up to some degree, giving yourself a little edge. And you need to make sure the coin isn't spinning in the air. When a coin spins, it's adding in all these new forces to the calculation, which you don't want. And when it spins, you can't be sure how it's going to hit the plate. If it contacts that smooth surface with its edge, it's going to roll right off. But if it lands flat, well, you've got a chance."

"But not much of one." Magic sighed. "You've still got a bit of forward velocity to deal with, and you've got that incredibly slippery surface."

Charlie was amazed at how much was going on behind the scenes of something as simple as a carnival coin-toss game. Oiled plates? Stuffed animals hung in a way that was designed to lessen your chances of winning? It certainly didn't seem fair.

"So how do you get the coin to stay on the plate?"

Finn smiled.

"We add a little chemistry."

Then he did something that took Charlie completely by surprise. He reached down behind the counter and retrieved one of the gold coins, then held it up in front of his face, stuck out his tongue, and licked it.

"Ninety-eight percent water, about two percent enzymes that break down starches. A little mucus, a few other elements depending on your diet and your genetic makeup. Saliva, Charlie. It's a pretty nifty chemical, lots of cool properties that most people don't know about, and even more important, you've always got some with you."

He turned, gave the coin a flick with his wrist. It went up, up, up, just avoided the bottom of the googly-eyed zebra, then dropped down, sticking to the same plate that he'd landed the last coin on: *clunk. A perfect winner.*

"You put spit on the coin," Charlie murmured. Magic squeezed his shoulder.

"Works even better if you eat something heavy in dairy right before you play. Ice cream, maybe some yogurt, it increases the thickness of the mucus."

"On a microscopic level," Finn said as if he were giving a book report, "the enzymes in your saliva have all these protein-size attractor points that grip the tiny imperfections in the plate, the grooves you could only see with a microscope—"

"Friction," Charlie said. "You create friction by licking the coin. Just enough that if the coin hits the plate flat on—"

"It's going to stick." Finn grinned.

Charlie whistled low. "That's pretty cool."

Finn pulled his leg back over the counter and put his boots back to the floor. He stretched, then straightened the sleeves of his ever-present leather jacket.

"Yeah, it's cool. But even when you know what you're doing, it's not as easy as it looks. It takes practice. Lots of practice. A couple of hours a day, a few times a week, and maybe you'll be as good as me."

Physics and chemistry. Not strength, not even accuracy,

really, though you'd need to practice the motion until you had the skill, until you could get the arc right and keep the coin from spinning in the air. But physics and chemistry, that's really what it was. That's how you beat the game. Charlie felt like he was on fire, eager to get started, eager to teach himself how to throw the coins as well as Finn, maybe even better than Finn. He started forward toward the counter, but Finn stopped him with a hand.

"Being good enough to do this nine out of ten times isn't enough. Because it's all in the way you do it. That look on your face right now, the way you're going for the coins—Charlie, that's going to end this for you before you even start."

"What do you mean?"

"You've got to disguise your movements. You've watched me beat this game here and at Sherwood. You ever see me licking any coins? No, because I do it fast, easy, cool—in a way that nobody can see me doing it. You've got to learn to play it cool. You've got to hit the game, land the coins, then get out without the carny ever realizing what you've done. And if you're going to keep hitting the same game over and over, you've got to play different roles so he doesn't recognize you each time. We're not talking major disguises here, we're just talking wearing a hat, maybe a different jacket—"

"Fake names," Charlie said, eyes widening. "Fake personalities."

Magic leaned toward him dramatically.

"Second rule of the Carnival Killers. Always be in character."

"Is all that really necessary?" Charlie asked. "I mean, are they really watching over these games so carefully?"

Finn shrugged.

"It's better to be thorough than to get caught, right?"

Charlie swallowed. His throat felt a little tight.

"What happens if you get caught?"

Magic playfully punched his shoulder, laughing away Charlie's sudden tension.

"Spitting on a coin? Tossing the coin the correct way to win the game? There's nothing illegal about that. You're just using your brain to beat them. They won't like it, but they can't get you in trouble for it."

"Which doesn't mean you stick around if they do start giving you problems," Finn said.

"Which brings us to the third rule of the Carnival Killers," Magic finished for him. He took Charlie by the shoulders, spun him around so they were face-to-face, sneering at him, nose crinkled and teeth clenched in full view like a wolf threatening its prey.

"Always be ready to run."

Magic laughed again, but Charlie couldn't tell if he was kidding or not. Before he could belabor the point, Finn was ushering him out of Magic's grip and toward the second fair game, a counter of darts and a wall of balloons.

SHRINKING DOWN THE MOUSE · 147

10

CHARLIE WANTED TO CLOSE his eyes. He wanted to scream. He wanted to do anything but what he was doing—standing there, frozen in place, his arm out in front of him, palm up, watching with terror as the metal dart plunged down through the air, racing toward his skin.

"Wait!" he finally shouted, but it was too late.

The dart reached his palm and the cold steel hit his skin, directly in the center, the soft unguarded flesh, an inch from the base of his fingers, and he opened his mouth to let out a noise—

And then, nothing. The steel point creased his skin but didn't even come close to piercing. In fact, it didn't hurt at all. Other than the coldness of the metal and the pressure from the downward arc of the dart, there was little to no sensation. The thing was so dull that even though Daniel had jabbed it down at his hand with fairly good speed and accuracy, it hadn't harmed him at all. Which, obviously, was the point.

Charlie turned his attention from the dart to the freckled face peering down at him.

"And they're all like this," Daniel said, bringing the dart back up to eye level. "They grind them down to make them as dull as possible. But that's not even the worst part."

He gestured to Jake, the soccer kid, who was a few feet to his left down the counter. Jake picked up one of the other darts and tossed it toward the balloons affixed to the wall. The dart hit one of the balloons dead on, and harmlessly fell to the floor. The balloon continued to wobble after the dart disappeared, a trembling blob of bright yellow. Charlie couldn't help wondering which of the kids had spent the necessary hours blowing up all those things. There had to be thirty, forty balloons attached to the wall.

"The balloons are only about three-quarters full. The latex is loose, nowhere near stretched to capacity. Which means that when a dull dart hits it, ninety-nine out of a hundred times the dart is going to just bounce right off."

Charlie nodded, still listening to Finn and Magic's coins clinking loudly against the plates. He tossed a glance over his shoulder, back toward where Miranda was still sitting in one of the drafting chairs, scribbling in a notepad. He wondered if she was taking notes about the teaching session for the paper she was going to write about their team.

The more Charlie learned about how even these supposedly "beatable" fair games worked, the better he felt about what he was getting into. With the darts and balloons, the deck seemed stacked heavily against the player. Under-filled balloons? Dulled darts? Like the oiled plates and the low-hanging stuffed animals, it seemed that the fair games were anything but fair. Carnival Killers? If the carnivals were so rigged against poor unaware kids who spent their allowances trying to win prizes—well, didn't the carnivals deserve to get killed? Was it cheating to even the odds of an unfair game?

"So how do you beat the balloons?" Charlie asked, narrowing his eyes.

Daniel smiled, the freckles around his mouth dancing like orange raindrops across a pasty white windowpane.

"I like your attitude."

He showed Charlie the dart, then did something bizarre. Without a word, he slid the dart down into his pocket. He held the dart there for a few seconds, then brought the dart back up, swung on his heels, and hurled it toward the balloons.

There was a loud pop as one of the balloon burst into a million pieces.

"Wow," Charlie said.

"Yeah, wow," Jake responded from a few feet away. He brought a dart out of his pocket and flung it toward the balloons. Again, another loud pop, another balloon bursting emphatically.

"What the heck is in your pockets?"

Daniel reached in and pulled out a small white piece of material that looked like a thick gauze bandage. He held it out toward Charlie.

"Careful, now."

Charlie raised an eyebrow, reached forward to touch the bandage, and jerked his hand back. The thing was hot. Not searingly so, but enough to make him wince.

"It's a heat wrap," Daniel said. "You know, the kind you can find at any drugstore. People use them for pulled muscles or aching joints."

Charlie had seen heat wraps many times before. His father had gone through a racquetball phase when

Charlie was in fifth grade. Before that, it had been pickup basketball with a few of the other professors at MIT. His father had worked through so many heat wraps, ace bandages, and Advil bottles, sometimes his medicine cabinet looked like the Celtics' locker room.

"You use them to heat up the darts," Charlie said.

Daniel nodded. Charlie instantly understood. Again, it was physics and chemistry mixed together to beat bad odds. His father had explained how the chemical filled heat packs worked, because Charlie had essentially been born naturally curious. Heat packs were actually made up of two separate compartments, one filled with liquid, usually water, the other with chemicals such as calcium or magnesium sulfate. When the pack was opened, the two compartments were combined, causing a chemical reaction that released energy via heat.

"The second law of thermodynamics," Charlie continued. "Heat always moves toward an equilibrium. The atoms excited by the chemical reaction give off energy, which travels from atom to atom through anything it touches, heating up the cooler materials until everything is an even temperature. In other words, you hold the dart against the heat pack, the metal heats up. And when you throw the dart at the balloon, that heat is transferred to the atomic structure of the latex, breaking those bonds—"

"And popping the balloon," Jake finished, tossing another dart that hit with another loud pop.

Again, physics and chemistry, the science of ballistics meeting the laws of thermodynamics. But this time, unlike with the coin toss, Daniel and Jake had added something that wasn't really part of the game—the heating pack. Charlie wasn't sure, but it felt like that was a little more like cheating.

Then again, the game was unfair. You couldn't really win the way the game was designed. And what were you really adding? You weren't throwing anything but the dart. You weren't moving closer to the balloons or really breaking any rules that Charlie could name. You were adding heat, which wasn't even something physical or quantifiable.

It was pretty ingenious, actually. The heated darts flipped the odds of the game on their head. Nine out of ten times, you'd probably pop those balloons. They were easy to hit, and with the heat reacting with the latex material, well, there would be a whole lot of popping going on.

Charlie was eager to give it a try himself. He was about to reach for one of the darts when Daniel caught his hand, then pointed over his shoulder.

"There's still one more game to beat," he said.

Charlie followed the kid's freckled finger. Greg was standing at the base of the rope ladder, arms crossed against his chest, a bored look on his face. Behind him, halfway up the ladder, Sam smiled toward Charlie, then gracefully scrambled up the last few feet along the sway-ing rope material and hit the bell with an outstretched hand.

11

THE RINGING IN CHARLIE'S ears seemed to continue even after the bell had stopped trembling; he used the few seconds it took to get from the balloon-dart counter to the base of the rope ladder to clear his head. He wasn't sure what it was about Sam that seemed to continually catch him off guard, but every time she looked at him, it was kind of like getting splashed with water.

By the time he reached the base of the rope ladder, she had clambered back down from the bell and was standing next to Greg, who still had his arms crossed, a smug look on his face. His shirt was bright green with a designer label, the collar starched so high it nearly touched his ears. Sam, in contrast, was in an oversize

sweatshirt and ripped jeans. Her outfit would have gotten her sent home during regular school hours, but this
late, nobody would be roaming the halls other than ath-
letes on their way home from various practices and the
odd musical prodigy coming back from one of the practice rooms on the school's lowest floor.

Charlie was surprised to see that she wasn't even
breathing hard; she'd gone up and down the rope ladder
in a near blur, so fast he hadn't even seen where she'd
put her hands and feet. The ladder was still swinging
a bit behind her, and the way it rocked back and forth
sent chills down Charlie's spine.

Like the other games in the room, he'd tried the
rope ladder before a few times in his life, at various
fairs and carnivals that his parents had taken him to
over the years. The results had always been the same.
Charlie knew his limitations: He wasn't a good athlete,
he didn't have great balance, and though he could do
math and science on a high-school level, the strength of
his arms and legs was barely beyond that of a toddler's.
He'd always sucked at all things physical. His father
had told him that those things only mattered until you
were eighteen, and then it all reversed, and all anyone
cared about was what you could do with your brain.
Charlie had suspected that that was the sort of thing

fathers always told athletically inept sons. Maybe it was true, maybe it wasn't, but eighteen years seemed like a heck of a long time to wait for the tables to turn.

Greg's eyes seemed to be telling Charlie the same thing as he looked him over.

"I guess we better get this over with." He sniffed, waving Charlie toward the still-swinging ladder. "Let's see what you've got."

Charlie looked from him to Sam, and she gave him a thumbs-up and an encouraging smile. Charlie took a deep breath and stepped past the two of them, then surveyed his competition. The ladder was exactly the same as the few he had tried before: two thick ropes leading about fifteen feet at a steep angle up the wall, bisected by a dozen or so wooden rungs. A foot above where the ladder reached the wall was the bell that Sam had rung so easily. *Simple*, Charlie said to himself, *just take a deep breath and give it a go.*

He reached for the second rung, gripping it tightly with his right hand. Then he put his left foot on the first rung, and lifted his weight up onto the ladder—

And that was as far as he got. The ladder lurched right, then left, then flipped upside down. His hands came open and he dropped, his stomach lurching as he plummeted the few feet to the floor. He hit with a huff of air, then realized, thankfully, that he'd landed on a thick blue gym mat. Nothing bruised but his ego. Greg and Sam peered down at him, laughing. Greg's laugh was cruel and hearty and went on a lot longer than Sam's.

"Pretty much what I expected," he said. Sam gave Greg a push, then stepped forward and reached out a hand. Charlie took it, letting her help him back to his feet.

"I gotta say, I'm not sure how math or science is going to help me with this one. It just seems really hard to do."

Sam laughed. Then she pulled Charlie next to her and turned him so he was facing the ladder with her, side by side. He was getting warm beneath his shirt but did his best to ignore the feeling.

"Charlie, tell me what you see."

Charlie raised his eyebrows, wondering if it was some sort of trick question.

"I see a ladder."

"And that's exactly why you can't do it. Because this one, well, it's really a matter of perception."

"What do you mean?"

Greg stuck his head over Charlie's right shoulder.

"You see a ladder, genius, so you reach for the

rungs. In the normal, physical world, that's how a ladder works. And that's exactly what the carnival thugs want you to do."

"But see," Sam said, leaning forward to grab one of the ropes that ran up the side of the rungs, "this isn't a ladder at all, actually. Your brain is fooling you. This is just two ropes hanging up a wall. The rungs are irrelevant."

Charlie looked at her and felt realization creeping in; he was starting to understand what she was saying. And if she was correct, well, he had been wrong—science was involved.

"The center of gravity—"

"Isn't where you think it is," Greg finished for him. "Your mind is telling you that this is a ladder, so the right place to put your hands and feet are on the rungs. But the real center of gravity is divided between the two outer ropes."

Greg stepped forward, put his hands on the ropes, felt his way up a few feet, then carefully placed his feet where his hands had been.

"You never touch the rungs. You move both sides of your body as simultaneously as you can, and zoom, zoom, zoom."

Smooth as silk, Greg skittered up the rope ladder,

hands and feet working in tandem. Even though he was much bulkier than Sam and a head taller, his movements seemed just as graceful. Now that Charlie knew what he was doing, he could see how the older kid avoided creating torque—the physics term for twisting, or spinning, around a center—by evening his weight out across the real centers of gravity, the outer ropes. When Charlie had tried to do the ladder, he'd placed his weight right in the center because he'd thought that's how a ladder was supposed to work, that's where the center of gravity was. He had been wrong.

A matter of perception, and really, of physics. Torque versus gravity, a problem of Newtonian physics. Gravity was pulling your body down; by spreading your weight between the two ropes, you could avoid the torque that would normally spin you around the center, flipping you off to the floor.

It took a barely a few seconds for Greg to reach the bell. This time, the ringing seemed loud enough to shake the blacked-out windows. Then Greg was back down the rope and up on his feet, holding his palms out on either side like a magician completing a difficult trick. Charlie heard applause from behind, and turned to see Miranda standing behind him and Sam. It seemed, for the moment, that the lesson was over.

Charlie was glad; even though he now understood what he'd done wrong, he wasn't exactly eager to try the rope again in front of everyone. Perception and practice were two very different things.

"I think you get the idea," Miranda said, her fingers lacing together as she gave Charlie as warm a look as she could manage with eyes cut from ice. "These are the three games we'll play, because these are the three games we know we can beat. For the next five weeks, we'll practice here every chance we get: after school, during lunch, during recess. And then we'll head to Incredo Land. The Solar Avenue games will open at seven a.m. on November third, and we'll have twelve hours to win as many tickets as we can."

The other kids came forward as she spoke, forming a small semicircle around her. She turned to open herself up to all of them, her gaze moving from face to face.

"Between the seven of you, we should be able to put together quite a collection. Everyone will take turns hitting these three games; we'll space it out so that the carnies running them won't notice how often you're winning. Then we pool the tickets, give them to Charlie. Charlie turns them in, wins the contest. And gets a shot at spinning the wheel."

Charlie could hear his heart thudding in his chest

as all the attention shifted from Miranda to him.

"It all comes down to that," Miranda continued. "Charlie, you'll have one chance. One spin."

Charlie cleared his throat. It felt like the room had frozen around him.

"And you think I can beat the wheel."

There was a cough from his right. He was pretty sure it was Greg, but he couldn't be certain. Then he felt Sam touch his hand with a reassuring finger. It was a tiny motion, the littlest of connections, but it took some of the tension away.

"I *know* you can beat the wheel," Miranda responded, smiling like a Cheshire cat. "And so do you."

Charlie looked from her to Finn, who was tossing one of the gold coins from hand to hand. For a moment, he watched the gold flashing in the low orange light, the way it seemed to dance between Finn's skilled fingers.

Charlie took a deep breath. He had been going over and over it in his head for the past twenty-four hours, ever since he'd agreed to join the team. Joking and jawing with the Whiz Kids in the library, riding the bus home next to Jeremy, absentmindedly chatting his way through dinner with his parents, slogging through two hours of homework before bed, alone in the dark under his covers, restlessly shifting back and forth until dawn, his mind had been on overdrive the whole time, working it out.

And the truth was, after all that thought, he knew that Miranda was right.

Unlike the games spread out across the back half of that art room, beating the wheel wasn't going to take skill, or perception, or even practice. Beating the wheel wasn't going to be a matter of group cooperation, subterfuge, or the sneaky use of simple chemistry. Beating the wheel was actually, in a way, much simpler, for a kid like Charlie Numbers.

Because beating the wheel, at its heart, was just a matter of math.

12

AND THEN THERE WAS darkness.

A thick, soupy, pitch-black darkness filling every inch of the voluminous auditorium, like a velvet dome weighing down every molecule of air, so full and heavy Charlie found it hard to even take a breath.

And suddenly, light. Or more accurately, *lightning*.

A flash so sudden and fierce that it seemed to crack the very air, followed by a bolt of terrifyingly white electricity running in a single, jagged streak across the center of the auditorium, leaping upward in daggers so sharp, it reminded Charlie of the serrated edge of a hunting knife, or the borders of an angry scar. In that instantaneous glow of the lightning bolt, the auditorium became momentarily visible, a scene illuminated so fast, it was like looking at a single movie frame frozen beneath a sheet of glass. Down at the center of the vast room, the two giant Textolite columns, six feet in diameter, rising twenty feet right out of the floor, capped by the massive double spheres of the Van de Graaff generator: perfectly round, shiny aluminum, melded together at the center, each fifteen feet tall, reaching halfway to the curved ceiling. The bolt of lighting had erupted right off the surface of the aluminum, rising up above the crowd—a frozen blur of wide-eyed faces staring straight up in equal parts awe and terror. Most had probably never seen anything like the display in front of them; assuredly, they had no idea how the Van de Graaff generator worked, or even that it was the largest air insulated Van de Graaff in existence. That it had been donated by MIT to the museum more than half a century ago. To most of the audience, it was an object of awe and maybe even magic.

Charlie trembled as he watched the streak of white leaping from the generator to the telescoping grounding beacon attached near the high curved ceiling of the auditorium. To him, there was no magic in this room; he knew exactly how the Van de Graaff worked. He knew that one of those massive columns contained a rubber conveyer belt, moving at about sixty miles per hour, carrying high voltage DC current to the aluminum of the hollow spheres. He knew that when the aluminum reached a high enough voltage, the energy leaped from the sphere to the grounding beacon—homemade lightning, as fierce and real as anything a cloud could produce.

This wasn't the first Sunday afternoon Charlie had found himself in the Theater of Electricity at the Museum of Science; the place was sort of a ritual for him, his first stop whenever his parents took him to the brick-and-glass, multifloored city landmark that squatted on a particularly pretty curve of the Charles River. Charlie had always loved the Museum of Science. As he'd aged, his interests had traveled from exhibit to exhibit. As a toddler, he'd been obsessed with the Discovery Center, which was filled with things you could touch and throw and build. When he was a little older, he'd gravitated toward the dinosaurs on the lower floor of the museum; he could remember many Saturday afternoons spent cowering in the shadows of the great T. rex that dominated the Mesozoic exhibit, wondering how something so huge and terrifying could have ever inhabited the same world that now catered to beings as fragile as humankind. After the dinosaurs, he'd moved on to the exhibit called Science in the Park.

which was still his second favorite area of the Museum, after the Van de Graaff generator. Usually overrun with kids his age, Science in the Park was like a playground that had been built specifically for Charlie: swings that helped you calculate and understand harmonic motion, a race track for marble-size balls to teach you about gravity and potential energy, a seesaw to analyze mass and pivot, even a massive pulley system that let you lift hundreds of pounds, breaking down the magic of leverage. If, as Finn had basically said, magic was science you didn't yet understand, the Science in the Park exhibit was like pulling the curtain back on a dozen magical things at once.

Standing there in the darkness that Saturday afternoon, staring up at the bolt of lightning, Charlie realized that's exactly what the Carnival Killers was, the place behind the curtain, the science behind what looked, to the uninitiated, like magic. For four long weeks, Charlie had been living behind that curtain.

Over those four weeks, Finn and the rest of the group had guided Charlie through intense practice sessions; three times a week, they'd met after school in the darkened art room, moving from game to game until Charlie had mastered the techniques they had taught him. Even though he'd understood the science behind the techniques from the beginning, actually performing the feats had taken a surprisingly immense amount of training. Getting the gold coins to arc just right, steep enough to counter any forward force but low enough to avoid the stuffed animals, was tough, but even tougher was managing to lick the coins without being so obvious that any carny within ten feet would see what you were doing. Likewise, hitting one of the balloons with the dart was pretty simple; the way the balloons covered the wall, it was actually harder to miss one of the brightly colored things than to hit one. But getting the dart into your pocket and holding it there long enough to let the heat wrap do its thing took skill, speed, and a lot of grade-A acting.

In truth, that was the biggest lesson that Charlie had learned through all that exhausting practice—there was a lot of acting involved in being a Carnival Killer. You couldn't just master the skills of the games; you had to be able to pull them off under watchful eyes. Finn and Magic, but just as often Greg, Daniel, Jake, and Sam, would take turns playing the parts of the carnival workers, standing beneath the stuffed animals, engaging Charlie in mindless conversation, always seeming to watch what he was doing, always keeping an eye on his hands and the expression on his face.

He'd learned early on that to truly master these games, you had to become a character. Confident, calm, cool, because if you looked nervous, then you looked suspicious, and when you looked suspicious, people watched you more carefully. If you were joking and smiling and playing like you didn't have a care in the world, nobody noticed when a hand went into your pocket for a few seconds or a coin flashed close enough to your face to touch your tongue.

On top of that, Charlie had begun to develop his own characters—fake personalities that allowed him to pull off the necessary acts without raising any attention. His favorite was Chucky the Easily Amazed—a kid who approached the games like it was his first time seeing them, blown away by every little thing he saw: *Wow, these coins are cool, you throw them at the plates, just wow, let me look at this thing up close, okay, here I go, watch it go high up, up, up in the air! And these darts, how cool, they're so heavy, can I throw two at a time? No, okay, I'll put this one back on the counter, oh here's the other one—pop! Wow I did it on my first try? No way!!*

After mastering the basics of the games and developing a handful of characters that helped disguise his play, it was just a matter of practice, practice, and more practice. Coins, darts, rope ladder, over and over again. The rope ladder was the most physical of the games, and it had taken Charlie more than a week of falling on his bum—sometimes from high enough up the ladder to cause real bruises—to get the balance right, but he'd eventually been able to get over his fears and master the balancing of his weight on the two ropes to get past the ladder nearly every time he tried. Sam had been exactly right; it was really a matter of perspective. Once you stopped concentrating on the rungs and thought about the dual centers of gravity, it was like unlocking a secret code. That was a good way to describe everything he had learned—unlocking a code—but even so, all the games seemed equally exhausting after the hundredth time. More than once, Charlie's father had commented about Charlie's bleary eyes and near catatonic state on the drive home from "math club," and if Charlie hadn't been so tired, he'd have felt worse about the lies upon lies he was telling to mask what he was really up to.

But the subterfuge involved in fooling his parents in the late afternoons and evenings to allow him those hours of practice time was minor compared to what he'd been forced to do during the day at school. For as long as he could remember, the Whiz Kids had shared everything, from Marion's first trip to the emergency room after eating a cookie made with sesame oil, to Jeremy's mother's pregnancy and the birth of the little diaper-filler he called a sister. From Kentaro's spelling-bee awards, to Crystal's tracking down of one of the rarest shades of granite. In the lunchroom, at recess, in the front hall, waiting for the bus. Those moments together, where everything was fair game and nobody kept anything back, had always been sacred.

But for the past four weeks, Charlie had been a ghost, disappearing as soon as the lunch bell struck, only to reappear at the very end of recess, or rushing off the moment that classes ended, invisible in the hallways and byways as he hurried over to the art room for more practice. Even worse, when he was with the Whiz Kids, he was always monitoring himself to make sure he didn't say anything to blow his cover. Finn called it the cardinal rule of the Carnival Killers; on top of all the other rules was the need for utter secrecy. The school might not understand what they were up to, and Miranda had made it clear that it was fundamentally important to her paper on them that they remain an island unto themselves.

At first, for Charlie, that meant lying almost daily about where he went, about Finn and Magic. And then there were the other sort of lies, when he passed one of the other Carnival Killers in the hallways, pretending he didn't know them, pretending he wasn't glancing at them when he thought nobody was looking. The worst moments were the few when he and the Whiz Kids strolled past Sam on the way to a class or to the library; forcing himself to look the other way taxed every muscle in his neck and jaw.

Charlie knew that his friends were the smartest kids in the school; the slightest slipup would open Charlie up to an inquisition. He was always one step away from finding himself under a microscope, like a specimen in Crystal's vast rock collection, pelted and prodded and poked, until he crumbled like so much basalt. To avoid that, he'd kept himself quieter than usual, hardly joining in with the daily banter that was so much the food of their lives. Some days, he didn't say anything at all, and he could tell that his silence and withdrawn mannerisms were driving a wedge between him and the rest of the group. He knew that by keeping a secret as big as the Carnival Killers from the Whiz Kids, he was endangering the very essence of who they were: a group of geeky, nerdy, genius kids who had found one another, and in so doing, had built a world where they all belonged, where they had protection from the harsh realities of the jungle world that was middle school.

Just two days ago, Jeremy had actually put Charlie's fears to words while they stood shivering in their down jackets on the sidewalk that bordered the circular school driveway, waiting for their bus.

"If it's something we did," Jeremy had started, without any pretext, his eyes downturned, concentrating on a crushed milk carton he'd been bouncing from one booted toe to the other, "you should say something. We can take it. We've been called everything in the book."

At that, Charlie had almost told Jeremy everything. He felt so bad about lying to the Whiz Kids, about keeping something so important from them, and especially keeping it from his best friend—that was harder than anything he had learned from Finn and the rest. Particularly the fact that if Charlie made it through to the end of his training, Jeremy was going to be coming along with him to the Cheeriest Spot in the Universe. But Miranda's icy eyes and perfectly chiseled lips were in his head. He could only sigh and mumble an apology.

"It's nothing like that. I'm just tired. Maybe overextended with homework and the science projects I'm working on with my dad."

It was another little lie, one he'd been using to explain the afternoons he couldn't spend with Jeremy at the park or wandering the creek behind his house. But it was obvious Jeremy wasn't really buying it anymore.

"Yeah, I know about tired, remember? There's a six-month-old sharing my bedroom and my dad works a night shift three days a week to pay for these stupid boots. But that doesn't mean I disappear at lunch every day and treat everyone I know like trash. If you've found new friends to hang out with, you should just be honest. We'd all understand."

Charlie had almost broken at that, but then the bus had mercifully pulled up to the sidewalk, and Jeremy had kicked the carton of milk hard enough to send it bouncing off one of the bus's big rubber wheels. They'd ridden to their shared stop in silence, and Jeremy had let the matter drop. Another week, Charlie'd told himself, and it would all be over, they'd be on their way to Incredo Land, and Jeremy would forgive him. And when Charlie got to the wheel, when Charlie *beat* the wheel, he promised himself he would tell Jeremy and the rest everything, no matter what Miranda wanted. She'd have her paper, the rest of the group would get their lifetime tickets to the amusement park, and Charlie would have his Whiz Kids back, with a couple of those lifetime tickets to share for the rest of their lives.

Of course, Charlie thought as the lightning thundered even louder overhead, causing the crowd to gasp in near unison, getting to the wheel and beating the wheel were two very different things. Now that he'd had four weeks of practice and that he'd seen what the Carnival Killers could do, he was pretty sure that getting to the wheel was something they, as a group, could achieve. But beating the wheel was going to be up to him.

His eyes shifted from the jagged, brilliantly white bolt of lightning to the giant aluminum spheres, then down to the enormous cylinders at the center of the stage. When he closed his eyes for a brief second, he could picture the immense rubber fan belt spinning within one of those cylinders, carrying the current up to the aluminum in a blur of mechanical speed. The science behind the magic, that's exactly what Miranda was expecting from him.

Would he be able to give it to her? He was just a skinny kid who was good at numbers. He didn't have a magic wand or a wizard's hat. He didn't have access to any magic spells.

But what he did have was even more powerful than magic. He had math. Or specifically, a mathematical formula. With just four pieces of information, he could calculate how long it took a ball to roll down a bowl.

Four pieces of information. The diameter of the

bowl. The time the ball was dropped into the bowl. The time the ball finished its first rotation. And the time the ball finished its second rotation. With those four pieces of information, those four numbers, he could calculate when the ball was going to stop. Or, metaphorically, where a satellite was going to land.

Or even more metaphorically, where a spinning wheel was going to stop spinning. Because really, Charlie now understood, a spinning wheel was no different from a marble in a salad bowl or a satellite going around the earth. The arrow at the top, clicking its way from section to section, was akin to the marble or the satellite. The wheel was the bowl, or the earth.

So all he really needed to beat the wheel was to know the diameter of the wheel, the time at the moment the wheel started spinning, and then, as it went around, the time as it finished its first revolution, and then, infinitely slower, its second revolution. At the moment, he wasn't sure how he was going to find out the exact diameter of the wheel at Incredo Land, or how he was going to record the time that the wheel started spinning and the two other important marker points, but those were just details. The important point was, Charlie could, theoretically, beat the wheel.

Charlie shifted his gaze from the Van de Graaff

generator back to the magnificent lightning in the air. *From theory to practice, from an idea on a piece of paper to terrifying bolts of pure white energy flying through a pitch-black auditorium.* From theory to practice was really just a matter of mechanics, of muscle and sweat and strategy. A process, boxes to be checked off a list, emotionless obstacles to overcome.

The thought brought him back to the previous day, his last afternoon of practice, because in one more week, he was either on his way to Florida or back to being a normal sixth grader. He'd just finished climbing the ladder for a seventh time in a row, and even his palm hurt from slapping that darn bell at the top of the ropes again and again. He'd half walked, half crawled to the pod of beanbag chairs someone had piled in a corner of the art room, right beneath one of the blacked-out windows. Because it had been late, nearly nine p.m., all the other kids had gone home one by one, and Charlie had suddenly realized, as he lowered himself into the bulbous beanie cushion, that the only other person in the room was Miranda, seated at one of the drafting desks.

Charlie had realized that in four long weeks together, this was the first time he'd been alone with her. At the moment, most of her face was obscured by her jet-black hair as she leaned forward over the desk, but as he settled into the beanbag, she had suddenly looked up, showing him a sliver of white enamel between the ruby lines of her lips.

"Charlie," she'd said, her voice piercing the air. "I think you're ready."

Charlie hadn't been able to disguise the pride that had washed over him. It wasn't just the feeling of belonging that had come with being part of the Carnival Killers; it was Miranda's approval, the fact that Charlie had earned her respect.

He knew, deep down, that his parents probably wouldn't have liked Miranda—in her perfectly tailored pencil skirt and cherry-red pumps; her manicured nails and perfectly styled hair; her flowing white blouse, knotted at the throat; and her shiny, sparkly watch—she was nearly an adult, and yet there she was, spending her evening helping a group of kids learn how to beat carnival games. And even though, over the four weeks, she'd let Finn and the rest do most of the guiding, she'd always been there, a presence you couldn't avoid.

She was doing it for a paper, and the tools they were using were physics, chemistry, and math, but still, it was a scheme practiced in secret, which they were going to use to win a prize. Charlie's parents wouldn't have understood.

"Sunday afternoon," Miranda had continued. "Finn will make the arrangements. If everything goes as planned, we'll know you're ready for Incredo Land."

It was strange to think that Ms. Sloan would not have made the arrangements herself, but the inner workings of a finely tuned machine were palpable—each member had their designated role, and it was clear that Finn was the head.

Now, two days later, standing in the darkness, watching streaks of lightning tear through the air, Charlie tasted sparks on his tongue, and an involuntary shiver ran down his spine. But though the oxygen around him was supercharged by the voltage spewing through the auditorium, the electricity in his veins didn't come from a Van de Graaff generator.

Sunday—tomorrow afternoon—Charlie was going to have to prove himself.

A trial by fire.

13

IT WAS TEN MINUTES past two in the afternoon, the sky was a deep and blustery gunmetal gray, and Charlie had just come to the undeniable conclusion that there was no cool way to walk through a crowd while eating an ice-cream cone. It didn't help that Crystal had ordered him the Triple-Decker Halloween Scoop: almost half a foot high of vanilla and chocolate swirl, covered in orange and black sprinkles. Or that she, Jeremy, and Kentaro were all wielding similar cones. Charlie doubted that even Finn could have pulled off a suave stroll through the Sherwood fairgrounds behind a phalanx of brightly colored sprinkles.

Crystal had lunged toward the ice-cream booth the minute they'd ditched Jeremy's dad in the parking lot.

Crystal was paying because she'd gotten twice her regular allowance the day before to make up for the fact that her mother had inadvertently vacuumed up part of her lava-rock collection, which her cat had knocked off her desk and onto her bedroom carpet. Charlie would have seemed really out of character telling her he didn't want free ice cream, even though it was hard to play it cool with a face full of sprinkles. It was precisely the same reasoning that had forced him to arrive at the scene of Miranda's test with three quarters of the Whiz Kids in tow. When Jeremy had called to tell him his dad had offered to take the crew to the fair on the last Sunday before Halloween, Charlie couldn't have refused.

"Marion shouldn't have been so concerned about his face," Jeremy remarked as they continued away from the ice-cream stand and out into the bustle of the fairground. "He'd have fit in perfectly with all the goblins and ghouls out and about this fine afternoon."

Charlie faked a laugh. It was eight days before Halloween, which meant that the Sherwood Fair was in full swing, right in its sweet spot. The parking lot had been completely full, and it had taken Jeremy's dad a good twenty minutes before he'd found a muddy pocket on the tire-ploughed field to stash his UPS van. He was lodged so tightly between two sparkling SUVs, Charlie had nearly had to climb out the window to get free. And Jeremy was right: Nearly half of the people cluttering the main glade of the Halloween Fair were in costume. Goblins, ghouls, witches, ghosts, the more popular television and movie characters, presidents past, present, and maybe future, and of course, vampires—so many flipping vampires, you needed a wooden stake and a clove of garlic just to navigate down the dirt path that ran through the center of the fair. The only costume that even came close to rivaling the vampire in popularity was the similarly ubiquitous zombie. Marion could have fit right in, especially with the zombies. The next time a deliveryman brushed him with a bouquet of roses in the elevator at his dentist's office, and his face exploded in firecracker hives like the sky above the Charles River on the Fourth of July, he could hide in plain sight at the Sherwood Halloween Fair.

Instead, Marion had stayed home, and the rest of the Whiz Kids were moving aimlessly through the park, trying to avoid the vampires, zombies, and especially the older kids who might think it was funny to see orange and black sprinkles spread out across a sixth grader's cheeks.

Lately Charlie was the quietest of the bunch. Inside, his nerves were so twisted into knots, he was using every ounce of energy to appear calm and normal; a large part of him wanted to turn and head right for the exit. He hadn't expected to be so tense. After all, he'd been practicing for this moment for what felt like an eternity. The muscles in his arms twitched as his fingers opened and closed over imaginary coins, and both pockets of his jeans felt thick with the still-cool heating pads that were hidden inside. He'd bought the pads at the local Walmart that very morning, telling his dad that he'd pulled a calf muscle chasing Kentaro up a flight of stairs at school.

"I think we should visit the face-painting booth first," Crystal said as they got deeper into the park. "And then the Ferris wheel. But this time I'm not sitting with Kentaro. It took me a week to get the vomit out of my shoes last year."

"I told you," Kentaro shot back, jabbing at her with his ice-cream cone, "that had nothing to do with the Ferris wheel. I had stayed up the whole night before working on a violin recital—"

"You can be such a stereotype, man," Jeremy said. "Just own it. When I vomit, I do it loud and proud. Crystal, I'd love to sit with you on the Ferris wheel."

"Not on your life," Crystal spat. She grabbed at Charlie's hand. "Charlie, sadly you're what's called making the best of a bad situation. Okay?"

Charlie felt a pang inside, a burst of warmth at her sudden touch; a part of him truly wanted nothing more than to ride the Ferris wheel with Crystal. But he wasn't there for fun, and he knew he had no choice. He was trying to come up with a witty answer when his eyes settled on a familiar swath of color: the peak of a midway tent, squatting about twenty yards away down the crowded path. Another few steps, and he could make out the huge sign, the scrawl of Old English:

Midway Games

He took a deep breath, and without looking, stretched out his arm and dropped his half-eaten ice-cream cone into an overflowing garbage can.

"Maybe a little later," he murmured as his mind suddenly clicked into gear. "But first I'd like to try my hand at a few games in there."

And with that, he was moving forward at double speed. He could hear his friends calling after him, but he kept going. It was as though he had blinders on like a horse pulling a cart; he knew exactly what he was supposed to do. As he went, he reached into his back pocket and yanked out a rolled-up baseball cap, then pulled it on his head so that the lid hung down low over his eyes. He knew he didn't have much time before the Whiz Kids caught up to him, but they were barely registering now that he could hear the clink of coins against plates, the clang of darts hitting the floor.

He reached the entrance to the tent, took another deep breath, and moved quickly inside. As he went, he kept repeating to himself what Finn had told him, for what had to be the hundredth time, at their last practice: *You do it fast, easy, cool.* That's how Charlie had to play the games, and that's who Charlie had to be. Mastering the techniques had been easy compared to mastering his own nervous system. *Fast, easy, cool.*

And then he was moving right up to the coin-toss counter, his eyes taking in every inch in front of him, making note of every aspect of his surroundings. The three high-school girls to his left, laughing as one of them missed every plate on the floor with ridiculously errant tosses. The bored, smug-looking carnival worker, unshaven, in shoddy, torn jeans and a Sherwood Fair branded sweatshirt, absentmindedly poking at one of the stuffed animals hanging above the plates as he watched the girls. And there, at the very end of the counter, standing there with his arms crossed nonchalantly against his chest, pretending to count pennies out of the change section of a Velcro wallet, Greg. For a brief second Charlie asked himself why in the world it had to be Greg, his least favorite of the Carnival Killers, but then it was past the time for thought. He had reached the counter and it was time to play.

He caught the attention of the carny and slapped a pink ticket onto the counter. The carnie sighed, turning away from the high-school girls long enough to take Charlie's ticket and exchange it for three of the oversize gold coins.

Charlie faked a smile, taking the coins into his hand. A dollar spent from his weekly allowance, but that didn't matter either, because Charlie was no longer Charlie. He was no longer a nerdy sixth grader at Nagassack Middle School with practical parents and an affinity for numbers.

"Wow, this is so cool, I bet I'm gonna hit every plate!" He coughed, in full Chucky the Easily Amused mode, as happy and smiling as a giant clam, shaking the coins in front of him like they were dice. The carny glanced at him, the smug smile digging deeper into his face. He'd seen idiots like Chucky a million times before. So many times that he didn't even notice as Charlie quickly and smoothly flicked one of the coins really close to his lips, touching one side thickly with his tongue. He was completely unaware of Charlie, who swiftly lowered his hand, then flicked his wrist in a perfect upward motion, releasing the coin at exactly the right moment. He didn't even notice that the coin arced almost straight up, barely missing the bottom of the lowest stuffed animal by an inch. He didn't notice anything, in fact, until the coin landed with a loud clack on one of the center plates.

"Hey." Charlie gasped. "Look at that! I hit a plate."

The carny glanced down and realized that, indeed, Charlie's coin was sitting on a center plate.

"Yeah, great, kid. That means you get one of the small animals," he started, but Charlie was already throwing the second and third coins in rapid succession. They both arced up and landed with equivalent clacks. All three on the same plate, bunched next to each other like the three holes of a bowling ball.

The carny opened his mouth, then closed it. Inside, Charlie was on fire. He could feel Greg watching him with approval, but he didn't acknowledge the other member of his team. Instead, he grinned and pointed to a huge stuffed giraffe hanging from the ceiling.

"I guess I get one of the big ones now, don't I? I'll take the giraffe. My sisters aren't going to believe this! I never win anything!"

The carny didn't say a word as he struggled to unhitch the giraffe from the ceiling. It was obvious he wasn't used to getting the big animals down, because it took him a full minute to get the thing loose. Then he handed it over the counter to Charlie. Charlie couldn't help but notice the admiring stares of the high-school girls as he tucked the stuffed animal under one arm and turned away from the counter.

Still grinning ear to ear, he started for the exit. Then he noticed Jeremy, Crystal, and Kentaro coming through the opening, still eating their ice-cream cones. They saw Charlie and the giraffe, and all three registered surprise. They'd all played enough carnival games over their lives to know how hard it was to win one of the big prizes. Even stranger, Charlie was wearing a baseball cap and grinning like a toddler.

Charlie quickly crossed to them, and before even Jeremy could get a word out, he handed the giraffe to Crystal.

"Here ya go, now you've got a partner for the Ferris wheel, one I guarantee isn't going to throw up on you."

Then he walked right past them, his heart pounding in his chest. He exited the tent, letting the crisp October air flow down his throat and into his lungs. It had only been one game, three coins, one prize—but this wasn't some mock-up in a deserted classroom; this had been real, live, under true carnival conditions. He'd still have to go back in and hit the balloon darts and the rope ladder, but even so, he'd already proven to himself—he could do it.

He was three yards past the flaps of the tent when he caught sight of Finn, standing by a barrel-shaped garbage can, flicking what looked to be pecan shells into the trash. Another yard and he saw Daniel, leaning against a bright blue Porta-potty, pretending to read a Spider-Man comic book. And there, in line for the same Porta-potty, three people deep, Jake, jumping from heel to heel as if he really had to go. Farther back, Magic, his face painted in bright yellow and red, juggling tennis balls to the great amusement of a group of third graders who had gathered just outside the face-painting booth. And a good ten feet behind Magic, Sam, her hands jammed deep into the pockets of her tight jeans as she pretended to kick a soda can against the fence that separated the fairgrounds from the parking lot.

But it took another minute, a few more steps, before Charlie caught sight of Miranda standing in the middle of a crowd of high-school kids dressed as vampires. Like the others, she pretended that she was a complete stranger, just a college girl spending an afternoon at a carnival.

And then, for the briefest of seconds, she broke character, looked right at him—and smiled. Then she turned, her jet-black hair fanning out behind her, and she was gone, lost in the sea of high-school vampires.

Charlie trembled. He shifted his eyes, back toward Finn and the rest, but they had faded away as well, vanishing into the depths of the Halloween Fair. Charlie felt the energy rising inside of him.

He had passed the trial by fire. He was officially one of them now.

And he was on his way to Incredo Land.

14

EYES CLOSED, IT WAS all physics and math, written in the language of engineering: steel and fiberglass, titanium and aluminum, iron bolts and copper screws. Eyes closed, it was an equation turned corporeal: spinning fan blades feeding air into twin gas turbines, where the air was compressed, sprayed with jet fuel, then ignited by an electrical spark. Eyes closed, it was theory turned to practice: a two-thousand-degree controlled conflagration, gasses expanding in a confined space, then forcefully funneled through an exhaust cone, creating thrust. *Equal and opposite reactions, Newtonian physics, the Second Law of Thermodynamics.* Thrust became momentum, forcing more air spiraling up the curved, retractable flaps of the wings, and momentum became lift.

But eyes open, it was an entirely different story. Charlie was loosely strapped to an uncomfortable vomit-green chair, clutching a plastic bottle of apple juice he had bought in the kiosk adjacent to the gate. Sitting there on the plane, beads of sweat started to form on his forehead as he thought about how he was enclosed in a veritable coffin-shaped, one-hundred-sixty-thousand-pound hunk of oblong metal that was hurtling thirty thousand feet above the ground, at almost six hundred miles per hour.

The logical portion of Charlie's brain was no match for the pure, terrifying magic of modern flight, and his fingers whitened against the plastic bottle of juice as the 727 worked its way through the last canopy of clouds on its way to its predetermined cruising altitude. To make things even worse, the oval, tempered glass to Charlie's right had gone dark a few minutes after take-off, and now all he could see when he peered into the porthole-shaped window was his own pale reflection staring back at him.

He hadn't always been afraid of flying. When he was younger, he had loved traveling by plane, and even though his parents had taken him on only a few short trips to New York and Washington, and once to Florida, he'd always looked forward to that feeling of flight: the rush as the engines growled to life, the thrill as the plane galloped down the runway, that indescribable, unique lightness as the plane lifted off the ground and took to the sky.

But now that he was older, his nerves had taken over. Which was ironic, because now that he was smart enough to know the science and the statistics, he knew, logically, that there were few places on earth safer than the cabin of a commercial airplane, and that a plane was literally built to stay in the air. But even so, he couldn't shake the feeling that such a very large, heavy object shouldn't be able to fly.

A matter of perception. Despite his fear, he couldn't help smiling to himself as he imagined Sam mouthing the words. He fought the urge to crane his neck around to search for her toward the back of the cabin; when they were boarding, he'd caught a glimpse of her putting her black backpack into the overhead compartment five rows behind where he was seated, but he'd been well trained. He hadn't even acknowledged the quick glimpse she'd thrown in his direction. Not that Jeremy, in a state Charlie could only describe as pure euphoria, would have noticed if he'd dived down the aisle and given her a great big hug.

As the plane finally broke free of the seemingly

magnetic grip of the last few clouds and straightened into a thankfully smooth flight line, he shifted away from his reflection and looked at his lanky friend, splayed out in the aisle seat to his left. It was like looking at a giant, redheaded grasshopper made out of maniacally twisted pipe cleaners. Amazingly, only ten minutes into a three-hour flight, Jeremy was fast asleep.

Charlie envied his friend's state of bliss. No doubt, Jeremy was out cold in part because he'd spent the past three days literally skipping to and from school; even asleep, a wide smile pulled at his chapped, slightly orange lips. He'd been smiling and skipping from the very moment during morning study period, three days ago, that Warden Walker had informed him that Jeremy's name had been chosen, at random, to receive free passage to Incredo Land with the class trip, the result of a promotional campaign tied to the park's anniversary celebration. To Jeremy, it was like winning the lottery, and when Charlie had told him that his own parents had agreed to send Charlie along since his best friend was going, Jeremy had been too excited to even question the out-of-character largesse of Charlie's "practical" mom and dad. Charlie had used the same line on his own parents—that his name had been chosen at random for the free trip—and it had done the job.

Jeremy had been floating ever since. At the airport, as they'd been slogging their way through security, meeting up at the American Airlines gate with the other eighteen students who had signed on to the trip, they were getting a short, sweet lecture from Warden Walker. Walker was the main proctor for the four-day excursion—he had rules for every little detail—but his biggest pet peeve was public misbehavior. And to Jeremy, rules were meant to be broken, so when Warden Walker wasn't looking, acting exactly opposite to how you would behave at school was par for the course. Jeremy had been like a filament in a lightbulb, electrified to the core, bouncing on the balls of his feet, laughing at just about everything, and prone to hug anyone within two yards of his elastic arms.

He hadn't registered even a note of curiosity as Warden Walker had introduced the two other adults who would be proctoring the trip. Mrs. Cauldwell, an eighth-grade English teacher with short blond hair and a penchant for dressing more like a teenager than the much older woman that she was; and a teaching assistant with flowing, ink-black hair, angular features, and a smile so blindingly white, it could have powered a jet turbine.

Of course, Charlie knew that Miranda's position as

one of the proctors of the class trip was no more random than Jeremy's being chosen to receive the "promotional" free ticket to Incredo Land. Charlie had no idea how she'd managed to trick Walker into believing the story behind Jeremy's ticket, or how she'd gotten herself assigned to the trip, but then, Miranda wasn't the sort to leave anything to chance. She'd probably guaranteed herself a spot on the class trip the minute she'd begun training her team.

On the plane, Charlie reached into his pocket, his fingers touching two distinct objects, one small and round and very familiar, the other rectangular, smooth, and utterly wrong. The feel of the gold coin calmed his nerves, forcing the rumble of the plane's engines and the shudder of the fuselage moving through light turbulence into the background. His fingers, and the muscles of his hand and wrist, knew the coin intimately. He had practiced so much over the past few weeks, the coin was like an extension of his body. He no longer had to consciously calculate the proper arc or the amount of strength he'd need to flick the thing to land on a plate every time—his muscles just knew. Muscles had memory, and if you did something enough times, it became ingrained in the connective tissue. The coin, and the dart, and even the ropes of the ladder, these things were all in his muscles now, as much a part of him as his very DNA.

But the other object felt nothing but foreign. He considered taking it out of his pocket, but even though Jeremy was asleep, he didn't want to risk his friend seeing the device and asking about it.

Just a little white lie, a borrowed iPhone, and now Charlie had almost everything he needed to beat the wheel. All he still needed, in fact, was one more piece of information—the diameter of the wheel itself. On the Carnival Killers' last day of practice, just twenty-four hours ago, Miranda had assured Charlie that she had a plan to get that information, but hadn't given him any details, just a confident smile and an almost maternal pat on the head.

Still, her confidence and the pride he'd gotten from pleasing her by being good enough to be a part of the Carnival Killers only partially made up for the fact that he'd borrowed the phone from his father and that he would have to lie to him to cover up that act.

A slippery slope, and he had the feeling he was about to slide right off the edge.

A quiet *ding* interrupted his thoughts, as the seatbelt light went off over his head. Although to Charlie, there wasn't such a thing as a "comfortable" cruising altitude, he decided to use the opportunity to stretch his legs, to take his mind off the borrowed phone and the black void beyond the window to his right.

Getting past Jeremy's sleeping form and out into the aisle was a bit like climbing a jungle gym, but eventually, Charlie found himself shuffling between the rows of seats toward the back of the cabin, his eyes rapidly adjusting to the dim lighting. He recognized faces on either side, nodding at the handful of kids who recognized him back. Twenty among a coach class that seated a hundred and twenty wasn't a high percentage, but twenty middle schoolers would have stood out in a crowd ten times their number. Even above the constant rumble of the jet's engines and the rush of wind against the wings, Charlie could tell that the noise level was higher than usual; kids laughed, kids yelled, kids kicked at the seats in front of them and pounded their shoes on the floor. Charlie wasn't sure where Warden Walker, Mrs. Cauldwell, or Miranda were sitting, but they obviously were avoiding the back of the plane, where most of the kids were gathered. The deeper he went into the cabin, the more it felt like a school bus with wings.

A few steps farther down the aisle, and he passed by Sam's row. Again, he fought the urge to acknowledge her. Her face was bent over a magazine, something glossy and filled with pictures of women who looked like Miranda and dressed like Mrs. Cauldwell. Then he was past her row, moving closer to the pair of lavatories that took up the last few feet of the plane's tail. He didn't really have to go, but he figured a little water splashed across his face would help his nerves. He took another step toward the tail.

And then he was tumbling forward, hands out in front of him, panic in his eyes. At first, he thought something had gone wrong with the plane, then he saw the leg stretched out across the aisle at ankle level, and heard the unmistakable, deep guffaw from the seat directly next to where he was falling.

Luckily, he caught himself on an armrest at the last second and managed to steady himself in a half kneel. He glanced up to see Dylan Wigglesworth beaming down at him, his eyes pinpricks in the thick, doughy rolls of his face. Next to Dylan sat Liam, and in the row directly in front of Liam, Dusty. Charlie's stomach dropped as he pushed himself back to his feet. He hadn't noticed the three thugs in the airport; they must have been in the front of the group as they'd entered the jetway. In retrospect, he shouldn't have been surprised that Dylan and his coterie were on the class trip; Dylan's father was an investment banker in Boston and was one of the sponsors of his pituitarially challenged son's Little League team. Tickets to Incredo Land were probably nothing to the Wiggleworths, and besides, even for his parents, getting Dylan out of town for a few days was probably worth any amount of money. Unfortunately, that meant Charlie was stuck going on vacation with his bully in tow.

"Whoops," Dylan chortled, giving Charlie a hard poke to the stomach. "Gotta be more careful, Numbers. Unexpected turbulence, and all."

Charlie fought the urge to turn and run back down the aisle toward his seat. Instead, he tried to think of a comeback, and was about to say something about unexpected morons being much more dangerous than unexpected turbulence when he heard someone clear his throat a few rows ahead and saw Finn waving at him. Finn was in his usual outfit: leather jacket, distressed jeans, boots hanging out in the aisle. There was an empty seat next to Finn, and despite the unwritten rules of the Carnival Killers, he obviously wanted Charlie to join him. Charlie immediately forgot about Dylan and started forward, but Dylan grabbed his sleeve, pulling Charlie down so that Charlie's face was only inches from his own. Charlie could tell by the angry look in Dylan's eyes that he had also seen Finn a few rows back.

"Keep in mind," Dylan snarled, his breath reeking of tuna fish and maybe even a little tooth decay, "Incredo Land is a big place. Maybe we get a chance to hang out without your bodyguard butting in. Wouldn't that be fun, Numbers?"

And then he let Charlie go with a little shove. Charlie stumbled the next few rows to where Finn was waiting, and dropped into the empty seat with a huff of relief. Finn grinned at him.

"Even at thirty thousand feet, you attract the nicest element, Charlie."

Charlie had to laugh at that. He rubbed a hand through his hair. Dylan was a nuisance and a bully, but lately barely factored into Charlie's thoughts the way he had just a few weeks ago. Charlie had much bigger things to worry about than avoiding getting stuffed in a locker or thrown into a garbage can.

Finn seemed to read his mind, gesturing around the plane with an open hand.

"This is something, isn't it? Incredo Land is a freaking kick, man. The flight down is always the same. Kids laughing, smiling, playing in the aisles. The flight back, it's like the saddest plane in the world. You'll see. The flight back, it's gonna seem like a funeral. Everyone on the verge of tears, except us."

The way Finn glanced at the other passengers, especially the other kids from Nagassack, he was dismissing them with his eyes. He and Charlie were in on a secret, and the rest of the kids were just civilians. Magic had used the term a few times, and it seemed apt.

"It's fun, isn't it?" Finn continued. "Being in on a secret."

Charlie nodded, but then he felt the weight of the iPhone in his pocket, and he shrugged.

"It's exciting, that's for sure. But—"

"Sometimes a secret feels a little bit like a lie, right?"

The cabin jerked up, then swiveled right and left as the plane hit a brief spot of turbulence. Charlie's reflexes kicked in, and he grabbed at the armrest, his feet kicking out, hitting Finn's backpack, which was tucked under the seat in front of Charlie. It was the same black backpack that Sam had been stuffing into the overhead compartment—the same one that both he and Jeremy, and all the other kids on the trip had been given when they'd met Warden Walker and the rest at the airport. The backpacks had been donated by a local sporting goods store and had the Nagassack school emblem sewn across a back pocket: the outline of a golden bear beneath a cartoonish-looking sun. Originally, the kids were all supposed to wear matching

Nagassack sweatshirts to make them easier to corral in the airports, but somebody had suggested the bags instead, because they were perfect for carry-on, and besides, sweatshirts didn't make a whole lot of sense in Florida. Beneath Charlie's bright red sneaker, Finn's backpack felt stuffed.

"You gotta relax," Finn said as the plane smoothed out again and Charlie found his breath. "And I'm not just talking about the flight. You know anything about Incredo Land, Charlie? I mean, apart from what they tell you in the brochures?"

"I know it's the cheeriest spot in the universe. Loopy Mouse and the Space Drop, the Haunted Moon ride and Solar Avenue and all that. Pretty awesome stuff."

"Sure. It's all those things. But it's got a history, man, like everything else, and it wasn't always such a happy place. In fact, before the Incredo Corporation and the people behind the cartoon turned it into an amusement park, Incredo Land was one big swamp. Thousands of miles of cheap marshland, full of alligators and snakes and spiders."

Charlie raised his eyebrows. He wasn't sure what Finn was getting at. But the intensity in Finn's eyes told him that it was something the older kid had given a lot of thought to.

"See," Finn continued, "the folks who invented Loopy the Space Mouse wanted to build something on a very big scale to take advantage of the popularity of the television show; they needed land, lots of it, and they wanted to get it all cheap. So they chose a big swath of swamp in a part of Florida that nobody gave a hoot about. A big, bug-infested dump of ground outside of Tampa."

"That's certainly not in the brochures," Charlie said. Finn smiled.

"Yeah, it wasn't public knowledge back then, either. See, they were smart. They knew that if they announced that they were going to buy all this swampland in Florida, everyone would know they were going to build a new theme park, and then that icky, worthless swamp would become really expensive. So they used dummy corporations with fake names to slowly buy it all up. Basically, they were tricking people into selling them the land for cheap."

Finn leaned closer, clearly impressed by the history he was retelling.

"In fact, not just the land—they even got the *dirt* dirt cheap. See, Boston University, yeah, the college in Boston, owned the mining rights to that land. So Incredo's owners created another fake company with a fake name, walked into BU, and bought the dirt rights from them for fifteen thousand dollars. Once they had all that swamp, they cleaned it out, gutted everything, and built the amusement park. You know how much Incredo Land made last year?"

Charlie shook his head. "I couldn't even begin to guess."

"Eleven billion dollars, give or take a few."

Charlie whistled. That was a lot of money for a space-based amusement park built on top of a swamp.

"You still feel bad about putting a little spit on a coin?" Finn added, suddenly digging right into Charlie's thoughts with pinpoint accuracy. "Or pressing a few buttons on a phone?"

Charlie paused, then leaned back against his seat. Finn made a good point. Most kids thought about Incredo Land as this magical, incredible place, but it was also a business. A very profitable business. If the Carnival Killers had a way of using their brains to give them an edge in the face of that business, could it really be that wrong? Pushing a few buttons on a phone. Finn knew it was much more difficult than that. Charlie had written the equation that the phone would use to calculate the deceleration of the wheel; he'd come up with the theory that would allow them to beat the game. He was the final piece in the Carnival Killers' puzzle, and

Miranda had recruited him for just that purpose. Well, actually, she'd sent Finn and Magic to recruit him, but most significantly Finn, because Finn was the sort of kid that you didn't say no to, the sort of kid that most would instinctively follow.

He wasn't just cool; in that leather jacket, those piercing eyes, that swooping hair, he was confident, but strangely down-to-earth in a boy-next-door sort of way. But even though Charlie had spent the past four weeks working closely with the older kid, he still didn't know very much about him. Finn was still a mystery, and that, more than anything, was hard to resist.

"Finn," he finally responded, his foot still resting on Finn's backpack on the floor in front of him. "Why did you quit the swim team? You were the best swimmer at the school. Maybe the best the school ever had. You would have won the national championship if you'd swum."

Finn's eyes narrowed, and for the briefest second, Charlie thought he'd somehow angered the older kid—and that terrified him. But then Finn shrugged, the genial smile back on his face. No matter how much Charlie prodded him, it wasn't something he was ready to answer. Two and a half hours of conversation later, he still hadn't answered. Then the fasten seat belt sign above their heads blinked on, and the captain's voice spilled through the cabin.

"Ladies and gentlemen, we're just beginning our initial approach into Tampa International Airport. Please take your seats as the flight attendants prepare the cabin for landing."

Finn gave Charlie a little wink.

"Saved by the bell. Time goes by pretty fast when you're having fun, doesn't it? You better get back to your seat before Warden Walker sees us conspiring together and turns us over to homeland security."

Charlie laughed, then rose, pushing himself back into the aisle. As he went, his trailing sneaker caught on the zipper to Finn's backpack, pulling the tines back a few inches, and Charlie saw a flash of green. It wasn't until he was halfway up the aisle, back toward the front of the cabin, that he realized what he'd seen.

Money. A stack of dollar bills, held together by a rubber band. He thought back to how the bag felt beneath his sneaker: bulging, full, lumpy. How many bills could you fit in a backpack? No doubt, Ms. Sloan had everything timed out to a T, and there wouldn't be time for ATMs. And dollar bills don't come up on X-ray machines, so getting the bills through the airport would have been easy.

Still, all that money; Charlie's eyes widened as he moved the last few rows to where Jeremy was now stretching, slowly coming awake. It was crazy to see it all in one place.

Charlie climbed over Jeremy and hastily strapped himself back into his seat. Jeremy was watching him, still rubbing the last vestiges of sleep out his eyes.

"Where you been? Out on the wing, taking in the sights?"

Charlie faked a laugh.

"Just doing laps. Ran into a nice flight attendant who got a bit chatty." His head was still whirling, dollar bills flashing behind his eyes.

The plane leaned hard to the left, then began to descend. Jeremy bent halfway over Charlie, trying to push his face right up against the window. The lights of Tampa were visible down below, pinpricks shifting and swirling beneath the clouds. Jeremy exhaled.

"I can almost see it, man. Incredo Land. It's all down there, waiting for us."

Charlie shivered as he watched the anticipation spread like a wildfire across his best friend's cheeks.

15

"WELL, YOU DON'T SEE this every day."

Charlie watched the swirling pinwheel of fire dancing dangerously toward him as he pressed his back
against the rough bark of a swaying palm tree. The beat
of the great tribal war drums reverberated through his
bones, and he fought the urge to push Jeremy in front
of him while he made a hasty retreat down the winding stone steps that led back into the main part of the
open-air lobby. He knew he was overreacting, but he
had to admit, the atmosphere was pretty immersive:
the oppressively humid tropical breeze rifling through
the fingerlike fronds of the palm trees that lined the
stone pathway; the rivulets of blue-green water trick-
ling down the craggy rock face of a twenty-foot cliff

directly ahead, the underbrush on either side so thick and green, it was like a waist-high carpet; the glowing tiki torches and multiple carved totem poles glaring at him from every angle, daring him to challenge the carefully crafted tropical fantasy.

And on top of all that, there was that flaming pinwheel, now only a few feet away, so close Charlie could feel the searing heat against his cheeks. It didn't help that the man spinning the torches—deftly guiding the twin flame-capped wooden poles around his wrists and palms like they were some sort of kerosene-infused propeller— was dressed only in a grass skirt and covered in bright red war paint. If this was supposed to be a tropical paradise, someone had a pretty twisted view of what the concept meant.

Then again, Jeremy wasn't the only witness to the scene sporting a ridiculously goofy smile as he clapped his hands together in beat with the throbbing drums. Charlie could count at least thirty other hotel guests gathered around the stone path, cameras flashing and cell phones recording as the spinning of the torches accelerated, faster and faster, until it seemed like the very air in front of the grass-skirted man was about to burst into flames.

Then suddenly, the drumbeat stopped. The man screamed something unintelligible—the fake language of Mercury, presumably, because the hotel, Mercury Palace, was supposed to be some fantasy take on a tropical space outpost on the tiny superheated planet. Charlie doubted that any of the gathered tourists would have noticed if he had been shouting in Japanese, Chinese, or even Klingon, for that matter. The grass-skirted man tossed the two torches high into the air and, like rockets of pure flame, they leaped higher, higher, higher, then plummeted back down. He caught them in one outstretched hand and in one swift motion, doused them with a spray of water from his mouth. A magician's trick, Charlie knew, what Finn referred to as "misdirection," a technique which used a simple distraction, such as a pair of flaming torches rocketing skyward, to disguise an action, such as surreptitiously filling your mouth with water from a pitcher hidden in nearby dense underbrush. But the crowd ate it up. The applause was twice as raucous as the drums had been, and nobody was clapping louder than Jeremy.

As the crowd finally disbursed, Jeremy placed a rubbery arm over Charlie's shoulder and turned him back toward the lobby, matching his friend's steps as they strolled down the winding stairs.

"And you thought that was going to suck. You could not have been more wrong!"

Charlie shrugged, because he knew better than to try to argue with Jeremy when he got like this. Besides, Charlie's heart wasn't really in it; even though all the other kids from Nagassack had done the sensible thing, heading straight to bed after the proctors had checked them in to the hotel and given each pair a set of room keys, Charlie wasn't going to throw water on Jeremy's euphoric mood. When he'd suggested that they swing by the nightly fire dance show, Charlie had acquiesced.

Jeremy was going to take in every sight, every sensation; even a faux-Mercury tropical paradise—as if the planet Mercury could even sustain such a place, as close to the sun as it was—was a thrill to him. He didn't care that everything around them was as manufactured as the fake volcano that dominated the hotel's outdoor swimming pool or the white sand beach on the other side of the craggy waterfall. It didn't matter to Jeremy that the guy in the grass skirt was just some guy they hired; it was all part of the experience. The Mercury was one of the two original onsite properties that Incredo Land had opened, situated on the Sea of Tranquility Lagoon. It was like a gateway to the futuristic amusement park, and for Jeremy, a place for the magic to begin.

Strolling along with his friend through the kitschy

hotel lobby, past the wicker chairs, half-coconut-shell sconces, and overgrown, lush indoor hedges, Charlie couldn't help but feel proud of himself to have gotten Jeremy there, even though his friend had no idea that Charlie had anything to do with it. The past few hours had almost made up for the distance that had grown between him and the rest of the Whiz Kids over the past five weeks. Jeremy was on cloud nine, and from there, the view was spectacular. "I bet I could do that," Jeremy continued as they moved out of the lobby and out onto the path that led to the hotel's cabinlike rooms. The rooms were in two- and three-story sections that encircled the main part of the hotel, which contained the lobby, a few restaurants, and a handful of shops hawking Incredo Land merchandise, magazines, and toiletries. "I'd be great at torch spinning. I've got the hands for it."

"Right," Charlie countered. "I've seen you almost set yourself on fire toasting marshmallows."

"Yeah, but deep down I think I was supposed to be an alien."

They stepped over a low hedge and then moved up a set of stairs that led to the two-story section that contained their room. Jeremy fumbled the keys out of his pocket, catching them right before they fell to the ground. He grinned sheepishly.

"You've got the hands for it all right," Charlie said.

Jeremy unlocked the door to their room and ushered Charlie inside with a dramatic flourish. A stiff breeze from the high-powered air-conditioning system hit Charlie in the face as he stepped through the threshold to the wood-colored room. It was pretty much in line with the lobby decor: a lot of wicker and bamboo, a textured carpet, fake tiki lamps instead of lights, and a sliding glass double door taking up one whole wall, which led out onto a small porch with more wicker furniture. Beyond the wicker, there wasn't much of a view, just more tropical hedges and dense underbrush. Charlie guessed that beyond all that green, paths led to the monorail stop that would take them to the park, and maybe beyond that, you might be able to get a glimpse of the giant Space Station perched high on the horizon, but from where he was standing, it was wicker, grass, and Jeremy, who had suddenly launched himself across the room and into the closest of the two double beds.

Charlie shut the door behind him, noticing as he did so that the bellman had placed their luggage on a low table by the bathroom. Then he turned toward the other bed, seeing that Jeremy had left him the one closest to the sliding glass doors.

"I get the bed with the view? How generous of you."

Jeremy was splayed out flat on his back, his head resting on his hands, his elbows out to either side like the bent cords of a crossbow.

"Actually, that bed already had your name on it."

Charlie looked at the empty bed and saw the envelope on the center of one of pillows. Even from across the room, he could read his name in bright red block letters across the front of the envelope.

Curious, Charlie crossed to the bed and retrieved the envelope. It was as thick as a deck of cards, and had some weight to it. Curiouser and curiouser. He used a finger to break the seal, tore the flap open—and then his eyes went wide. He quickly shifted his body so that his back was turned toward Jeremy, then opened the envelope wide and peered inside.

Wow. Dollar bills, in a thick stack, held together by a rubber band. He rifled through them with his fingers, counting as quick as he could. *Two hundred dollars, give or take a few.* It was a small fortune. Even though there was no note inside the envelope, no instructions or anything, Charlie understood exactly what he was looking at.

This was his stake. Tomorrow morning, the Carnival Killers would be hitting Incredo Land. The midway games would cost money to play. Probably one or two dollars a game, and he'd be playing all day long. His head swam as he leafed through the bills again. His thoughts immediately flashed to Finn on the airplane and the backpack beneath his feet. Of course, Finn had been playing the Sherpa, carrying their stake from Logan to Tampa. All in dollar bills, because dollar bills made more sense than higher denominations. A twelve-year-old walking into a carnival with a handful of twenties would look pretty suspicious. Nobody looked twice at one-dollar bills.

Another thought hit Charlie. If he had gotten two hundred dollars in an envelope—well, that meant the rest of the team had probably gotten similar stakes. *Seven kids, fourteen hundred dollars.*

Had Miranda put up all that cash? For a paper for her graduate school program? It seemed curious, a little hard to understand. Had she gotten some sort of grant to do the paper? Or was she just spending the money out of her own savings?

"Is it a love letter?" Jeremy called out, still on his back. His voice sounded heavy, as it was now well past ten, and they'd had a heavy dinner of burgers and fries at the airport after the flight. "I bet it's a love letter. Did Crystal sell off some cheap rhinestones to make sure it was the last thing you saw before you went to sleep?"

Charlie resealed the envelope and shoved it into his pocket.

"It's a note from Warden Walker, actually. My dad called him about his cell phone—you know, how I accidentally packed it along with my stuff."

Another white lie, which Jeremy had amazingly seemed to accept, because his eyes were already closed and he was minutes from a good, heavy snore.

Feeling the weight of all two hundred of the dollar bills in one pocket, the "borrowed" iPhone in the other, Charlie doubted that he himself would be sleeping soundly anytime soon.

In less than ten hours, Charlie and the Carnival Killers were going to take on Incredo Land.

16

WARDEN WALKER WAS FIGHTING a losing battle. There was simply no way a gaggle of sugar-infused, over-stimulated sixth, seventh, and eighth graders were going to pay attention to a red-faced, bespectacled middle-school principal reading names off a clipboard, while a futuristic air train whiffed along an elevated track, twenty feet above the shiny crown of his rapidly balding head.

"Quiet down!" Walker piped, but his words were lost in a sudden burst of the train's laser cannon, which seemed to crack the very air. "Mrs. Cauldwell's group will include Michael Thompson, Peter Crockett . . ."

Even Charlie had trouble concentrating on the names as Walker droned on from the clipboard; Charlie's gaze, like everyone else's, was drawn to the buglike, glass-

and-steel docking station that served as the entrance to Incredo Land, and the glistening curves of the air train, which was passing directly above Warden Walker as it slid along to the starting point of its circular route around the amusement park.

When Charlie looked past Walker to the bank of turnstiles that led into the wide tunnel piercing the heart of the docking station, an artery pumping brightly clothed tourists into the park at a steady pace, even at eight in the morning on a bright, sunny Thursday, it was obvious that that was exactly what the creators of the park were going for. An enormous, three-dimensional movie come to life. The monorail, the docking station, the turnstiles—you were about to take part in a real live movie, but like with a movie, you had to wade through the previews before you got to the big reveal.

"And lastly," Walker continued, raising his voice ever louder as the train caterpillared by "we have Ms. Sloan's group. Daniel Gordon, Jake Tucson, Greg Titus, Sam Ashley, Finn Carter, Michael Buster, and Charlie Lewis. Okay, everyone, that's it, so line up behind your proctors and we can enter the park. And no pushing!"

Hearing all their names in a row like that was sobering, and Charlie was awed by how carefully Miranda had planned everything, down to the last detail. Since the kids would all be separated from one another, each group with a single adult proctor, nobody would be witness to the Carnival Killers as they plied their scheme. *One less level of subterfuge,* Charlie thought to himself. Then he heard Jeremy sigh next to him as the kids started to separate themselves into the three groups to head into the turnstiles.

"Shoot, maybe I can trade with someone," Jeremy mumbled. "It's not going to be half as fun riding the Space Drop without watching your screaming mug in the seat next to me."

Charlie was pretty certain nobody from his group was going to trade with Jeremy.

"It will be okay," he said. "And we've got three days; maybe they'll change up the groups tomorrow."

"Yeah, but it's still going to suck."

Jeremy pointed to the row of kids lining up to their right, in front of Mrs. Cauldwell, who was positively beaming in tune to her bright yellow halter top and white skinny jeans. Charlie immediately caught sight of Dylan's hulking form between the simian shapes of his two cackling buddies. Jeremy was in for a long day, but that couldn't be helped.

"Just do your best to stick close to Cauldwell." Charlie shrugged.

"Thanks, you're a big help," Jeremy shot back glumly. Maybe he was angry that Charlie didn't seem more sympathetic, or that Charlie hadn't offered to trade with someone himself. Charlie felt truly bad about how he was acting toward his friend, but what else could he do? Charlie tried to think of something else to say, but Jeremy had already moved away, finding a place in his line behind an eighth-grade girl with a long blond ponytail and Hello Kitty purse, and a seventh grader in cargo shorts and a Nagassack athletic T-shirt.

Nothing to be done about it, Charlie thought to himself. He had to be strong. If Jeremy was back to being angry with him, that was something he'd deal with when this was all over. He did his best to wipe his mind of Jeremy as he strolled into his own line, taking up position right behind Finn and Magic, who were helping Miranda dole out the admission tickets to her group of seven. Then they were headed to the nearest turnstile. Miranda stood to one side as they each moved through, one at a time.

When it was Charlie's turn, she reached forward with a manicured hand and pushed the cool metal bar of the turnstile for him. Her face had become intense, her features narrowing into something truly feral. Leaning close, her breath was like a hiss against his ear.

"Pace yourself. Just picture yourself back in the art

room. Concentrate on what we're here to do. Everything else is a distraction."

And then she was back to her amiable self, waving Charlie through as she gave Warden Walker, at the head of his own group a few yards away, a cheery smile over the bank of turnstiles.

A moment later, Charlie was moving through the tunnel in lockstep with a veritable mob of Nagassack kids and babbling, bubbling tourists, inching his way into the park by way of Solar Avenue, or as Loopy called it on the cartoon, a little taste of Earth at the gateway to the stars.

Ten feet of shuffling his way through a crowded tunnel beneath the docking station, and then a sudden, instantaneous hundred-year dive forward in time; Solar Avenue was jarring to Charlie's senses. A blast into the future, everything was brightly lit and made out of shiny chrome, steel, and bulbous glass. The sidewalks moved, like at the airport, though most people were walking anyway, in a rush to see as much of the shiny avenue as quickly as possible

The first thing Charlie noticed was the smell. The very air was sweet: a potent blend of cotton candy, chocolate cake, ice cream, even popcorn. Finn might have cynically pointed out that the scented atmosphere wasn't an accident; every morning before the visitors arrived, the sugar-tinged air was pumped out of vents above a futuristic-looking candy store. But Charlie didn't care how the air was flavored; for this one brief moment, he wanted to experience the place the way it was designed.

Stepping deeper into the circular courtyard that served as the base of Solar Avenue, he tried to take everything in at once. The electronic music that seemed to throb right out of the moving sidewalk below his feet; the wonderfully futuristic-looking storefronts on either side, beginning with the Space Explorer's Outpost, a general store peddling everything from Loopy the Space Mouse umbrellas to state-of-the-art recording equipment; the Lunar Theater, with its half-moon-shaped windows and neon marquee, showing the first Loopy cartoon that started it all, "Loopy Goes to Mars"; the Space Cake Bakery; the extraterrestrial architecture of the Alien Trading Post, from the twisting arch of its gilded laser tower to the saucer-shaped mock spacecraft visible in the open docking port.

It was all perfect, designed to evoke wonder in the adults and to create an attitude of awe in the children. To Charlie, strolling behind Finn and Magic, Miranda a few steps ahead, everything seemed fresh and magical.

It was everything he could have imagined: astronaut ice cream, hot dogs shaped like rocket ships, park employees dressed in shiny futuristic garb.

From the giant, welcoming, green-skinned Martian that stood guard in front of a meteorite store to his left, to the supercooled ice sculpture of astronaut Buzz Aldrin standing outside the rocket-ship hot dog restaurant to his right, all of it represented a look into the future. And Charlie was so swept up in the experience, he didn't realize that Finn, Magic, and the rest had stopped walking until he stumbled right into Greg, nearly knocking them both over. Greg shot him a glare, while Magic laughed and wagged a finger.

"You still haven't mastered the First Rule of the Carnival Killers, have you Charlie? Keep an eye on your surroundings."

Charlie started to mumble an apology to Greg, when he realized why they had all stopped so abruptly. Ten feet to their right, in an alley next to a brightly lit moon-boot store was the entrance to a striped circus tent.

From Charlie's vantage point it was difficult to tell how big the interior of the tent might be, but from the sounds emanating from inside, it was obviously vast. Bells, whistles, laughter, and the unmistakable sound of carnival barkers, hawking various games of skill and luck. Charlie's eyes instinctively shifted to the sign above the tent. It was neon and blinking:

Midway on Solar Avenue

Charlie had no doubt what he'd find inside. Miranda gave the team a wink, then sauntered a few feet away, reaching for her cell phone. One by one, the rest of the team moved toward the entrance. In a moment, only Charlie was still standing where they'd started, gathering up the energy to follow them inside. He was just about ready, when a voice from behind took him by surprise.

"Oh, that kind of sucks. Carnival games? You could have stayed home to play carnival games."

Charlie turned and saw Jeremy sauntering toward him. Jeremy's group was about fifteen feet away, still heading down Solar Avenue toward the park proper.

"You sure you don't want to sneak along with me?" Jeremy continued. "I think Allison Clark would switch groups; she doesn't particularly want Dylan yanking at her ponytail all morning, anyway."

Charlie didn't know what to say to that, so he just shook his head. Jeremy got a hurt look on his face, and stopped a few feet from Charlie. Then he shrugged.

"Yeah, okay. Whatever, man."

And then he turned on his heels and was moving back toward his group, his long legs pumping to catch up. Charlie almost ran after him—but again, forced himself to be strong. He turned away, toward the entrance to the midway games. The rest of the Carnival Killers were gone. He tossed one last glance at Miranda and was surprised to see she was no longer on her phone. Instead, she was chatting with a young man wearing what looked to be a clerk's uniform: a tan collared shirt with a name tag on the lapel, and matching tan pants. The guy was obviously a park employee of some sort. He had a scruffy, scraggly halo of spiky brown hair, and an easily visible, mean-looking scar above his lip. He was grinning as Miranda spoke to him, and when she leaned close to say something particularly important, he nodded vigorously, obviously excited, the greasy locks of his hair flipping about.

Charlie wondered who the guy could be. Probably nothing to do with the Carnival Killers, but still, the sight of the two of them made him strangely uneasy.

But before Charlie could run with that thought, Miranda was peering his way. She caught his eyes with her own, and with a determined flick of her head, reminded him where he was supposed to be.

Charlie nodded, took a deep breath, then headed through the entrance to the circus tent.

"WHO THE HECK IS this kid?"

"He's on fire."

"It's like he doesn't even look at the plates."

Charlie's eyes were near slits beneath the wide brim
of a Florida Marlins baseball hat as he leaned against the
counter, one elbow crooked to support his weight while
his other hand casually scooped a gold coin off the bur-
nished wood. It was true, he barely even looked at the
plates; his face was completely impassive, his breathing
regular and soft, and he let the muscles of his wrist do
the rest. It was strange—in real life, the thought that at
least a dozen kids were gathered behind him, pointing
and gawking and analyzing his every move, would have
filled him with anxiety. Especially since about half of

them were girls, varying in age from ten all the way up to seventeen. But at the moment, he felt nothing. He was cool, he was calm, he was totally in control.

Clank. The coin hit the plate as if it was magnetic, sticking so solidly that he half expected the carny to scoop it up and look at the underside for glue. Instead, the guy, who was in his mid-twenties, dressed in a shiny silver vest, matching suspenders, and a cone-shaped hat that was supposed to look vaguely spacey, just grinned at him and cupped a hand around his lips.

"Another winner! Give the Frisco Kid another ticket!"

Charlie wasn't sure when the guy had started calling him that. He knew the reason; one of the characters he had invented was a lonely boy from San Francisco, left to his own devices while his family took an older sister on rides he was too scared to ride. But the past eight hours had blended together into one big, frenetic mishmash. That's how it was, when you were living at ten thousand RPMs.

When he closed his eyes, all he got were glimpses. Slices of the day caught like images in front of a flashbulb.

Nine a.m.

Just thirty minutes from the moment he'd followed

the rest of his team through the entrance to the tent, and it was like he'd been there all his life. Even to Charlie, it was amazing how fast his training had kicked in; to the uninitiated, that first step inside that tent would have been like leaping off a cliff into a world of absolute chaos. The whole place was like a carnival on steroids, larger than life.

Except, when Charlie let it all sink in and allowed the logical, mathematical portion of his brain to digest what he was seeing, it was all a brilliant and beautiful facade, much like the rest of Solar Avenue. The place was more crowded and architecturally more vast than Sherwood, but at its heart, it was the same set of midway games. Once his senses acclimated to the science-fiction setting, it took Charlie only a few minutes to find the three games he could beat. Then it was just a matter of navigating through the thick crowd of kids, changing his face as he went, pulling the baseball cap out of his back pocket and rehearsing the characters he was going to cycle through as he moved from game to game: the lonely kid from San Francisco; the spoiled dentist's son from Arizona, who was so bored by all the rides that he'd come to the midway games to blow through his ridiculous allowance; the sickly child who'd spent the day before vomiting his way from the

Space Drop to the Haunted Moon, and was now rele-gated to the midway tent by his two brothers, who were sick of getting kicked off rides because of his weak stomach.

He didn't even pause as he reached his first target, the coins and plates, the game he felt most comfortable with, the one he had learned first and fastest. Working his way between a clutter of kids pitching coins hap-lessly in every direction, he slapped two dollars onto the counter, smiling eagerly at the carny as the man replaced his bills with golden coins.

Without even seeming to pause for breath, Charlie hit six plates in succession. *Clang, clang, clang, clang, clang.* The carnie stared at him for a beat, then reached up and rang an electronic bell.

"Winner, winner, winner, winner, winner, winner!"

And just like that, everyone at the counter was look-ing at Charlie, who was laughing like an idiot and going on about how his friends in San Francisco were never going to believe what had just happened, how his sib-lings were going to be so jealous that they'd spent the day on stupid rides. When the carny tore off a set of six white tickets with pictures of Loopy the Mouse stitched across the center of each, Charlie raised his eyebrows as if surprised.

"No stuffed animals? What, do we change these in for prizes?"

As the carnie explained the contest, Charlie pretended to listen and shrug. Meanwhile, he was taking in the reaction of the other kids around him. Some of them were well aware of the promotion, were even playing in groups to try to win a shot at the wheel themselves. Many others were just playing for the fun of it. Either way, it didn't matter. Charlie had tested the waters, and he knew now that it was just a matter of continuing what he'd started.

He palmed the tickets, thanked the carny, and strolled away from the counter. Jake Tucson passed him as he crossed beneath the blinking orange and black lights. Neither acknowledged the other. Just two kids at a carnival, strangers passing beneath the folds a circus tent. Jake took up Charlie's old position at the coin-toss counter, and Charlie worked his way to the spot at the balloon-dart game where Jake had just won a half dozen tickets of his own.

Eleven a.m.

The balloon-dart area had gone positively rowdy—shouts, cheers, arms pumping up and down. Charlie could barely stay on his feet as he was good-naturedly jostled back and forth by hands as big as mitts. It had happened suddenly: A busload of bigger kids had surged around him just as he was settling in to his third hour of straight play. In fact, his hand had just emerged from his pocket with its folded-up twist of heating pad inside, a warmed dart poised to fly, when he was surrounded and nearly lofted right up over the counter. Charlie didn't need to listen hard to overhear who they were; he could have just read their matching sweatshirts. A junior high football team from Miami on a class trip similar to Charlie's own. The two ringleaders of the group, a heavy-set African-American kid in a bulky gray sweatshirt and Adidas sweatpants, and a loudmouthed blond kid in jeans, matching sweatshirt, and high-top sneakers, had taken an immediate liking to Charlie because of his hat. And beginning right after his next three throws—the balloons popping like fireworks—they started cheering like maniacs with every throw.

The football kids were providing Charlie with natural *misdirection*, almost as perfect as flaming sticks tossed toward the sky. By the fifth balloon he'd popped, Charlie was grinning beneath the brim of his baseball cap; the carny wasn't even really looking at him as he tore off more prize tickets and slapped them on the counter next to more darts.

By the twelfth balloon, Charlie was enjoying himself so much, he didn't even notice that Greg was now standing about three feet to his right, also in the jumble of junior-high football kids. And Daniel, his red head stuffed beneath a wool cap that was part of a Brooklyn-hipster persona that Magic had dubbed "more dip than hip," was a few feet to his left, also half swallowed up by a crowd of gray sweatshirts. Like Charlie, they'd recognized the natural cover of the crowd. Nobody was going to notice them in the loud mob of junior-high kids. Charlie didn't even see his teammates until all three of them happened to throw darts at the exact same moment. The three balloons exploded at once, right next to each other in the center of the board.

Bang. Bang. Bang!

The football players erupted in shouts. The two big ringleaders grabbed Charlie under his arms and lifted him right off the ground, shouting at the carny in unison.

"Winner, winner, winner!"

Charlie, feet dangling as he smiled helplessly, looked back and forth around the counter, and for the briefest of seconds his eyes met Greg's, then Daniel's. All three stifled grins.

"Do it again!" yelled the football player in the high-tops.

Charlie laughed. He certainly wasn't going to disappoint his fans.

Three p.m.

Back at the coin table.

Charlie was chewing on a granola bar that Jake had shoved in his pocket on their last pass across the tent, as he pushed through a set of what looked to be triplets grouped around the closest corner of the game counter. The three brothers were all chubby and red-faced, obviously frustrated with the way their day was going. Charlie could easily see why: They were throwing coins almost in unison, and every time, the result was the same. The coins skipped and scattered their way from plate to plate, disappearing to the floor— and yet again and again, the triplets kept hurling away, putting their thick biceps into it as they wound up like they were pitching for the Red Sox. Charlie waited until they were finished, their faces getting even more radishy as they finally ran through their last few dollar bills, and then leaned over the counter himself, flashing six singles to the carny. It was a different man than before—Charlie had counted at least two shifts gone by since the morning hours. Counting the shifts was another piece of Charlie's training; each change in shift meant a new carny, a new set of eyes that hadn't just watched you win way more than you were supposed to, which meant you could do it all over again without much worry of getting noticed. This time, the carny was as thin as a pipe cleaner, with a high beak of a nose and eyes like beads. He had an exasperated look on his face, and Charlie immediately saw why.

Directly across the gaming pit, beyond the sea of clinking plates, at the counter right across from Charlie, he saw a group of high-school girls gathered around Finn. Finn actually had his back to the game, leaning so nonchalantly he was almost sitting right up on the counter. He was chatting to the girls, obviously charming them with his eyes, his manner of speaking, the smug way his lips turned up at the corners; as Charlie watched, one of the girls even reached out and touched Finn's jacket.

Then she laughed, and he held a gold coin to her lips. Without even turning toward the plates, he flicked his wrist back over his shoulder, sending the coin into a perfect arc. It hit a plate and stuck, and all the girls burst out in applause. The carny just stared at Finn's back, then shrugged and reached for another winning ticket from the roll attached near his electric bell. Finn didn't even turn as the man put the ticket on a pile that already looked to be thirty tickets thick.

What a jackass, Charlie thought, and then he grinned. It was time for the Frisco Kid to get in on some of that action.

He kissed one of his own gold coins as if for good luck, and gave it a perfect toss toward the waiting plates.

Six thirty p.m. Just a few minutes before the close of the day's games.

"Ten. Nine. Eight. Seven . . ."

Charlie was eight feet above the ground and moving like a spider monkey, hands burning against the thick twists of rope, shoes barely glancing against the sides of the ladder as he shimmied forward. At the moment, all he saw were numbers, flashing around his head as he moved up the ropes—translucent and green, flashing behind his eyes as his body automatically calculated angles and weight, pivot points and torque. The numbers were everything—how his weight countered the natural spin of the ropes, how his center of mass had to be measured against the rotational pull of gravity. The numbers were his weapon, his strength, his own personal magic spell, and he could wield them like nobody else.

"Six. Five. Four . . ."

A few more feet, weight shifting back and forth, body smoothly moving up, and then there, right in front of him, was the little button by the bell. His right arm shifted up, palm out, as his left arm moved in tandem, balancing those numbers, perfecting the equation, and then—

"Three. Two. One!"

His palm hit the button and the bell exploded in metallic ecstasy. The crowd of onlookers cheered, and Charlie's head cleared; the numbers sped back into the computer of his mind. He was staring straight down through the top two rungs at the rubber mat that covered the ground now ten feet below. His heart thudded, and for a brief second he almost lost track of his arms and legs, almost twisted over and sent himself plummeting down. But then, above the shouts, he could hear both Sam's and Finn's voices, and he fought back against the torque, refusing to let himself fall. He slid back down the ropes, hands and feet working together as he had been taught, and then righted himself at the base of the ladder.

The crowd was dispersing as the carny handed him another winning ticket. When the man turned away to take payment from the next kid in line for the ladder, Charlie suddenly found himself face-to-face with Magic, who was smiling from beneath what looked to be a turban. The turban was a heck of a contrast to

Magic's tie-dyed T-shirt and cargo shorts, but then, in the cultural smorgasbord that was Incredo Land, nothing was really out of place.

Before Charlie could say a word, Magic shoved a large plastic bag against his chest. Magic leaned close, whispering into his ear.

"This is for you. Don't spend it all in one place."

Then he walked right past and headed toward the entrance to the tent.

Charlie waited until he was gone, then opened the top of the bag and peered inside.

Tickets. Jumbled together in thickets ten and twenty deep. He couldn't know for sure, but from the weight of the bag and what he could see, it had to be more than five hundred of them, maybe even closer to six. That meant that they'd all been winning at about the same rate, each of them winning more than ninety percent of the way through their matching budgets. Even if other groups of kids were also pooling their tickets, Charlie doubted he was in much danger of losing. Even though there were still a few more minutes left in the day, obviously the team felt pretty confident they had it in the bag. Everything had gone according to plan.

And the truth was, he had loved every minute of it. His skin felt like it was on fire, and his heart was still pounding from the rope ladder. He hefted the bag up, holding it tightly against his chest like he was holding his favorite pillow, and fought the urge to laugh out loud.

"Charlie! Drat, man, you've been in here all day?"

Charlie turned to where Magic had just disappeared, catching sight of Jeremy as he bounced through the threshold of the tent. For the moment, at least, Jeremy's anger at him from the morning had seemed to disappear; Jeremy's face was a study in pure joy, from his bright red cheeks to the clown-size smile drawn across his lips. His red hair was matted with sweat, and his arms were pumping happily along as he crossed toward Charlie.

"We had the best freaking day. We hit the Space Drop three times, the Haunted Moon twice, and Saturn's Rings broke down halfway into the ride, so they let us stay on as long as we wanted after they got it going. I think my brain is still spinning around in my skull. Man, you got stuck with the worst group."

Charlie's attention shifted halfway into Jeremy's monologue, as loud cursing erupted from directly ahead. It took him less than a second to realize where the cursing was coming from. Even without the theatrics, Dylan was hard to miss; at the moment, the big thug was bouncing from foot to foot, his fists pounding against a gaming counter as he shouted words that would have gotten him kicked out of school for a week. Charlie looked past Dylan's angry, heaving shoulders, and saw that his nemesis was standing at the milk-bottle game, and it was plain what had just happened. Ten feet ahead of Dylan stood two obstinate milk bottles, one of them barely rocking in place, next to four downed bottles. Dylan was yelling at a carny who was just shrugging and shaking his head as Dylan's two buddies, Liam and Dusty, cursed right along with their leader.

Charlie stifled a grin and was about to turn back to Jeremy, when he noticed Sam standing a few feet to Dylan's right, also watching the display with an amused look in her gray eyes.

Charlie felt something inside of him click.

He turned back to Jeremy and handed him the plastic bag full of tickets.

"Hold this for me? I'll be right back."

And then he was strolling forward toward Dylan and the milk bottle game. His adrenaline was pumping, but he kept his limbs from shaking as he slid up to the counter a few feet away from Dylan, and signaled to the carnie. The carny leaned toward him, and Charlie whispered into the man's ear.

"Set it back up, but this time, put the heavy bottle on top."

The carny stared at him.

"Sorry?"

"You heard me. Look, I know how this game works. And if you don't want everyone else to know, put the heavy bottle on top."

The carnie thought for a moment. Then he shrugged, walked over to the bottles, and restacked them into a pyramid. Charlie steeled his nerves again and strolled over to where Dylan was standing.

"Hey, Dylan. You mind if I try one throw?"

Dylan, Liam, and Dusty turned as one. Dylan peered down at Charlie, and then a huge laugh burst from his mouth.

"Hah! You, Numbers? This is hilarious! You couldn't knock over an empty soda can! Sure, give it your best shot!"

Dylan stepped back, palms out, sarcastic look in his eyes, as if he was handing Charlie the keys to the world. Charlie grabbed a baseball from the counter, squared his feet, took aim, and then let fly.

It wasn't a great throw by any means, but it was straight, just hard enough, and it hit the bottles near the base of the pyramid. The pyramid wobbled back, then suddenly collapsed, all six bottles tumbling down. There was a moment of silence, and then laughter and applause from all around. Dylan stared at Charlie in utter shock.

"How the heck did you do that?"

"I don't know," Charlie responded over the rush in his ears. "Like you said, I just gave it my best shot."

Without another word, he strolled back to where Jeremy was standing and took the plastic bag from his aghast friend. Jeremy stared at him, trying to find words. Charlie glanced back toward Sam, and even better, she was covering her mouth because she was laughing so hard.

Charlie gave Jeremy a friendly punch in the shoulder, then tucked the bag of tickets under his arm and headed for the exit. In his head, it was like a dozen carnies were shouting at him at once.

Winner. Winner. Winner!

THE SKY WAS A dull purple by the time most of the crowd had filed out of the midway tent and down the few remaining yards of Solar Avenue to the steps of Moon Base Alpha. As settings went, the Moon Base's steps were as official a place for an awards ceremony as Charlie could have imagined; the imposing pyramid-shaped building gave off a feeling of importance. From where Charlie was standing next to Jeremy in a crowd of kids at least twenty thick, everything felt very real and intense.

"Come on, man," Jeremy mumbled, for what had to be the hundredth time. "We're going to be late for the monorail, and Warden Walker is going to have our butts. What the heck are we doing here, anyway?"

Charlie didn't answer. Instead, he glanced around the crowd, picking out the faces of the rest of his team. Finn and Magic were together a few feet to his right, and Greg, Sam, Jake, and Daniel were behind them, below the bottom step. Charlie didn't see Miranda anywhere, but he assumed she was watching from somewhere. None of them would be there without her, of course; she had to be savoring the moment.

"I mean, you can't really care about some stupid midway game contest, can you? Some kid's gonna win a free T-shirt or something, and we're all standing around waiting to shake his hand?"

Again, Charlie didn't answer, because something was happening beyond the top of the steps; the main doors to the Moon Base slid upward, and out stepped two men. The first, Charlie recognized: gray curly hair, a dark suit, a wide smile, and friendly green eyes. He was the same man from the YouTube video that Miranda had shown Charlie the first time he'd been introduced to the Carnival Killers. This time, instead of standing near the Loopy Wheel, he was strolling along, holding a thin envelope in his right hand.

The second man he didn't recognize: tall, dark-haired, with wire-rimmed glasses and a jaw that ended in an almost perfect triangle. He walked in step with the gray-haired man, but instead of an envelope, he held what looked to be a heavy burlap sack. The sack was imprinted with lettering, dark and clear, that Charlie could read even from that distance: INCREDO LAND CHARITIES. Charlie wondered what a sack like that could possibly contain, and what it had to do with the ceremony.

He wouldn't have to wonder long, because as soon as the two men reached the lip of the steps, someone handed the gray-haired man in the suit a wireless microphone. The man smiled at the crowd, then cleared his throat.

"Thank you all for coming, and for a wonderful day at the midway tent. As you all know, our annual promotion has now come to a close, and I'm here to announce the lucky winner who will get a spin at the Wheel of Wonder!"

A smattering of applause rang out. Jeremy sighed, rather loudly, but Charlie ignored him. The man pinned the microphone under one arm, causing a loud spike of feedback but freeing his hands. He then tore into the envelope and pulled out a little piece of white paper. He read the name on the paper to himself, and then retrieved the microphone.

"And our winner, with six hundred and thirty prize tickets: Charlie Lewis, from Nagassack Middle School in Newton, Massachusetts!"

Jeremy gasped. Jeremy hadn't even seen Charlie turn in all his tickets; Charlie had handed them over to a booth attendant on the way out of the midway tent, filling out his name and school affiliation while Jeremy was busy getting photographed next to a bulgy-eyed space alien.

Charlie's stomach flipped over, and then he was being pushed forward by a hand in the small of his back. He heard Finn whisper a hearty congratulations, and then he was moving up the steps, as if on autopilot. When he reached the top, the gray-haired man shook his hand, then handed the microphone to the stranger with the glasses and the burlap sack.

The stranger smiled at Charlie.

"Young man, congratulations. Tomorrow morning, nine a.m., you'll be spinning the wheel for a chance at a wonderful prize."

Charlie stared out at the crowd, savoring the moment. He was barely listening as the man continued, his mind already speeding ahead to that wheel and what it was going to be like standing there, spinning it, surreptitiously reaching for the iPhone in his pocket.

"Eight lifetime tickets to Incredo Land, which in itself is a priceless prize. But on top of that, we have a special, surprise announcement to make. This year, Incredo Land will be making a donation to the Tampa chapter of the American Red Cross. And as part of our promotional effort to raise awareness for this wonderful cause, we're also matching that donation with a cash prize for today's midway game winner. Something as spectacular as the future itself! This!"

With a flourish, he overturned the burlap sack, spilling its contents onto the porch at his feet. A hush went through the crowd, and Charlie's eyes shot open.

"Fifty thousand dollars!" the man crowed into the microphone as Charlie and the rest of the crowd took in the banded stacks of hundred-dollar bills. Two Incredo Land lackeys in gray work shirts moved to scoop up the bills and shove them back in the sack as the man continued to talk. "Donated by our corporate headquarters this year, and this year only, to celebrate the fact that the Tampa Red Cross raised over two million dollars in the Tampa area over the past twelve months! On the stage tomorrow, next to the wheel, we'll have a box set up to take donations for the Tampa Red Cross, but right now, it's all about you, Charlie! Congratulations!"

Charlie's throat constricted. *Fifty thousand dollars.* He watched as a pair of photographers began photographing the money, obviously for publicity purposes. Cash made a much better picture than a check in an envelope. It was doubtful they'd be handing that kind of money over to a kid; they'd be giving it to the kid's parent or guardian for safekeeping. Charlie felt his face flush from the inside.

Miranda had mentioned there would be a cash prize, but she'd said it was nominal, something small and unimportant, and that it would be donated to charity—specifically, to her education program. *Fifty thousand dollars?* That was real money.

"That's right, Charlie," the man continued. "Tomorrow morning, you'll be spinning the wheel with a chance to win those tickets, and fifty thousand dollars in cash!"

Charlie's head swam. He looked out into the crowd. Jeremy was still staring at him, mouth wide open, awed. Finn, Magic, Sam, and the rest were clapping, surprised as well, but obviously thrilled. He blinked hard, not knowing what to think.

So much money. When it was just tickets, and maybe a trivial amount of money given to charity, well, it was easy to see it all as an exciting caper, mind over matter, using their brains to beat a beatable game. But this kind of prize changed everything. And using his iPhone tomorrow to beat the wheel, for fifty thousand dollars in cash . . .

Charlie blinked again, and suddenly, right in the center of the crowd, he saw her. Those dark bangs glowing in the blue light from the castle looming in the distance, those cat eyes flashing as they stared right into his own, those white teeth gleaming in that frighteningly perfect smile.

Miranda. She was looking right into his mind, and for a brief moment, her red lips straightened, and her head nodded, imperceptibly. She was proud of him, but more than that, she was telling him that he wasn't finished yet, that tomorrow morning he was going to spin that wheel. The one missing piece, the diameter of the wheel, which Charlie needed to know to make his equation work, that was just a detail, one that Miranda had a way of providing. Because it was obvious now, Miranda had thought all of this through. Every step.

The dark-haired, bespectacled man continued into the microphone.

"Tomorrow morning, Charlie, you'll have a one in five chance of winning it all."

Charlie shivered, because he knew the truth. The man was wrong. With the diameter of the wheel and his dad's iPhone in his pocket, it wasn't going to be a one in five chance.

It was going to be a mathematical certainty. Numbers doing what numbers were supposed to do.

Winner. Winner. Winner . . .

19

YOU GOT TEN MINUTES, lovebirds. If you hear me whistle, get out, fast."

Charlie pressed his back against the brick wall, watching the shadows play across the narrow alley. He could hear Sam breathing next to him in short, nervous gasps as she slid along the wall next to him, feeling her way over the rough bricks with the palms of her hands. Charlie was happy to let her lead. He'd never been all that coordinated, and his night vision was pretty near pathetic. Even in the dull blue glow from the Castle in the distance and the drifting neon light from Solar Avenue just a dozen yards behind them, he was pretty near blind. The scruffy-haired park employee moving through the alley ahead of them, leading without ever looking back, was just a shape in the darkness; Charlie couldn't make out the spikes of his hair, let alone the scar above his lip. If he'd known the guy's name, he might have called out to him to slow down, but then again, he probably wouldn't have had the guts. He didn't want to talk to him any more than he had to. He still wasn't sure what the man's job was at the park, or what Miranda had offered him to get him to help them, but Charlie was certain that he wanted very little to do with the guy. He was pretty sure Sam felt the same way, because she hadn't gotten closer than three feet to him since he'd let them into the park through a back gate in a shadowy corner of the docking station. When he'd brought them to the alley, just a few buildings down from Moon Base Alpha, and pointed toward the warehouselike structure where they'd need to go, they had simply followed, wordlessly, staying as small and invisible as possible. Nobody would think twice, seeing a park employee wandering around after closing, but two kids would be a lot harder to explain.

"And if you touch anything other than the wheel," the scarred man said, stopping halfway down the alley and jabbing a hand in their direction, "you're gonna be in big trouble."

He shifted the same knifelike hand toward the

brick wall, pointing at a window, which was at about the man's shoulder level. As Charlie and Sam inched closer, Charlie could see that the window was halfway open. It was too dark to make out anything inside, but Charlie guessed that if a screen had been there, it was now gone. Scarface had taken care of everything. Or more accurately, had done whatever Miranda had asked of him.

Charlie trembled, as Scarface gave them one last look; then the man hurried back down the alley toward Solar Avenue. A second later, Charlie and Sam were utterly alone, both of them still pressed against the wall, listening to the breeze play across the gravel beneath their feet. It was strange, being in that place after dark. And especially being alone with Sam. Being next to her like that in the dark made his pulse quicken; it was a strange feeling, one he couldn't quite define. Sure, sometimes Crystal had made him lose his words—when she did something particularly cute, or laughed just the right way—but this was different. This was something much more palpable, in his gut. Everything about this moment had him on edge, tingling like he was about to catch fire.

Just an hour ago, the last remaining tourists had been happily strolling their way down the Avenue on the way to the park's exits, but now that the park was closed, Charlie felt like he and Sam were in the middle of some sort of alien planet. Incredo Land just didn't feel right after hours. In the first place, it was just too freaking quiet. The electronic music was gone, but even more noticeable was the lack of ambient sound. Now, Solar Avenue was like a corpse, facades instead of real live buildings, a shell without a soul.

Sam reached the window first and stretched her arms over her head. Even at full extension, she could just get her fingers over the sill. Charlie stood next to her, shaking his head.

"Shoot, that jerk could have at least given us a boost. We're never going to get up there without some sort of ladder."

Before he could finish the sentence, Sam's fingers had gripped the edge of the sill, and she swung her legs up, a study of pure grace. A second later, her feet were through the open window in a perfect tuck, then the rest of her, until only her head remained in the alley. She smiled down at Charlie.

"You're next."

She held out both hands, leveraging her body against the inside of the windowsill. Charlie swallowed hard; obviously Sam had some gymnastics training. He felt even more uncoordinated than ever, but he didn't want to embarrass himself in front of her. He had to at least try. He reached up and put his hands on hers.

Her grip was incredibly strong for such a small girl; using his feet against the bricks while she pulled, he managed to scramble up the wall with surprising ease. Getting himself through the half-open window was a bit trickier; Sam had to move out of the way, and Charlie found himself wriggling through like a caterpillar attacking a leaf. Hands feeling the darkness in front of him, he let himself drop into the room on the other side of the window—thankfully feeling carpet against his palms, then rolling into a clumsy ball. Sam helped him back to his feet, brushing dirt from the sill off his borrowed jean jacket.

The jacket had been Magic's; Charlie hadn't planned on sticking around the park after dark, when the breeze, combined with the humidity in the air, turned the temperature cool enough to bring goose bumps to his skin. Truthfully, he hadn't planned on being involved in this part of the game at all. Breaking into a building to measure a giant wheel was not his idea of using his brain to beat the system. But when Sam had volunteered, and Miranda had asked who she'd want to come along to help, and Sam had looked at Charlie, well, he hadn't had much choice. His mind had already begun to figure out a way to sneak away from Jeremy, pretending he had to call home to go over some old science project with his dad. He had no idea why Sam had asked for him. Likewise, at first he'd been surprised that Miranda and the rest of the group had even let Sam herself volunteer. But seeing her lithe form slink away from the window and into the dark room, Charlie realized she was incredibly athletic, and from the way she'd gone through the window, she seemed to have a catlike agility.

"This isn't going to be as hard as I thought," Sam whispered, pointing ahead into the darkness.

At first, Charlie couldn't see anything, but as his eyes adjusted, he began to make out shapes. They were in a storage room, with cavernous walls and a high, barely visible ceiling. There were steel shelves lining the walls to his left and right, covered in objects of all sorts of sizes and shapes, and a big glass cabinet on the other side of the room, by the interior door that led to the rest of the building. But Sam wasn't pointing toward the shelves or the cabinet; she was pointing to a huge shape standing in an alcove, directly across from them. Even in the darkness, Charlie knew exactly what he was looking at.

At least twice Charlie's height at its peak, at least two feet deep, draped in a heavy sheet—the thing was enormous, and made to seem even bigger because it was up on a huge motorized metal dolly with rubber-soled wheels. The frame of the dolly was all steel piping, with a high iron cage reaching up behind the sheet. Charlie had no idea how much the thing weighed, but he did know that to adequately measure the thing, there was going to be some serious climbing involved. Even to reach the monstrosity's halfway point, one of them was going to have to monkey up the side of the dolly.

"It looks way bigger than it did on the video," Charlie murmured as Sam crept forward toward the alcove. She seemed to be calculating something as she moved, her gaze measuring the carpet in front of her, the distance between her feet and the dolly.

And then suddenly, she leaped forward into a perfect front handspring. Her palms barely touched the floor, then she was flipping over in the air, landing softly on the edge of the dolly, her hands tight against the steel bars.

"Wow!" Charlie gasped. "You're like a superhero."

It was a pretty dumb thing to say, but Sam just laughed. She hauled herself up along the bar, then reached out, grabbing a section of the heavy sheet, and gave it a yank. The sheet slid halfway down, revealing the top part of the great wheel. As Charlie moved closer, he could see the outline of Maddy the Turkey Hawk in one section, and a piece of the Frog.

"Actually, I always wanted to be a superhero," Sam whispered as she traced one of the wheel's sections with a finger. "I've been a gymnast, going on about five years now. Started when I was eight. I was originally enrolled in ballet dance class, but I hated it. I begged my mom to let me do gymnastics instead."

Charlie reached the base of the dolly. He thought about trying to climb up next to her, but decided getting through the window had taxed his abilities enough. Instead, he reached into his pocket and retrieved the heavy-duty tape measure that Miranda had given him for the job.

"My mom was against it at first," Sam continued, her expression invisible in the darkness. "She thought that little girls should take dance. But I convinced her that gymnastics would help with my math homework; I was already kind of obsessed with the science and math behind the moves. How many steps it would take to get to the vault. What was the proper force and angle necessary to jump off a springboard and stick a front handspring. The rotational kinetics of the parallel bars."

Charlie felt himself growing more and more impressed by her as she reached down and took the tape measure from him. She really was a geek like him, even if her overall package had nothing geeky about it.

"I even wrote a paper about it," she added. "When we moved from New York and I had to transfer schools, my mom sent the paper along with my admission package. I think that's partly how I got into Nagassack as a seventh grader. They're pretty picky for late arrivals, you know."

Charlie nodded, and then something struck him.

"That's probably how Miranda found you. Your essay."

"Yeah, I figured that out a while back too. When Finn and Magic first approached me to join the team. I'd just transferred in from New York, and Miranda had made it seem like she was interested in me because she was from the City as well, and she knew how hard it could be to adjust to the suburbs, but I knew it was more than that."

Charlie watched as Sam slowly extended herself out to reach the far edge of the wheel with one hand.

"So it was Finn and Magic with you, too," he said.

"Yeah, well, mostly Finn. He has a special relationship with Miranda. I think she's friends with his family.

They kind of grew up together. At least that's what I've gathered."

That was something new. Finn had never mentioned that he'd known Miranda beyond the Carnival Killers. Charlie had assumed that he had been recruited because of his school record as well.

"What do you think of her? Miranda?"

Sam shrugged in the darkness.

"She's pretty amazing. And intense. But I admire her a lot. She's smart, and she's also beautiful, and she doesn't seem to be scared of anything. She's kind of a role model for me. She can be a little scary, but I think her heart is in the right place."

Charlie pressed his lips together. They had just climbed through a window into a dark warehouse room to secretly measure a wheel. He wasn't sure he agreed with Sam's thinking.

"The money, the fifty thousand dollars."

"Yeah, It's a whole lot of money. I guess we were all surprised by that. Miranda as much as any of us. Last year it was a few hundred dollars, which went to charity."

That's exactly what Miranda had said, when the group had gathered by the monorail, right after Charlie had won the contest. The money was a big surprise; just as the man on the steps had said, nobody could have known that there would be such a huge prize. Miranda had promised that she'd find a good charity to put the money toward, since her school program wouldn't be able to accept a donation that large. It was crazy and shocking, but they would do something good with it, she'd insisted, that was what mattered.

"I don't think it changes anything," Sam whispered. "Every one of us got into this because we love math and numbers. For me, it was gymnastics. For Finn, maybe swimming. You were the last piece in the puzzle. So whatever Miranda really thinks, no matter what her real reasons, I think the important thing is that she got us together. It's a once-in-a-lifetime kind of thing."

With a sudden motion, she flicked the end of the tape measure toward Charlie with her fingers. The tape spat out like a lizard's tongue and Charlie just managed to catch it before it smacked into his chest.

Sam grinned at him through the darkness, then extended her body out across the dolly, stretching her long, lean arms toward the far edge of the wheel. . . .

20

IT WAS TEN MINUTES past eleven in the evening, and waves of soft violin music drifted out through the crack under the locked door, cresting softly against the faux wooden walls of the narrow hallway. When Charlie closed his eyes, he could almost see the layers of air vibrating outward and washing over him in great, bulbous, concentric circles, the near atomic molecules vibrating back and forth as they clambered through his ears, varying the air pressure against his eardrums, reverberating against his microscopic skin cells at wonderfully specific frequencies: 440 Hz, a beautiful, searing A, sliding all the way down to 220 Hz, another A an octave lower—and then, almost to nothingness, and back again, rising, rising, rising. Charlie's mother had always told him that the violin was the most perfect of instruments, because it always told the truth. Charlie had never really understood what she'd meant by the comment. Standing there in the hallway, waiting for Miranda to open the door, he thought maybe his mother was right; he couldn't imagine what it would sound like to hear a violin tell a lie.

Another moment passed, the violin the only sound in his ears. He glanced back over his shoulder at the empty hallway; the rest of the resort had gone quiet as a tomb. Eleven p.m. wasn't that late in much of the world, but in Incredo Land, it was certainly the middle of the night. People went down early because they couldn't wait for the next day to begin. Tonight, Charlie didn't want to go to sleep for precisely the opposite reason—he wanted to put off the next day for as long as he could.

He hadn't intended to stop by Miranda's room to give her the measurements from the wheel; after all, she didn't need the precise numbers, she already knew how Charlie's equation worked. But when he'd returned to his own room to find Jeremy fast asleep in one of the double beds, and three missed calls from his parents on his dad's iPhone, he'd felt awash in guilt about all the white lies he'd told, to his parents, his friends, and especially to himself. Sneaking into a warehouse to measure the wheel with Sam had been thrilling, but it had also been wrong, and no amount of rationalization would make it right.

He'd come to the conclusion that he needed to tell Miranda what he was thinking. If anyone could help him through his concerns, it was her. Sam was fascinating and brilliant, but she was totally invested in what they were doing, and obviously looked to Miranda as a guiding force. Finn and Magic didn't seem to have any qualms with any of it, and Charlie doubted they even cared about the bigger picture. Finn had quit the swim team on the morning of the biggest and most important meet of the school year. It was obvious he had developed his own personal sense of right and wrong.

But Miranda was nearly an adult, and she was their leader. So Charlie wanted to hear it one more time from her. Before it was just him, alone, facing the wheel.

He set his jaw, reached out, and knocked on the door for a third time. But again, there was nothing but the soft tug of the violin strings. He could see a sliver of yellow light beneath the door, but no motion inside, no shadows or footsteps. Either Miranda was a heavy sleeper, or she wasn't home.

Charlie considered heading back to his room. He was sure he could get into his bed without waking

Jeremy, but he doubted he'd be able to fall asleep. Too many things were battling within in his head.

Looking at the locked door, listening to the dutifully honest tone of the violin, he came to another, sudden decision.

There weren't many adults who could resist a crying twelve-year-old, and the poor, harried woman behind the front desk was no exception. She was middle-aged, a little overweight, with a frayed bun of dyed-blond hair on her head and glasses hanging from a cord around her neck. By the time Charlie got the decibels up to a low wail, she was primed to give in to just about anything Charlie could have asked for. In fact, she looked like she was about to start crying herself, but that might have had more to do with being two hours into an overnight shift behind a desk with an empty faux jungle of a lobby splayed out in front of her. There were only so many times you could withstand listening to alien jungle noises pumped through speakers disguised as totem poles and tiki torches, while tourists wearing Velcro fanny packs took photos of the combination waterfall/ gift shop, before you lost your mind.

"I just don't know how I lost my key," Charlie bleated, rubbing his eyes hard enough to cause real tears. "And if I knock on the door and wake the baby, my mom's gonna kill me. I was only supposed to step out for a second to get ice from the ice machine, but then I wanted to go see how the volcano by the pool was lit up at night, and then I lost track of the time."

"It's okay, kid, I'll make an exception just this time—"

"And I've been trying my hardest to be good all week long, and my baby brother just cries all the time—"

"Look, kid, here's a duplicate key! Everything's gonna be just fine!"

Charlie sniffed, taking the electronic keycard from her, then grabbed the empty ice bucket he'd taken from a janitor's closet to use as a totally unnecessary prop, and headed back toward the lobby exit.

"Thanks, lady, you saved my life," he choked out over his shoulder. But the woman had already gone back to the trashy celebrity magazine she kept hidden behind the front desk. Charlie's hysterics were just another unfortunate memory, and she had six more hours to go on her shift.

Key in hand, Charlie's sobs morphed into a grin; not only had he learned how to beat carnival games, but he'd picked up some Oscar-worthy skills along the way.

• • •

Miranda's door came unlocked with a supple mechanical click, and Charlie cast one final glance behind himself to make sure the hallway was still empty before using both hands to carefully nudge the door open just enough for him to slide inside. He knew what he was doing was wrong; sneaking into someone else's hotel room was a step beyond little white lies to his parents and friends. But he didn't see any other way to figure out what was going on.

The hotel room was similar to the one he and Jeremy shared: two double beds covered in vaguely jungle-floral prints, a set of glass doors leading out to a small patio, a few pieces of wicker furniture, a potted plant by the door, a flat-screen TV. But Miranda's room also had a sort of kitchenette, which consisted of a low counter supporting a coffeepot, a small cubic stainless-steel microwave, and a compact minibar. The minibar door had been left partially ajar, and Charlie could see that a fair number of its contents were already missing. Then he noticed the three empty miniature bottles standing like a tiny platoon of AWOL transparent soldiers behind the microwave, and a shiver of nervousness moved through him.

He didn't know where Miranda had gone, but from the state of the room, he doubted she'd be gone long.

Not just the minibar and the empty bottles—on a second glance across the room, he saw that her suede jacket was hanging on the back of a chair parked by the TV table, and she'd left a stack of papers sitting on the small desk by the doors to the patio. She was probably nearby, maybe meeting with Finn or the others, or taking a quick dip in the pool. Which meant he was going to have to act fast.

He was about to head straight for the stack of papers to see if they would shed any more light on Miranda when something else caught his attention. A flash of smooth black leather on the floor beside one of the beds. A little bigger than a paperback book, with a shiny chrome clasp and a designer's scroll across one side. Miranda's purse. It must have bounced off her bed when she'd tossed it there and now it was right in front of Charlie, like a gleaming invitation.

As bad as sneaking into Miranda's hotel room was, going into her purse seemed even worse; if there was one thing Charlie had learned about women from his mother, it was that a lady's purse was completely off limits. But Charlie didn't see any other choice. He was ten hours away from spinning the wheel, and he needed to know more about the woman behind it all.

As the violin music blended with the sound of the

blood rushing through his ears, he quickly crossed the room to the purse and bent down on both knees. It took him a second to figure out the clasp, and then he was inside, leafing through her possessions. Makeup, a little plastic mirror, a key chain, a few slips of paper with numbers written on them. And a little leather card holder, folded tightly closed. Charlie flipped it open and counted through six credit cards, all of them gold, with Miranda's name stenciled on each. That seemed like a heck of a lot of credit cards for an eighteen-year-old teaching student, but then, maybe she was from a rich family. She'd been able to front them each two hundred dollars and pay for their trips; maybe the money had come from one of these cards. He was about to shut the card holder and continue sifting through the purse, when a picture of Miranda caught his eye. It was a school ID card; she looked just as perfect under glossy plastic as she did in real life, those pitch-black bangs like a dagger over her icicle eyes. Charlie glanced past the picture and noticed a lot of red and gray writing— and then he paused, blinking hard. He suddenly realized that the card wasn't a Northeastern ID at all; above Miranda's picture it said Massachusetts Institute of Technology. His eyes narrowed, and he continued reading her ID. Beneath her photo were the words

DEPARTMENT OF MECHANICAL ENGINEERING, followed by a student ID number.

Charlie shook his head. That didn't make sense. Miranda had told them she was a teaching student. Heck, she was a teaching assistant at Nagassack, getting credit for assisting the teachers there with grades seven and eight. Why would she need teaching credits if she was an engineering student?

His face paled as another thought hit him. She'd told the group that she had formed the Carnival Killers because she was working on a paper about group dynamics in middle schoolers. Would a mechanical engineering major at MIT be working on a paper on middle schoolers?

And what about her original claim that whatever little money came along with the prize for beating the wheel would go to her teaching department as charity. If she wasn't a student at Northeastern, had she simply been lying to them?

Charlie didn't know what to think. He stared at the ID card, frozen in place, listening to the Vivaldi in the background, feeling each vibrating violin string as if it was slapping against his face—

And then suddenly, the violins stopped. The room went dead silent.

Charlie hastily shoved the card back in the card holder, flipped the purse and let it fall back to the carpet, then leaped to his feet.

Miranda had entered the room but had her back to him as she fidgeted with the TV, choosing a new music channel. Charlie had no idea if she had noticed him in the room or not, but from the way she was swaying, he was pretty sure she had added to the three empty mini-bottles she'd consumed before heading out. He decided not to stick around to find out.

He leaped forward, his feet barely touching the carpet, and dove through the still-open door. He hit the hallway at full speed, nearly careening into the opposite wall, then found his balance and raced toward the elevators. He didn't look back until he was inside, hitting the down button with his thumb as hard as he could. Just as the doors shut, he caught a glimpse of motion from the direction of Miranda's room, a spray of jet-black hair, a flash of alabaster skin in the dim light from the hallway ceiling, and then the elevator doors clanked shut.

He was breathing hard as the elevator descended. If she'd seen him, well, he wasn't sure how he'd explain himself. But even more pressing, something was going on, and it wasn't good.

Miranda had lied. Charlie wasn't sure why, but he

intended to find out. It was now nearly midnight, which meant he only had a few more hours, and he wasn't going to be able to go any further without help. Which left him with only one option.

He was going to break the Cardinal Rule of the Carnival Killers.

21

THERE WERE FEW THINGS more peaceful-looking than a gawky, redheaded kid in Spider-Man pajamas, splayed out faceup on a still-made double bed, cheeks splotched with chocolate from a half-eaten Toblerone bar, snoring away in the dim glow of a flat-screen TV. The pajamas were an inside joke; Charlie had convinced his parents to buy them for Jeremy for his eleventh birthday, insisting that the pj's were all that Jeremy had asked for, and Jeremy had been forced to smile and thank Charlie's mom and dad, all the while cursing Charlie under his breath. Two years later, the pajamas were now more than two sizes too small; they barely came down to his calves, and were frayed into nothingness right around his elbows. Spider-Man himself had faded almost into oblivion; he was now more dull, reddish blob than well-defined superhero. But the funny thing was, over the years Jeremy had actually grown to love them, and wore them as often as he could, especially whenever Charlie was sleeping over.

Seeing him lying there, snoring away, a smile from the day's excitement still on his chocolate-covered lips, Charlie almost felt bad about what he was about to do. But then he flashed back to Miranda's room and the college ID, and he knew he had no choice. He needed his friend, and he needed him alert and awake.

Charlie held the glass of ice four inches above Jeremy's face, and then flipped it over. There was a moment's pause, and then Jeremy's eyes snapped open like window shades, and he jerked upward, sending the Toblerone bar and television remote skittering across the room.

"What the heck! Hey, man, I was sleeping!"

"I can see that," Charlie said as he lowered himself onto the side of the bed. Jeremy was sputtering, slapping pieces of ice off of his face, neck, and chest. One piece managed to find its way under the material of his pajamas, and he wriggled back and forth to try to work it free. "You look like a big ginger snake trying to shed its skin. Sorry I had to use extreme measures, but I need your help, and it can't wait until morning."

Jeremy obviously heard the change in Charlie's tone; he could tell that his friend wasn't joking, and despite all the distance that had grown between them in the past few weeks, Jeremy didn't brush him away. Charlie felt even worse about all the lies and subterfuge; but that was over with now.

"I'm here for you, you know that. And I'm dressed to impress."

That got a little smile out of Charlie, but his tone remained serious.

"I'm going to tell you something, Jeremy, and it's going to sound crazy, but all of it is true. All I ask is that you wait until I'm finished talking before you respond."

Charlie took a deep breath, and then began at the beginning.

Ten minutes later, Jeremy was leaning back against a pillow, his hair like a demented red halo across the pillow-case. Every last vestige of sleep was gone from his eyes, and the chocolate on his cheeks had blended in with the burst of blush on his face.

"Holy cow, Batman. That's a crazy story."

Charlie nodded.

"So you see why I've been acting so strange, and

why I couldn't tell you anything. I wanted to. But yeah, it's all pretty crazy."

"And cool. It's also very cool. Finn, Magic, and that girl, Sam? Wow, man, it's like the Whiz Kids on steroids. Beating carnival games with math. I freaking love it."

Jeremy was literally bouncing on the bed, and Charlie was worried for a moment that his friend had missed the most important part—that Miranda had probably lied about who she was, and thus, why she had brought the team together. But then Jeremy got serious again, leaning forward off of the pillow.

"Obviously, we need more information. This Miranda chick, she's not at all what she seems. She's a facade. We have to knock down that facade and find out what makes her tick."

Charlie nodded. It was exactly what he wanted to hear. Jeremy had sifted right through to the crux of the situation; he was Charlie's best friend, and in many ways, he was like an extension of Charlie's personality. Charlie felt whole, talking it through with him, and again, he regretted not bringing Jeremy into the scheme earlier. But it didn't seem to matter to Jeremy; he was ready to help. The question was, what could either of them do?

"And how do we go about that? It's after midnight.

I'm supposed to spin the wheel in, like, eight hours."

Jeremy looked him right in the eyes.

"There's only one option, dude."

Charlie stopped. He realized what his friend was saying, and shook his head.

"Like I said, it's after midnight—"

"One option," Jeremy repeated, lowering his voice.

Charlie's head stopped shaking, because he knew that his friend was right. He had been trying to avoid coming to the same conclusion, but Jeremy had zeroed right in. It was the one and only thing they could do.

Without a word, Charlie reached into his pocket and retrieved his dad's iPhone. He wasn't thrilled about what was coming, but it really was the only way.

"Code Blue," Jeremy said, putting words to both of their thoughts.

"Code Blue," Charlie repeated. "And, boy, is she going to let us have it."

And then he started to dial.

"OKAY, HERE'S HOW THIS is gonna work. Electromagnetic crampons attached to woven steel gloves. We work our way up the side of Building 10, draped in highly reflective glass-mail cloaks to confuse angles of vision from the street below. Then we reverse rappel up the Great Dome with retractable aluminum claws, and use a chemical solvent on the iron joints that attach the skylights to the top of the dome. Once through the joints, we string high-tensile wire down through the opening and shimmy down into the lobby. Ten feet above the floor, we set off a ring of cordite satchels we've previously placed, in a parallel series along Mass Avenue, to draw the attention of the security guards. Then we drop down, using spring-loaded pressure pads attached to the bottom of our boots to absorb the kinetic energy. When we're on the ground, we blanket our approach with military-grade sulfur smoke bombs, and we make our way to the file room. In and out, twelve minutes, minus how long it takes to get the materials and set up the cordite. Yippee-ki–yay!"

Kentaro crossed his arms against his chest, breathing heavily from the monologue, his miniature chest ballooning forward with pride. Marion, next to him in the dark recess of the alley that jutted off of Mass Avenue, shadowed by the multistoried building that seemed to stretch on forever in front of them, nodded vigorously, his thick cheeks jiggling beneath the black knit cap he'd pulled down over his curly hair. The hat matched his clothes; some sort of bizarre black jumpsuit, halfway between sweats and a ski outfit. Kentaro's outfit wasn't much better: black long johns on top and bottom, and bright green rubber kitchen gloves.

Crystal stared at the two of them for a full beat. Then she pulled a plastic card out of the back pocket of her overalls and waved it in front of them.

"Or, we could try this."

She shoved the card into a slot by the nondescript green door in front of them, and there was a high metallic click as the electronic lock opened.

Kentaro and Marion glanced at each other, then back at Crystal.

"I guess that might work too," Kentaro mumbled.

"If you want to take the boring approach," Marion added.

Crystal groaned to herself as she twisted the doorknob, pulling the green door open. Three descending stone steps led to a second door with a matching security slot.

"If you'd rather blow the interior door with cordite, be my guest," she said, waving Kentaro ahead. He shrugged sheepishly.

Idiots, Crystal thought to herself. The two worst covert operatives in history, and she was stuck with them. Even worse, the three of them were embarking on the most dangerous Code Blue in the history of the Whiz Kids—with almost no warning, no preparation, and only the barest understanding of what the heck they were getting themselves into.

But in truth, there hadn't been any choice. Charlie had called the Code Blue in from Florida, and no matter how infuriating he'd been over the past month, it was their duty to respond. And, to be fair, in the six years since the Whiz Kids had come up with the term, it had only been enacted once before. And that had been nearly four years ago, when Marion had accidentally let his sister's cat out of his house when his family was away at the mall. An officially called Code Blue was supposed to be a matter of life and death, but then again, Marion's older sister was quite a beast, nearly twice Marion's size, with dyed-blue hair and an ever-present lacrosse stick gripped in her meaty right hand. Rumor was, she had once nearly decapitated an eighth grader who had made fun of her hair—and that was when she was nine! So that first and until now only use of Code Blue had been confirmed, and Crystal, Charlie, Jeremy, and Kentaro had spent an entire afternoon helping Marion dig through bushes, climb trees, and sneak into unlocked garages searching for a mangy Siamese who answered to Tiffy, if she deigned to answer at all. They did, eventually, find Tiffy, hanging upside down by her claws from a telephone pole three blocks from Marion's house. But by the time they'd returned with the escaped feline, Marion's sister had already stationed herself on his front porch, lacrosse stick in hand. Only a sudden outbreak of cracked, bleeding hives had saved him from a beating.

Tonight was different. First of all, it was nearly one in the morning, which meant all of them had been fast asleep when the call had come in, and they'd had to figure out ways to sneak out of their homes, way past bedtime. They'd previously come up with the process to call a Code Blue after hours: Charlie had dialed each of their homes—landlines, of course—and let the phone ring three times, then hung up and called again, hanging up before anyone answered. But it was up to each Whiz Kid individually to figure out a way out of the house. Crystal had snuck through a first-floor bathroom window. For all she knew, Kentaro may have crawled through a doggy door. Marion had gone out through his garage—beads of sweat lubricating his chubby form as he squeezed between his parents' matching BMW X5s.

After a quick stop at Charlie's house to retrieve Charlie's father's MIT key card and ID, which Charlie had told her she could find in the glove compartment of his Volvo, spare keys for which his father kept in a magnetic case in the rear wheel well, they met on a nearby corner, made a call from Crystal's cell, and all cabbed it to the address just off of Mass Avenue. They were pretty young to be taking taxis by themselves, but that was really just a matter of convincing a tired, overworked driver in the middle of a night shift that a parent would be waiting for them when they reached their destination.

And the danger was multiplied by the sheer fact that all three of them would probably be applying to the school one day, because for kids like them, the

Massachusetts Institute of Technology was like a mother ship. The university was dedicated to geeks, geekdom, a full on bastion of nerds like them learning to inherit the earth. Looking up at the shadows of the enormous Great Dome that served as the university's architectural center, just a dozen yards around the corner from where they were standing—a mountain of stone, glass, and noble gothic pillars rising high into the air—well, it was beyond awe-inspiring. *Even if that pinprick Kentaro was still imagining blowing much of it up with cordite satchels.*

Crystal steeled herself and hurried down the small flight of stairs. She used the card again, listened for another mechanical click, then opened the second door and ushered her two overeager accomplices inside.

The hallway beyond the door was halfway between tunnel and corridor; it had an institutional feel, with a shiny linoleum floor, off-yellow walls, and a low ceiling. The hallway stretched in either direction as far as the eye could see, lined on both sides with numbered doors.

As infinite as this hallway seemed when she peered ahead, it wasn't the actual Infinite Corridor of MIT fame; that was a couple of levels up, above their heads, an eight-hundred-and-twenty-five-foot cavernous corridor that cut through the spine of the university. Even now, even in the middle of the night, when the air outside was still bearable and the snow had yet to fall, Crystal knew that the Infinite Corridor would be crowded with students moving one way or another, heading to the nightly extra help sessions and club meetings, bouncing off one another and the walls like electrons in a hadron collider. In many ways, the Infinite Corridor was the center and source of MIT student life, a circulatory system pumping brilliant people between the different organlike departments. Day or night, the Infinite Corridor was the true artery of MIT.

If the Infinite Corridor was the circulatory system, then this hallway was quite possibly the bowels. It was mostly devoid of students, a veritable shaft beneath the mine, which kept the circulatory system pumping.

Janitorial rooms, storage facilities, maintenance alcoves, this was where the guts lived. Crystal glanced at the closest door, reading the number above the knob. Then she turned to Marion.

"Show me the blueprint again," she said. There had never been any question about who would be leading the Code Blue; if the two buffoons had been in charge, they'd all have probably ended up in the Charles River by now, after trying to scale the Great Dome.

Marion opened the zipper of his jumpsuit and

removed a small rolled-up piece of blue paper. He handed it to Crystal with a flourish, even bowing slightly. Crystal fought the urge to punch him in his knit cap. It helped to look at the blueprint; as she unrolled the blue paper, she had to admit that Marion had his uses. He'd known exactly where to look to find the architectural blueprint, and ten minutes with his parents' computer had been all he'd needed.

Crystal drew a finger along the etched lines on the blueprint; it wasn't so different, really, than reading the schematics of an iron- or copper-ore mine, something she did quite often, actually, as a break from cataloguing and lovingly recataloguing her mineral collection. It took only a few minutes to find what she was looking for. Then she started forward, moving at such a brisk pace that Kentaro, with his little legs, had to jog to keep up.

"If someone sees us," the overly imaginative pip-squeak peeped, "we're on government business. The military gives a lot of money to MIT, there's a lot of top secret defense research going on around here."

Crystal rolled her eyes.

"You're an idiot. The government doesn't hire twelve-year-olds."

"How do you know?" Marion countered, huffing

and puffing as he staggered along next to her, counting the numbered doors with moving lips as he went. "I have an uncle who's a federal employee, and he once told me—"

"Your uncle works for the post office," Crystal cut in.

"Okay, but he says that government agents are getting younger every year. Because of the hackers, you know. They need young people to infiltrate the hackers."

"Well, when they start trying to infiltrate chimpanzee gangs, I'm sure they'll get you two."

"Hey, that's not very nice."

Crystal stopped short, hands outstretched to block her fumbling escorts. Her hand bounced off Kentaro's head and caught Marion right in the chest. She grimaced, noticing that his jumpsuit felt like it was made of velvet. Then she pointed to a numbered door.

"This is the undergraduate file-backup room, according to your blueprints. Most of the data is electronic, so it's in the cloud, but there should be some hard copies of things—registration forms, dorm leases, filed complaints, stuff like that."

She reached out and tried the doorknob, but it was locked, as she suspected.

"You got a magic card for this one too?" Kentaro asked.

"Magic is science for morons. I've got something better."

She started down the corridor again, passing two more doors and then stopping in front of what looked to be a ventilation grate planted about waist-high along the wall. As Kentaro and Marion followed, she retrieved a Phillips-head screwdriver from the side pocket of her overalls. She tapped the still-open blueprint with the head of the screwdriver.

"You were right about one thing, Kentaro. MIT and the US military do have a close relationship, and a lot of defense department money flows through these buildings. Peaking around WWII, this place was like an engineering factory for the military. Just a few hundred yards from here is where geeks like us developed microwave radar, guidance systems for aircraft, sonar, even early computers and much of the hardware and software used in ballistic missiles."

"And this is relevant—" Marion started, but she shut him up with a look.

"It's relevant because it's going to get us inside that file room. See, a lot of this architecture came about through military R & D grants, which meant there were certain safety precautions that had to be met in the case of an enemy attack, or some sort of homegrown sabotage. During the seventies, there were a lot of sit-ins that turned into near riots, on account of the military presence on a fairly liberal campus."

Kentaro and Marion's eyes had glazed as she lectured them, so she poked the handle of the screwdriver against each of their chests.

"Anyway, if either of you'd actually looked over these blueprints, you'd know that most of the rooms on this hallway were built with positive pressure ventilation systems. Basically, the air in these rooms is kept at a higher pressure than the environment surrounding it. Which means that if there's some sort of chemical leak, the rooms can be vented immediately, keeping these rooms environmentally secure. To do this, there are powerful fans in large ventilation ducts leading in and out of all the rooms on this side of the hallway."

She tapped the grated opening.

"This leads into a central air-pump room, with more ducts leading to each individual room. We get in here, we're in the system."

Kentaro grinned.

"Old-school hacking. A screwdriver instead of a wireless modem. I love it."

"I'm glad. Because you're the only one who's small enough to crawl through the ducts. Shouldn't take you more than a few minutes to get to the file room, and then you can open the door from the inside."

Kentaro's curses and complaints were music to Crystal's ears as she went to work on the screws that held the grate in place.

Ten minutes later, Crystal leaned back from the aluminum filing cabinet, her brows furrowing as her eyes followed a cone of orange light across a heavily lined sheet of paper. She was controlling the cone with her lips; a small flashlight hung from the corner of her mouth, and as she read through the text, she skillfully shifted the light down the page. It was a trick she'd picked up over many evenings spent scouring beaches, quarries, and even her own backyard—sometimes you found the best minerals at night, because the precise glow of a flashlight threw off sparklelike reflections you didn't get from a blanket of daylight.

At the moment, she was getting some pretty startling sparkles of a different nature; rather than the rainbow arcs of silicon, graphite, or quartz, she was seeing bright red flicks of ink and jagged daggers of a pen.

Once she'd located the correct filing cabinet, it hadn't taken long to track down Miranda Sloan's undergraduate file. The drawers of each cabinet were segregated by department, and since most of an undergraduate's life was now online, each folder of backup paperwork was quite small—some as short as a single sheet, like an insurance form or a signed tuition bill tucked inside a manila folder.

But Miranda Sloan's file was at least twice as thick as anyone else's in the mechanical engineering drawer—and from the very first sheet Crystal pulled, it was easy to see why. The circled blank squares and Xs next to unsigned bars told a story that was surprisingly easy to file.

"Unpaid tuition bills," Crystal murmured around the flashlight as Kentaro and Marion crowded around her, trying to see over her shoulders. She didn't feel a need to add their eyes to hers. She'd honed her investigative ability over a lifetime of analyzing rocks, ranging from some so small you could only see them under a microscope, to boulders you had to use a ladder to ascend. Compared to that, this was like finding silicon salt on a beach. "She's at least three of her payments behind. Adds up to almost twenty thousand dollars. She's on her third mailed warning; another letter like this, and she's going to be out on her butt."

"Maybe that's why she took a teaching job at Nagassack," Marion tried. "I mean, that doesn't explain why she lied to Charlie, but maybe she just needed a little cash."

"A teaching gig at Nagassack isn't going to cover these bills."

Crystal kept scanning through the folder, looking for anything else that might be useful for Charlie. She was through to the last sheet of paper when she paused, the flashlight tight against her teeth.

"What is it?" Kentaro asked, hopping from foot to foot in the darkness behind her. "A picture of her boiling rabbits for sport? Or holding a smoking gun?"

"No. But now I've got her dorm-room number. Looks like she's got a roommate. Maybe we should pay her a visit, see what else we can find out."

It took about five minutes of aggressive knocking before Crystal heard movement on the other side of the door to Miranda's dorm room, but she was pretty sure that had less to do with the late hour than with the loud music from behind the door. It hadn't been particularly hard to find the modern four-story dorm building just a few blocks through Cambridge behind the Great Dome, nor had it been much of a task getting past the security desk on the first floor. There were some benefits to being twelve, one of which was that everyone pretty much believed any story you told them. The security guard looked like a college kid himself, probably making extra money on the side while catching up on his studies via the large textbook Crystal could see braced against his lap on the other side of the low security desk. He certainly didn't want to deal with a crying twelve-year-old who'd snuck out of her sister's dorm to buy some candy from the lobby candy machine, forgetting to bring her sister's ID card with her. The guy didn't even bother calling up to the dorm room to check her story; he just waved her by, as she'd suspected he would. Kentaro and Marion had given her thumbs-ups from outside the glass front entrance to the building, where they'd be waiting for her while she completed her mission.

Though it was a little scarier being on her own, it was better than letting the two goofballs loose in a college dorm building. When the door to Miranda's room finally flung inward, revealing a two-bedroom suite, she was doubly grateful that she'd left Kentaro and Marion downstairs. The woman standing in the doorway, a plastic phone jammed against her left ear, was barely wearing any clothes. A little pink tank top, a pair of matching boy shorts, and nothing else. Her blond hair was rolled up on top her head, and her fingers and toes looked like they'd just been painted. Bright red and glossy, like the talons of a bird that had crash landed in a Ferrari-painting factory.

The girl stared at Crystal, then raised an eyebrow, speaking into the phone while the pop music blared out around her from speakers lost somewhere in the chaotic room behind her.

"No, Billy, it's just some kid. You know you're the only guy I'm interested in. No, don't be stupid, you don't have to come over here and beat anybody up. It's just a little girl. Hold on a second."

The girl covered the phone with a palm and leaned toward Crystal.

"Can I help you?"

Crystal blanched, because there wasn't much she hated more than being called a "little girl," especially by someone who she doubted could tell the difference between a piece of marble and a chunk or rhyolite. But she wasn't there to make a scene.

"Um, I'm not sure I'm in the right place. My cousin, Miranda Sloan, told me to stop by after my family got to town, but our flight was crazy delayed, and my parents' phone ran out of batteries so I couldn't call first."

"Miranda isn't here. She won't be back until Monday, actually."

Crystal made her eyes wide.

"Really? Oh no, I guess there was a miscommunication. She's out of town?"

"Florida," the girl said hastily, obviously trying to get back to her phone call, and the "charming" brute on the other end of the line. "Wow, she's quite the family girl this week. She's down there playing Mother Goose to a nephew and a bunch of his friends. Knowing her, hitting every mall in the state, right?"

Crystal faked a smile. *A nephew.* From what Charlie had told her, that had to be Finn. And combining the overdue tuition bills from Miranda's file with the shopping comment, along with what Crystal could see of the dorm room—a jumble of expensive furniture and accessories right out of a catalogue or off a showroom floor—Crystal was getting a better picture of the woman Charlie was dealing with and her possible motivations.

"I guess I'll have to come visit another time," Crystal mumbled, backing away from the door. The girl winked at her with heavy, overdone eyelashes, already bringing the phone back to her ear.

"Sure, swing by next week! Miranda says she's going to throw one heck of a party when she gets back in town. She says she's finally going to pay off her missed tuition bills and her credit cards, so we can charge, charge, charge again another day! I don't have to tell you, that girl has more lives than a cat, and the cat has got her claws into a golden goose!"

With that, the girl disappeared back into the room, chatting away into the phone with Billy the Pig, shutting the door behind her. Crystal was left alone in the hallway, the pop music echoing around her head. It was late, she was tired, but she was also pretty pleased with herself. As Code Blues went, it had been a very successful night.

Way better than the last Code Blue—although it would have been hard to do worse than a temperamental cat, bleeding hives, and a near beating with a lacrosse stick.

Twenty minutes later, Charlie hung up the iPhone and sank down against the bed, his mind whirling, Crystal's voice still echoing in his ears. Jeremy was shaking his head as he paced back and forth in front of the bed; Charlie had turned the phone on speaker once Crystal had gotten into the meat of the story, and even Jeremy, who tried his best to see the good in most people, couldn't ignore the obvious.

Miranda had known about the money the whole time. It seemed clear now; the park employee with the scar was her accomplice, and she had worked with him to concoct the scheme. He was probably getting a cut—there was certainly enough money to go around. That's what this was about, from the very beginning. There was no paper, the money wasn't going to charity; it was going to pay off Miranda's tuition and credit-card bills.

Charlie was Miranda's golden goose.

Playing chaperone to her nephew and a bunch of his friends. Sam had said that Miranda and Finn seemed to have known each other a long time. That made sense, of course, since they were related. Which meant that Finn might have known all along what Miranda was up to. Certainly, he knew that she wasn't a teaching student at Northeastern. In fact, she was an engineering student at MIT. She wasn't writing a paper; she was running a scam. It wouldn't have been hard for her to have fooled her way into the teaching position at Nagassack; crafting a fake resume and a few references would be child's play for someone as sharp as Miranda. And a few hours a week away from MIT wouldn't have been too difficult for her to pull off, even as an engineering student.

She had probably figured out the math and science on her own, then trained the team to bring down Incredo Land to the tune of fifty thousand dollars.

"She's smart," Jeremy said as he paced in front of the bed. "If you back out now, she'll find another way to get the money. Maybe put Finn up in your place, pay off more park employees, I don't know. She's freaking scary."

Charlie didn't think Finn had any chance of beating the wheel, but it didn't matter, because Charlie wasn't walking away from this. Not now. He'd already been used, lied to—heck, he'd lied himself, all for the group. He wasn't going to simply run away.

"I have no intention of backing out," he said, a sudden steel in his voice. I'm still going to beat that wheel."

Jeremy raised his eyebrows.

"You've got a plan?"

Charlie nodded, his mind still whirling behind his eyes.

Miranda had betrayed him, she'd betrayed all of them. But she'd also given Charlie and the rest a chance at doing something great; she had opened their eyes, let them in on a secret world. Charlie had become cool and confident in a way that would only grow with time. In a way, he owed Miranda.

So he was going to beat that wheel for her. And then, somehow, he was going to find a way to give her exactly what she deserved.

23

THREE A.M.

Flecks of moonlight glistened across the glassy surface of a meandering jungle pool as the artificial tones of an animatronic Macaw tore through the silent, humid air. Then a single figure cut like a serrated blade through the water—elegant, skillful strokes, arms sweeping in perfect arcs, legs kicking with practiced ease. The level of focus was almost frightening; from Charlie's vantage point, it appeared that to the kid in the pool, there was nothing else. It was as if all of existence had shrunk down to that moment, flesh against fluid, muscles contracting and expanding at a cellular level. And then, at the very last second, his hands shot forward, fingers gripping the concrete, and he came up, out of the water.

The smile on his face looked pure, unsullied by thought or pretense or even character. In that moment, he just was.

Charlie watched from within the shadows of the vast dormant volcano that rose up beside the curvy pool as Finn shook the water from his ears. When he couldn't contain himself any longer, he stepped out of the shadow of the volcano and sat on the edge of a reclining wicker patio chair.

"There's one thing I don't get," Charlie said, half to himself, as Finn turned to look at him. If Finn was surprised to see him there, it wasn't evident on the older kid's face. "I mean, I understand why Miranda set this all up. She needed the money, and she knew, with the right group of kids and enough practice, we could pull it off. And that nobody would suspect a bunch of middle-school kids of working a system like this—beating beatable carnival games."

Finn crossed his arms against the cement, resting his chin on a bicep, still watching Charlie, still smiling that pure, unsullied smile.

"But what I still don't get," Charlie continued, "is what's in it for you? A little piece of the action? Just helping a member of the family? It just doesn't seem a part of who you are, to do all this for money. But without you, none of this would have worked. You recruited us, one by one. You convinced me to join. You gave her credibility. Why? What's in this for you?"

Finn ran a hand through his longish hair. Then he sighed.

"You're a good kid, Charlie, but sometimes you think too much."

Charlie listened as the artificial Macaw chimed in from his perch in a twiggy roost halfway up the volcano, a high, melodic birdsong.

"I thought that's why Miranda wanted me. Because I know how to think."

"Double-edged sword, eh? Yeah, you know, I should tell you, Miranda actually didn't want to bring you in. She thought it would be easier just to take your project, reverse engineer it, and train one of us to pull it off. She was worried that you wouldn't have the guts to do what needed to be done. From your school file, she thought you were too much of a geek."

The breeze felt wet against the back of Charlie's neck, but he didn't move, didn't even shift against the wicker of the chair.

"But I'd seen you around school," Finn continued. "You and your friends, that chick with the rocks, the little guy, Mr. Allergies, Jeremy freakin' Diapers!—and

I convinced her otherwise. I could tell, yeah, you're a geek, Charlie, I don't think that comes as any surprise, but you've got a good heart, you're incredibly loyal, and you're stronger than you realize. I guess even I underestimated how strong."

"That's not an answer, Finn."

Finn paused, then cocked his head to the side. His smile seemed to change, turning crooked at the edges. His chin dug deeper into his bicep, his shoulders relaxing.

"On the plane, you asked me why I quit the swim team, the morning of the national meet."

Charlie's pulse quickened. This was going in a direction he hadn't expected. He glanced around the pool area, but it was still deserted, the shadows from the volcano obscuring everything beyond ten yards.

"For years," Finn said quietly, "for most of my life, really, I was obsessed with swimming. I'd wake up every morning at four, train three hours before school, then rush home after the bell, train another three. I was crazy about it; it was pretty much all I did. See, I didn't have great parents like you; my dad works all the time at the bank, my mom left us when I was three. But I'm not trying to get all 'after-school special.' It wasn't about that; it was about me and the water, and winning. See, I was good. Really good. And when I swam in a big meet and beat the other swimmers, it was the best feeling in the world. That feeling, it was everything. After a while, it was all that mattered."

Charlie wasn't an athlete, but that day he'd gotten a taste of that feeling, he knew what it was like to be better than everyone else, to win. It was an incredibly addictive thing.

"By the time of that national meet, I had been training so much, my muscles were on autopilot. I was swimming faster than I'd ever dreamed possible. I was unbeatable. Everyone knew it. The coach, everyone on the team, everyone at Nagassack. Even the other coaches and swimmers."

Finn was so low in the water now, Charlie could only see his eyes, heavily lidded, piercing green echoes of the moon.

"The night before the national meet, my dad had to work late. Really late. Around midnight, I couldn't sleep, so I biked over to the pool for one last dip in the water. The place was empty, I was alone."

Finn slapped a hand against the side of the pool, sending up a spray of drops. Charlie jerked back so hard, he almost fell off the chair.

"Suddenly, it all drifted into place. The way my

body moved, the water flowing beneath me, the speed, the energy, the focus. I realized then what everybody else knew—there was nobody who could beat me. The competition was over. And the next morning, for the first time in my entire life, I didn't feel like swimming. People came up with so many reasons. I was scared. I was injured. I was a head case, crazy."

Finn let his body float back from the wall so that he was barely hanging on to the edge with his fingers.

"But the truth is, I simply didn't need to swim. I already knew I could win. There was no point. I had nothing to prove."

Charlie stared at him. He wasn't sure he understood, but he could see from Finn's face that he was truly serious—maybe for the first time since Charlie had met him.

"For me, this isn't about the money," Finn said. "Or Miranda, or even the Carnival Killers. I'm doing this for me. I'm doing this to beat a beatable game. To prove that I can—to the only person I need to prove anything to. Myself."

Charlie felt his legs numbing as the wicker dug into the backs of his thighs.

"You didn't have a problem with any of it. I mean, when there wasn't any money involved, yeah, it's beating a beatable game to show that we can. But with fifty thousand dollars at stake—"

"It's a matter of perspective. I don't consider it cheating."

Charlie wished he could be so cavalier, but now, knowing what he knew, he simply didn't agree.

"Math to beat a beatable game, right? Brains to level an unfair playing field. But the wheel—well, that's not just gonna take brains, and you know it."

Finn looked at him for a full beat. Then he shrugged.

"You want to make me and Miranda the bad guys, Charlie? Okay. But I'm not the one with an iPhone in his pocket."

With that, as Charlie digested the words, Finn pushed off with his arms, sending his body into a perfect backstroke, his hands slicing through the moonlit water with soundless ease.

Finn had a point, of course. Charlie had the iPhone in his pocket.

But he also had the inklings of a plan.

24

THE HAWK WASN'T WEARING any pants.

It was a stupid, silly thought, yet Charlie couldn't clear it from his head; no matter how hard he tried, it just kept reverberating through his mind, jumping from cell to cell like a viral video across the web, pushing all logic out of the way as it threatened to consume every sparking neuron. *The freaking hawk wasn't wearing any freaking pants.* He had an electric-green hat with a little tassel, a red scarf, a shirt with buttons and cuffs—and then he was naked from the waist down. It didn't make any sense. He was a hawk and either he should have been totally nude, like in real life, or he should have been wearing pants. But there he was, beaky smile and jaunty crook in his tail, staring at Charlie from the lined-off section of the enormous wheel, two sections down from where the thick plastic arrow rested, ready to click away, waiting for the wheel to move, around and around and around . . .

"Anytime, Charlie. Just give it a good spin. No pressure. Forget the crowd, forget I'm standing here, forget the tickets and the money. Give it a good ol' spin. It's just a game of chance."

Charlie nodded. The man with the gray hair was wearing a similar suit from the day before, but his tie was bright red and covered in little pictures of Incredo Land characters; Charlie knew, without looking, that all five of the creatures from the wheel in front of him were there, tiny replicants made of twists of thread. Loopy. The Frog. Dandy the Squirrel. Boots the Kangaroo. And that darn, pantsless Maddy.

But standing there, trying not to look at the crowd that had swelled to at least a hundred people at the base of the stage that had been set up across the midway point of Solar Avenue, trying not to see the sack of money on the table in front of the wheel next to the big Plexiglas Red Cross charity box—the one the bespectacled man had referred to the day before, for new donations, with the inviting slot—*desperately* wanting not to feel the weight of the phone in his pocket, he knew that the man was *wrong*. It wasn't a game of chance at all. It was math, pure and simple. Numbers wielded like a sword, designed to kill any semblance of luck or chance.

It was almost too much to bear. Charlie felt his legs weakening, his knees threatening to buckle under his weight. Finn was wrong; he wasn't strong enough to do this. He was weak, a geek, a nerd, he was Charlie Numbers, and he didn't have the will to go through with it.

And then he heard a cough from the crowd and saw Jeremy, a head taller than the kids on either side of him, anticipation splashed across his freckled, reddish face. That was all Charlie needed.

He gripped the wheel with both hands, and using all his weight, spun it as hard as he could.

Up close, the *click, click, click* of the arrow was like machine-gun fire in his ears; the sound echoed through his bones, erasing the last trivial vestiges of half-naked water fowl from his thoughts. His eyes were intent on the wheel, the images in each defined section that blurred as it spun—but no so much so that he couldn't pick out where one ended and another began. Loopy, Dandy, Boots, Maddy, *there*. The first revolution, and in that instant, Charlie brushed his hand against his pocket again, hitting the screen of the iPhone. The information was entered into his satellite tracking program, and then his eyes were refocused, picking through the blur. Loopy, Dandy, Boots . . . *again.* Charlie touched his pocket a third time, marking off the end of the second revolution. Three little flicks, that's all it had taken, and in front of a crowd of over a hundred watching eyes. But nobody was looking at him, because right there, next to him, in swirling Technicolor, was the greatest misdirection one could ask for. A spinning wheel twice as tall as him, whirling round and round and round.

And then Charlie felt the vibrations against his thigh. Five little bursts, separated by a second between each one. It was his own design. He'd known that trying to actually look at the phone without anyone noticing would have been too risky, so he'd come up with a way that the phone could communicate with him secretly, using its vibrating ring. And now Charlie knew, for certain, where the wheel would stop. He looked over at the gray-haired man, who was smiling at him expectantly, and Charlie cleared his voice so that nobody would mishear:

"Maddy the Turkey Hawk!" he said loudly. Of course, it would have to be Maddy, Charlie thought sardonically. The gray-haired man repeated the words to the crowd.

The wheel continued to spin. Still a blur, but second by second, slowing down, the friction in the air and the tug of the wheel's axle eating away at its kinetic energy, joule by joule.

But by that point, Charlie was barely watching. He knew the math, he knew that the equation he'd plugged into the phone was sound, that the numbers wouldn't lie. He knew, for a fact, that when that wheel finally stopped spinning—

"Holy smokes!" the gray-haired man shouted. "You got it! Maddy! You win! Charlie Lewis, you just won fifty thousand dollars, and eight lifetime tickets to Incredo Land!"

Charlie turned back toward the wheel, and there he was, Maddy, bare tail feathers up in the air, right underneath the plastic arrow, frozen for everyone to see. Charlie had done it. The Carnival Killers had won. They had beat the unbeatable game.

And then, in that moment, everything seemed to happen at once.

Out of the corner of his eye, Charlie saw Miranda hopping up the steps that led to the stage. She was clapping her hands and smiling and saying something to the gray-haired man about being Charlie's guardian, his chaperone for the trip, and as he handed her the lifetime tickets, part of the prize for beating the wheel, she informed him she was going to hold on to them as well as the money until Charlie's parents could pick him up at the airport when they got back to Boston.

But before she reached the top step, Charlie was already moving as well. With a single motion, he swept his black backpack off the stage by his feet, ripped the zipper open, rushed over to the table where the money was piled up—and started shoving the stacks of bills inside. He didn't look up as he went, praying that the wheel and the gray-haired man were obscuring Miranda's view, ignoring the crowd that was now pointing and laughing at what probably seemed to them, his overdramatic antics. *Five thousand. Ten thousand. Twenty thousand. Fifty thousand.*

Only then, every last hundred-dollar bill safely in the backpack, did he look up. Miranda had just gotten free from the man with the gray hair and was moving toward him. Her gaze moved from him to the bag, and then her smile froze on her face.

Charlie yanked the zipper shut and hoisted the bag over his right shoulder. It was way heavier than he had imagined, but he didn't care. He gave Miranda one last look and then dove forward off the stage, taking the steps at full speed.

Miranda shouted something, frantic, high-pitched words that sounded like "Barry," or "Gary," followed by "get him!" But then Charlie was diving into the stunned crowd of people, his shoes churning against the ground, his body moving fast as a bullet, faster than he'd ever gone—

And then suddenly, he slammed headfirst right into Jeremy.

They went down in a jumble of arms and legs, both of them screaming as they went. The backpack flipped off Charlie's shoulder as he crashed into the ground, and then Jeremy was on top of him, trying to untangle himself.

"Hey, man, get off me!" Charlie shouted.

"Ow, you're on my ankle!"

"Just move!"

And then, less than a second later, Charlie was back on his feet. He reached down, grabbed the backpack out from beneath Jeremy, who was still down on one knee, and then Charlie was moving forward again. The crowd parted as he barreled through, and then he was speeding down Solar Avenue, feet churning as fast as they could go.

A few more yards, and then he dared to looked back—and that's when he saw the two impossible shapes moving after him.

One looked like a giant mouse. The other, a mutated frog in oversize moon boots.

Both were wearing pants. And both were coming after him, murderous looks in their giant cartoon eyes.

25

BACK PRESSED AGAINST THE locked steel door, heart pounding in his chest, face frozen in a rictus of pure fear, the sickly sweet tones of singing robot children echoing down the narrow corridor, the words themselves twisted and torqued by the steam pipes and rusting gears jutting from the cinder-block walls. Charlie held the backpack out at arm's length in front of him, his gaze pinned to the enormous headless mouse, and the even more terrifying frog, as they towered over him.

Loopy, or Barry, or Gary, or Scarface, as Charlie now thought of him, leaned forward so that Charlie could see the yellow of his teeth.

"Thought you could get away? That was real stupid,

kid. Miranda promised me ten percent of that stash. And Loopy's got to get paid. Understand?"

Scarface laughed at his own words, then reached out with a giant white glove and tried to grab the backpack by its strap. The huge hands swatted against the material, but the sausage-shaped fingers couldn't close. The man cursed, and Charlie heard a loud guffaw echo out of the Frog costume.

"You gotta take off the hands, man. Loopy's only got four fingers. Can't grab much with four freaking fingers."

Scarface glared at his buddy in the Frog costume, then went to work on the enormous gloves. It took him a full minute to get them unattached, then he flung them both to the cement floor.

"Let's try this again," he hissed.

He reached out and grabbed the backpack, this time getting the strap on his first try.

"Nice and heavy," he said. "I like that."

He showed the pack to the Frog, then grinned back at Charlie.

"Nobody beats the Mouse, kid. You should know that."

Then he attacked the zipper, ripping it open with a single yank. Still grinning, he flipped the backpack over, aiming its contents toward the ground—

And then his gasp echoed off the cinder-block walls. Instead of thick stacks of hundred-dollar bills:

Diapers. Dozens of diapers, raining down from the backpack, piling up on the cement floor . . .

Scarface stared at the growing pile, then back at Charlie. His hand opened, and the backpack fell to ground, landing right on top of all the diapers.

"How?" he stared. Then he shook his head. "I don't know what just happened here, but you better freaking start talking. Where's the money?"

Charlie swallowed. He hadn't exactly planned to get cornered like this; he'd hoped to just drop the backpack with the diapers somewhere in the amusement park, where security would eventually find it. The diapers had been Jeremy's idea, both to make the bag look as if it were still full of cash, and also add a nice personal flourish to the job. His plan had worked, everything but the endgame. He reached his hands behind his back, pressing at the cold steel door again. Still locked. He looked around, beginning to panic as the two men lurched menacingly closer.

And then a familiar, if shocked, voice echoed through the corridor.

"Charlie Numbers? Dude, what the heck is going on?"

The Frog and Scarface turned as one. Charlie looked between them, and saw Dylan standing in the corridor about ten feet behind the two men, flanked by his two bozos, Liam and Dusty.

The corridor went near silent; the only sound, besides the music from the ride, was Dylan's labored breathing. The hefty thug must have run pretty fast to catch up to Charlie and his pursuers. Charlie could see from the expression on Dylan's face, the scene in front of him wasn't at all what he'd expected. Obviously, Scarface and the Frog felt the same way. One kid in a desolate corridor they could handle, but a fifth of a school trip? This was more than either of them had signed up for.

Scarface looked back over his shoulder at Charlie and then spat toward the floor, missing the diapers by a few inches.

"Not worth it," he grunted. "You can keep your stinking diapers."

And then he turned and started back down the corridor. The Frog followed one big shoe-length behind. A moment later, they had squeezed past Dylan and his groupies, and a minute after that, Charlie was alone with his least favorite classmates. But for once, Charlie was more than glad to be facing his usual tormentor.

"I think you just saved my life." He gasped.

Dylan opened his mouth to respond, and then closed it again. His pasty cheeks suddenly filled with color. *My god*, Charlie thought, *he's blushing*. Dylan had been a bully for such a long time, he had forgotten what it felt like to help someone out. He looked completely overwhelmed and confused, but it was obvious he liked the feeling.

"First time for everything," he said. "I guess."

He glanced at Liam and Dusty, then over his shoulder, at the now empty corridor. Then he turned back to Charlie.

"You know what, Numbers? Today, you get a pass."

Then Dylan's wide, pasty face broke out in a grin.

"I mean, after all, it is Incredo Land, right? The Cheeriest Spot in the Universe?"

At the moment, Charlie couldn't disagree.

26

IT TOOK ABOUT TEN minutes for the crowd to dissipate, which wasn't surprising considering the bizarre scene Charlie had caused. Picturing the whole scene was such a bizarre thought—a skinny kid in red sneakers scooping money into a backpack, then diving off a stage, Loopy the Space Mouse and the Frog in hot pursuit. When Charlie had rammed right into him, taking them both down to the ground, it had looked so real that even Jeremy had a hard time believing they had planned the whole thing at three in the morning. But like Charlie had predicted, it had worked perfectly. In the ensuing chaos, nobody had noticed that Charlie had lifted the wrong backpack off the ground. Nobody had noticed anything except that crazy kid running down

Solar Avenue, a cartoon nightmare right behind him.

Still laughing, Jeremy gripped Charlie's heavy black backpack and strolled up the steps leading to the stage. The gray-haired man was gone, as was Miranda and just about everybody else. Jeremy had no idea where that conniving fake teacher had vanished to, but he truly hoped he never saw her again. Just watching her as her face had gone cold, seeing Charlie with the money, it was enough to give you nightmares. Reaching the top of the stage, Jeremy glanced at the huge colorful wheel, still frozen in place the way Charlie had left it—the hawk up top, beak open in a wonderful grin. Jeremy felt exactly as that hawk looked as he crossed to the big Plexiglas charity box. Then he unslung the backpack from his shoulders and undid the zipper.

As he pulled the first stack of hundred-dollar bills out of the backpack, he noticed a Midwestern-looking couple about five yards away down Solar Avenue, watching him. The man was portly, in jeans and a red sweater, and there was a look of awe on his face as he saw the green in Jeremy's hand. The woman was short, a little bit stocky, with thick glasses and a tight ponytail. She was saying something to her husband, and he shrugged back at her. *Well,* Jeremy thought to himself,

I'm on a stage. May as well have an audience.

With a flourish, he jammed the stack of hundred-dollar bills into the charity box. And then he dug back into the backpack for another stack.

It took about five minutes to shove all fifty thousand dollars into the slot. When he was done, he stuck his head into the backpack to make sure he'd gotten everything. Every bill, gone. He grinned, imagining what Miranda was going to think. Jeremy had cleaned out the entire baby shelf at the convenience store in the hotel lobby. It seemed like a fair exchange. Fifty thousand dollars for the Red Cross, and a backpack full of diapers for Miranda. If Jeremy had been looking for a definition of the word "karma," he couldn't have done much better than that.

He looked up from the bag, and noticed that the Midwestern couple had moved a couple of yards closer. The husband was still wide-eyed, and gave him a once-over, head to toe. Then the man shook his head.

"Wow," he called out. "That was pretty generous. And a whole lot of money for a kid."

Jeremy grinned back at him.

"I'm, like, an Internet millionaire. We seem to get younger every year, don't we?"

With that, he gave the Plexiglas box a gentle pat,

then slung the now-empty backpack over his shoulder and shot the Midwestern couple a wink. Then he started back down the steps, ready for another wonderful day of adventure, in the Cheeriest Spot in the Universe.

THE RAIN WAS COMING down in gray-on-gray sheets, spitting and splattering against the vast picture windows, droplets exploding against the tempered glass in rapid succession, miniature fireworks through a smoldering sky. Charlie leaned forward on his stool, his face so close that he could almost feel the November wind as it drove the sheets of rain. Down below, when he craned his neck, he could just make out the Charles River looping by, and could even see one of the infamous Boston Duck boats chugging along; from that distance, the awkward half boat, half bus looked more like a waterlogged slug than an amphibious WWII-era vehicle.

Charlie and the Whiz Kids had ridden the Duck

boats a few times over the years, but this particular gray Saturday, they were content to be inside, lodged happily at the back window of the Museum of Science's main dining area. They'd spent the entire morning racing from exhibit to exhibit, because each of them had his or her own personal favorite, and none intersected. Crystal oscillated between the fossils on the first floor and the geology specimens on the third. Kentaro, the History of Language, a traveling exhibit tucked behind the Butterfly Garden. Marion, another traveling exhibit, this one on ancient building techniques: From Pyramids to Igloos and Beyond. Jeremy, dinosaurs, of course, because one could never get enough dinosaurs. And Charlie had his lightning. In short, a trip to the Museum of Science with all five Whiz Kids was well beyond exhausting; which was why, for the past twenty minutes, they'd thankfully traded racing from exhibit to exhibit for the view of the rain over the river, pleasant conversation, and a bite to eat.

"You guys really wanted to blow up MIT?" Jeremy was saying from three stools over from where Charlie was planted. Jeremy had a half-eaten hamburger in one hand, a handful of french fries in the other. "I mean, that's a pretty stupid plan."

Kentaro, one seat to Jeremy's left, jabbed at the him

with a hot dog, sending a splash of mustard arcing up past Jeremy's head.

"Not all of it. Just a little cordite around the Dome. A distraction."

"That's not a distraction," Jeremy responded through a mouthful of burger. "That's an act of war. The next time we call a Code Blue, you and Marion aren't included."

Charlie couldn't help laughing, watching his Whiz Kids enjoying their banter-filled lunch at the window overlooking the Charles. Inside, he was incredibly grateful for what they'd done. Crystal, especially—he owed her big time. And even though she'd seemed pretty thrilled when he'd given her the agate charm bracelet he'd bought in the airport gift shop with a good portion of his allowance, he was still planning to do more. Maybe a real gemstone someday, something rare for her collection, if he ever saved up enough to purchase one she didn't already own.

"Well," Crystal said when she'd finished clapping, "the next time Charlie starts hanging out with mysterious seventh graders, why don't we just hit him over the head with Marion's sister's lacrosse stick and be done with it?"

Charlie laughed again. Although Crystal hadn't

actually said Finn's name; the mere mention had brought back memories of the airport, the last time he'd seen the seventh-grade leader of the Carnival Killers.

As they always seemed to appear out of nowhere in their mysterious fashion, Finn and Magic walked up behind Charlie as he'd come out of the airport gift shop. It was the first time he'd come face-to-face with Finn since he'd leaped off that stage, backpack full of money in hand. None of the group had spoken at all during the flight home from Florida. And Miranda, well, Charlie hadn't seen Miranda even once since that moment on the stage. She must have booked a different flight back.

Right after Charlie had returned to Solar Avenue with Dylan and his flunkies, Warden Walker had gathered all the kids from Nagassack together, explaining that Miranda had gone home suddenly with some sort of unexpected illness and her group would be divided up between Walker's and Mrs. Cauldwell's. So Charlie had, in fact, been able to spend the last two days at Incredo Land with Jeremy, screaming their way through nine rides on the Space Drop and three more on the Haunted Moon. It really had been the trip of a lifetime.

But seeing Finn and Magic outside the gift shop had nearly scared him right out of his shoes. He'd had no idea what they'd thought of what he'd done. When Finn strolled toward him, hands jammed into the pockets of his leather jacket, Charlie had half expected the older kid to punch him in the face.

Instead, Finn had pulled his right hand out of his jacket pocket and held up the gold-embossed tickets. Lifetime tickets, Charlie'd realized, to Incredo Land. The prize Charlie had won by beating the wheel, which Miranda had handed off to Finn to hold for safekeeping in the shuffle after the stage-diving incident.

Finn had smiled, handing a pair to Charlie. Then he'd held out an open hand for Charlie to shake.

"Good for you, man."

There was no mention of the money Charlie and Jeremy had donated to the charity, no mention of Miranda, no mention of the frantic scene on the stage. He didn't seem angry at what Charlie had done, or bewildered by the loss of Miranda; in fact, he seemed as cool and collected as he ever had. Finn had simply shaken Charlie's hand, and then he and Magic had turned and headed through the terminal. When they'd gone about five feet, Magic had turned once, giving Charlie a wild grin.

"And everybody says I'm crazy. I don't hold a candle to you, kid."

And just like that, they were gone. Charlie had been

about to head back to Jeremy, to tell him what had happened, when a hand touched his shoulder. He turned to see Sam standing next to him. Before he was able to say a word, she grabbed him in a warm hug. Sparks exploded inside his chest at her touch, that inexplicable feeling burning bright, then floating away. Cheek pressed against his, she suddenly whispered in his ear:

"We'll always have Incredo Land, right, Charlie?"

When she pulled away, she laughed at herself, then pointed a finger at him.

"And what happens in Incredo Land, stays in Incredo Land."

With that, she'd headed after Finn and Magic, leaving Charlie standing there, wondering what the heck she'd meant, or what, exactly, he had felt when she'd hugged him. In the end, he'd decided not to dwell on any of it; Sam was right. What happened in Incredo Land, stayed in Incredo Land. Sure, back at Nagassack, he'd see them all again. After all, it was middle school, everyone knew everyone, and they all ate lunch in the same place, even if at different hours. Sooner or later, they would run into one another. But it wouldn't be the same. *We'll always have Incredo Land.*

BRINGING DOWN THE MOUSE

by Ben Mezrich

About the Book

Charlie Lewis is a sixth-grade student at Nagassack Middle School in Newton, Massachusetts. He is nicknamed "Numbers" because he sees everything mathematically. He has a core group of friends nicknamed the "Whiz Kids." Charlie is recruited to be part of the "Carnival Killers," a group of students that train to beat carnival games to bring home the ultimate prize: Incredo Land lifetime park passes. Charlie soon realizes there is a reason he was chosen to be part of this elite team to win the passes to the best amusement park in the world. Will he risk his longtime friendships to complete the task?

Prereading Activities

1) Describe a time where you were involved in an activity that seemed to be considered cheating. How did you feel? What did you do after completing the activity? If you could go back to that day/time, would you do anything differently?

2) Describe a time when you were asked to keep information to yourself and not share with your closest friends. What did you do? Did you share this information? How did you feel during and after this event?

Discussion Questions

1) After reading chapter one, can you tell why the book is titled *Bringing Down the Mouse*?

2) Why do you think Charlie's parents are five thousand miles away in Newton, Massachusetts, when he is running from two characters in an amusement park?

3) How did Jeremy Draper get the nickname "Diapers"? How did Charlie Lewis get the nickname "Numbers"? Do you have a nickname that people use? How did this

nickname come to be given to you? How do you feel about having this nickname?

4) How did the "chip" incident play out for Charlie? Explain how being encountered like that at school or in public makes a person feel. Give examples to support your answer.

5) Why do you think Charlie is meeting Finn and Magic at the Sherwood Country Halloween Fair?

6) Describe Charlie's group of friends known as the "Whiz Kids." Your explanations should be detailed enough to give a person hearing them a picture in his or her mind of each friend.

7) Compare the show *Wheel of Fortune* to the carnival game of the same name.

8) What is the prize for winning the promotion at Incredo Land Amusement Park?

9) Explain why you might think twice about playing the claw machine the next time you encounter the game.

10) Would you play the milk bottle or basketball game? Explain why or why not.

11) What was the proposition made to Charlie by Miranda Sloan? If you were in Charlie's position, would you accept the challenge?

12) Why do you think Charlie was recruited by Miranda?

13) What was the one condition that Charlie presented to Miranda that had to occur in order to get him to agree to go with the Carnival Killers to Incredo Land? What does that tell you about Charlie's character? Explain.

14) How does Charlie learn to conquer the coin toss game? What obstacles stand in the way of winning this game?

15) Why aren't people able to win the dart game more often? How are these obstacles overcome?

16) How would someone overcome the obstacles that stand in his or her way of ringing the bell to beat the time on the rope ladder? Do you think knowing these tricks and using them is considered cheating? Explain your reasoning.

17) Explain Charlie's feelings about deceiving his parents and the Whiz Kids in regard to what he was doing during recess and after school. How would you feel if you were in Charlie's position? How would you feel if you were one of his friends?

18) How did Charlie prove he was worthy to go to Incredo Land?

19) What was Charlie going to use to beat the wheel at Incredo Land? Explain how this item would be used.

20) How was Jeremy told that he was going on the school trip to Incredo Land? Do you think this was the right thing to say to Jeremy? How do you think Jeremy would feel if he found out the truth?

21) What explanation did Charlie give his parents that allowed him to attend the trip?

22) Explain the characters that Charlie was playing as he made his way through the midway games.

23) How did Charlie conquer the milk bottle game? Why do you think he played it even though it wasn't on his list of three games to play?

24) What were Charlie and Sam doing at Incredo Land after closing hours? What does this say about how Charlie has changed from the beginning of the story?

25) Why did Charlie break into Miranda's hotel room? What did he discover when he was in there?

26) How did Charlie break the cardinal rule of the Carnival Killers? Why do you think he broke this rule? Would you have done the same thing if you were in that position?

27) What was the "code blue" that the Whiz Kids were involved in?

28) What did Crystal find out as she went through Miranda's student file? What was her response? What was Miranda's real reason for the trip to Incredo Land?

29) Do you feel that the Whiz Kids were breaking laws to discover information about Miranda and this quest? Explain your reasoning.

30) What was Finn's response to Charlie when he confronted him at the pool? How does Finn's reason for not swimming in the final meet explain why he wants to win this promotion at the amusement park?

31) Explain in detail the events that transpired as Charlie stood onstage to spin the wheel until he jumped off the stage and started running. How did he beat the wheel?

32) When was the backpack switch performed? What was in the pack that Loopy took from Charlie?

33) How did Dylan's role in Charlie's everyday life change on the day of the contest? Explain what this says about Dylan's character.

34) What did Jeremy decide to do with the $50,000? What would you have done with this amount of money in this situation?

35) What did Finn do when he met Charlie at the airport on the way back to Massachusetts? What does this tell you about Finn?

36) What did Sam mean when she told Charlie, "We'll always have Incredo Land"?

Guide written in 2014 by Christine Lavin, a fifth- and sixth-grade math teacher at East Brookfield Elementary School in East Brookfield, Massachusetts.

Just because you're a kid, it doesn't mean you can't solve crimes.

But it probably means you won't solve them well.

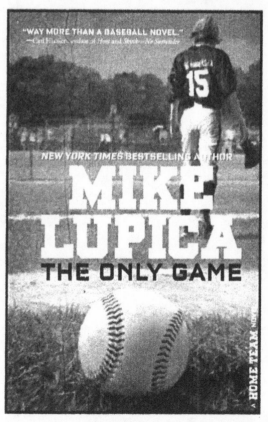